The After-Hours War

a 509 Crime Story

by Colin Conway

What is the 509?

Separated by the Cascade Range, Washington State is divided into two distinctly different climates and cultures.

The western side of the Cascades is home to Seattle, its 34 inches of annual rainfall, and the incredibly weird and smelly Gum Wall. Most of the state's wealth and political power are concentrated in and around this enormous city. The residents of this area know the prosperity that has come from being the home of Microsoft, Amazon, Boeing, and Starbucks.

To the east of the Cascade Mountains lies nearly two-thirds of the entire state, a lot of which is used for agriculture. Washington State leads the nation in producing apples, it is the second-largest potato grower, and it's the fourth for providing wheat.

This eastern part of the state can enjoy more than 170 days of sunshine each year, which is important when there are more than 200 lakes nearby. However, the beautiful summers are offset by harsh winters, with average snowfall reaching 47 inches and the average high hovering around 37°.

While five telephone area codes provide service to the westside, only 509 covers everything east of the Cascades, a staggering twenty-one counties.

Of these, Spokane County is the largest with an estimated population of 506,000.

*May we never go to hell
but always be on our way.*

- traditional drinking toast

The After-Hours War

PART I

Chapter 1

The cell phone buzzed loudly on the nightstand. Shane McAfee awoke, rolled away from the woman he was entwined with, and fumbled for it. He remembered he wasn't in his own bed when he knocked over a framed photograph. It clattered to its face.

The phone rattled once more on the nightstand before Shane picked it up.

Next to him, Emily Harris moaned, "Turn it off."

Unfortunately for Shane, there was no ignoring this call.

"McAfee," he said. He sounded like a bullfrog.

"Shane?" a woman responded.

He cleared his throat.

"It's Laura."

"Uh-huh."

"Are you awake?"

"No." His eyes remained closed.

"Well, get up. You've got a messy one."

"How bad?"

Emily groaned her displeasure and thrust her naked butt against Shane's hip. He set his hand upon her leg.

"It's a freakin' massacre—five bodies."

McAfee blinked into the darkness. He sat upright and flipped the cover away. "What happened?"

"Someone walked into a garage and shot up the place."

"A garage?" McAfee pulled the phone from his ear to check the time. His eyes couldn't focus, and he rubbed a knuckle into the right socket.

Emily grabbed the bedspread and tugged it back to its proper place. "Go in the other room," she muttered. "I've got class later."

"Is that her?" Laura asked. She sounded almost giddy. "Must be serious if you're spending the night. Or are you guys living together now?"

McAfee slid out of bed. He didn't bother dressing before padding out of the room.

Laura continued. "I hear she's pretty. All the guys have said it. You know, if you were on Facebook, I wouldn't have to wonder about these things."

He waited for her to comment on Emily's age, but Laura said, "She probably got her looks from her mother. My husband and I met her once. The mother, I mean. At a department event. We liked her. Super nice and real pretty. The father, not so much."

McAfee entered the kitchen and flicked on the light. "It's what—" He pulled the phone from his ear to recheck the time. He blinked a couple of times which brought everything into focus. "—barely after four. When did this thing go down?"

Laura clicked loudly on her keyboard. "Units arrived on-scene twenty minutes ago. Better get a move on, Shane."

God, she seemed in good spirits.

He found an erasable pen and prepared to write on the refrigerator's white board. "Where did it happen?"

She told him, and Shane jotted it down. His penmanship at that angle was atrocious. The address was on Willow Road in the city of Millwood—not too far from where he was in Liberty Lake. Maybe fifteen minutes at average speeds, but he had to stop at his home first to grab a change of clothes.

"Any suspects?" McAfee asked.

"None."

"Witnesses?"

"None."

"Survivors?"

"Everyone in that garage is dead. Like I said, Shane—"

He remembered her words. "A freakin' massacre."

"That's right."

He held a hand to his forehead. Laura was too chipper for this early in the morning. Dispatchers had the worst sense of timing.

Shane asked, "Why were people in a garage at four in the morning?"

"How would I know? You're the detective."

"Am I walking into a meth lab?"

"No, you're not. That much I can tell you. From what it sounds like, they were just hanging out."

"Anyone else on this one?"

"Chambers. He's already been notified, and you know how he is."

"Yeah, I know how he is." He stared at the address written on the whiteboard and did the math. Five dead. Two investigators. It was going to be a long day. "All right. I'm on my way."

"And Shane?"

"Yeah?"

"Don't go back to bed." Laura giggled.

Before he could comment, the call ended.

***

A lamp clicked on as McAfee was bent over, hunting for his second shoe. He'd already slipped on his shirt and pants. He straightened and eyed Emily.

She sat upright and leaned back against the headboard. Emily's blond hair was disheveled, and the bedspread was tucked around her. She rubbed her eyes with the palms of her hands. "You're leaving?" Her words sounded dreamy, as if she could easily tumble back into sleep.

"There was an incident."

"What kind?"

"A shooting."

Her hands dropped into her lap, and she frowned. "Was a deputy involved?"

"No." McAfee returned to hunting for his shoe. "No deputy. Go back to bed."

"Why couldn't they call someone else?"

"They did."

"And you still have to go?"

He nodded. "It's my job, and this is a bad one." He showed her the single shoe. "Do you know where the other one is?"

She waved a hand. "Try the bathroom."

"The bathroom," he said. "Why didn't I think of that?" He walked into the other room.

The shoe was there—upside-down and in the corner. He had no recollection of kicking it or tossing it there while in the throes of passion. Maybe Emily had.

"You think they'd give you a break tonight," she said from the other room.

"It's the morning."

McAfee grabbed the shoe and returned to the bedroom.

"But it was our night." She wiggled the engagement ring on her left hand as she studied it.

"They didn't know."

"Maybe you should have taken it off."

"This isn't the first time I've been called out."

"I know." Her lower lip jutted out slightly. Emily didn't pout often, and she only did it to get her way. McAfee found it oddly charming. No other girlfriend had done such a thing.

"And if I had taken the day off," he said, "I would have spent my morning alone because you've got class in a few hours."

"Just the one." Emily folded her hands together and smiled hopefully. "We would have spent the day together after that."

McAfee dropped the shoes to the floor and slipped his feet in. "I'll make it up to you."

Her eyes narrowed. "How?"

"What do you want?"

Emily's face brightened. Her smile was one of his favorite things about her. He couldn't help but return the pleasantry.

"We stay here again," she said. "Tonight."

McAfee's smile began to melt. He disliked staying at her apartment. He liked when they stayed at his place. "Fine," he said and forced his smile to return.

"And we drive through some new areas to look at houses."

McAfee knelt to tie his shoes and let his smile totally fall away. "What if nothing is for sale?"

"I don't care. I want to look at different neighborhoods to see if there are places we'd like to live."

He wanted her to move into his house, but she didn't like his neighborhood. Getting called out this morning was going to cost McAfee far more than lost sleep. "Fine," he muttered again. He stood and forced another smile.

Emily threw the covers back and slipped from the bed. She stood unabashedly naked before him. "I know you're only doing it for me, so I'll make it up to you." She kissed him and reached for his belt.

He broke the embrace. "I can't."

"Please."

McAfee patted her hip. "Go back to bed."

"Come with."

"I've got to go."

She thrust her lower lip out. "You're no fun."

"That's what I've heard."

Emily spun and hopped onto the bed. He lingered a moment to admire her. When she reached over and clicked off the lamp, it was time to go.

***

The sun was starting to come up as Shane McAfee pulled into the Millwood neighborhood. Even without the address, he could have found the house. Patrol cars from the Spokane County Sheriff's Office lined the street. A couple of unmarked units were there, signifying a sergeant and a lieutenant were already on the scene.

A cluster of evidence technicians gathered around a large cargo van. Several of them noticed McAfee and waved. They'd wait until the detective authorized them to proceed. He switched off the engine and watched them. Maybe things were breaking his way this morning. He'd already been assigned to work with Chambers. The man's meticulous nature would be welcomed on a multiple-victim homicide scene.

A woman with blond hair appeared briefly from behind the van.

"Ah, hell," McAfee muttered.

So things weren't breaking his way after all.

The blond woman said something to an evidence technician before the two of them climbed into the boxy vehicle.

He'd avoided running into her for a while now. Could he somehow continue to avoid her today? Maybe he could get Chambers to work with the evidence techs.

McAfee grabbed his portable radio and exited his car. He clipped the heavy plastic rectangle to his belt but left the sound off. He didn't like it squawking at him while on a crime scene. By the time he arrived, the danger surrounding whatever he was investigating was already gone—the responding deputies had secured the area.

He surveyed the neighborhood. To the east was Argonne Road. To the south was the Spokane River. This community seemed filled with older ranch homes and detached garages. Most of the yards were without fences. Only shrubs or trees marked some of the property lines.

It wasn't yet five in the morning, but most of the lights in the neighborhood blazed brightly. The residents of this ordinarily quiet burb were no doubt awakened by either the shooting or the noisy law enforcement response.

McAfee popped the trunk of his car and removed a sketch pad, some latex gloves, and booties. He returned home after leaving Emily's to change his clothes and swap his personal vehicle for the department-issued Chevy Impala. He closed the trunk and headed toward the cluster of patrol cars.

There were no sidewalks in this neighborhood. That's the way it was in much of the valley—the area comprised of the city of Spokane Valley, Millwood, and portions of unincorporated Spokane County. McAfee imagined that the rural communities that initially sprang up in the shadow of the more formal city of Spokane did so with a laissez-faire attitude. This resulted in streets without sidewalks and roads that often wound haphazardly about.

A late '80s blue Saab was parked in front of the house. It was maintained exceptionally well but not to the exquisite tastes that a car show might demand.

Two lines of yellow POLICE—DO NOT CROSS tape surrounded the target house. The first was at the edge of the property and designated the outer perimeter. The second was back at the garage and marked the inner.

The home was a single-level rancher painted white with red accents. The lights were on inside. McAfee could see through the living room window that a woman stood crying while a female deputy stood by.

"Look who it is." Sergeant Irvin Lee waited behind the first line of yellow tape and absently tugged at his mustache. He wore the department's tan and green uniform. A lanky man with a balding head, Lee looked the type who might have been cast as a villain in a Saturday morning kid's show. "Heard you had dinner with the mayor last night."

McAfee glanced around. "Is Chambers here?"

"He's already inside." Lee jerked a thumb over his shoulder. "Speaking for the residents of Spokane Valley, we'd like to know what you spoke with our community leader about."

McAfee ducked under the yellow tape and headed toward the rear of the property.

"No comment?" Lee walked beside the detective. "Because of you, the sheriff and the mayor are still sparring over the annual pay increases in the new policing contract."

"That's not what they're arguing about."

"Is that inside information?" Lee excitedly hopped once. "Did your girlfriend's father ask your opinion over hors d'oeuvres?" The sergeant pronounced it 'whores-da-fors.'

"No."

"So, it was a dessert topic, then?"

McAfee stopped. "Give it a rest, Irv."

The sergeant chuckled. "If you can't take the heat, get out of the mayor's daughter."

"Crude."

"Hey, you're the one dating an underaged girl. Not me."

Emily was twenty-two, but this was a topic that many in the department had razzed him about since his relationship came to light. And since Emily's father once shouted his feelings during a public meeting with the sheriff, everyone else seemed emboldened to make their comments known to McAfee.

Arguing with the sergeant about anything related to Emily was a losing battle. McAfee turned and continued to his destination.

"So, it's true?" Lee asked, hurrying to catch up. "You had dinner with the mayor last night?"

"It's none of your business."

"I'm a valley resident. It's certainly my business."

McAfee walked along the driveway. It could barely be called that. It was simply two strips of decaying concrete that ran from the street to the detached garage. The rest of the driveway was made up of compacted dirt. This type of set-up would get muddy during a Pacific Northwest winter and spring, but the concrete would allow a vehicle to traverse it without sinking in.

Several classic cars were parked in the driveway—an impeccable BMW, a shiny gray Mercedes, and a beautiful gold Oldsmobile that stood next to the garage. McAfee stopped to study the vehicles, and Sergeant Lee bumped into him.

"Well?" Lee asked. "Have you nothing to say?"

"Has anyone run the plates?"

"We're not incompetent, Shane. It's in the CAD report. The homeowner's name is Ahmet Dogan." He pointed to the Olds. "That's his. What happened at dinner?"

McAfee approached a younger deputy who stood at the next line of yellow caution tape. The man held a clipboard that contained an entry log. Anyone who entered the inner perimeter would be recorded. The detective nodded once at the deputy, then slipped under the tape. The deputy clicked the pen he held and turned his attention to the log.

The sergeant stayed on the other side of the tape. "This isn't done," Lee said.

McAfee glanced back. "With you, Irv, nothing ever is."

The sergeant's eyes widened, and his mouth popped open. "What's that supposed to mean?"

Chapter 2

McAfee stepped around the side of the garage to the open man-door. He studied the jamb—there didn't seem to be any forced entry. The door had an inlaid window with white vinyl lettering applied to it—*The Shisha Room.* McAfee stared at the words for a moment. He wondered who or what *Shisha* was. He jotted the word in the corner of his sketchpad so he would remember to look it up later.

Inside the garage were five bodies—six if he counted Detective Tim Chambers—but McAfee ignored them. It was the room he wanted to understand. The garage had been modified to become a living space.

Large swaths of lightweight fabric drooped from the ceiling. Heavy, colorful tapestries lined the walls. The concrete floors were covered with several large rugs.

A sizeable U-shaped couch took up most of the room. Its legs had been removed, so it rested directly on the floor. Vibrant pillows of various sizes were scattered about.

A short wooden table sat in the middle of the room. Its centerpiece was a large hookah—a glass device with five long hoses used for smoking. Each line appeared to be wrapped in a fabric, and the handles were made of polished wood. Scattered around the hookah were various glass tumblers of liquid, cell phones, wallets, and car keys.

A stereo rack stood against the east wall, which was the garage's roll-up door. A large drape hung before it, likely blocking any winter or spring chill. Next to the stereo was a white half-sized refrigerator and a small wooden shelf that held liquors. Two bottles—Grey Goose vodka and

Maker's Mark whiskey—were opened and sitting on the top.

McAfee's gaze traveled toward the ceiling. The garage door opener was gone, as were the metal rails; the large door was permanently affixed into place.

"What a setup," McAfee said.

Detective Tim Chambers stood near the refrigerator. He was about McAfee's height but was a few pounds heavier. He wore a green windbreaker, black jeans, and light blue booties over his shoes. His hands were tucked into his pants pockets. He grunted in reply to McAfee's appreciation of the room.

"You don't like it?"

"It's simple." Chambers took several steps forward and sniffed.

"Smell something?" McAfee lifted his nose and hunted for a smell.

Chambers cocked his head. "Not marijuana."

McAfee tucked the sketchpad into an armpit, then slipped the booties over his shoes. Before he stepped into the room, he visually inspected the nearby floor to make sure he wouldn't step onto any piece of evidence. He carefully moved into the garage and immediately noticed the aroma that Chambers must have been trying to decipher. "Tobacco."

"There's something different in the smell. It's not like cigarette tobacco." He looked over his shoulder. "It reminds me of something my grandfather smoked in his pipe."

McAfee sniffed again and tried to pick up the subtleties. "I'm not sensing it." He motioned toward the hookah. "I've never known anyone to smoke anything but weed from those."

Chambers turned his dark, examining eyes toward McAfee. "What do you see?"

It was then that McAfee paid attention to the bodies. There were five of them—all men who seemed to be in their forties and fifties. The group was a mix of races. Two seemed to be of Middle Eastern descent, two were black, and one was white. They were all dressed nicely in collared shirts, slacks, and dress shoes.

McAfee thought about the vehicles out front. They were classics and kept in excellent shape. What kind of men owned them? Judging by their ages and clothing, were they successful types? Or were they only men who liked to congregate over the shared interests of old cars, smoking tobacco, and a late-night rendezvous?

Most of the men had been shot twice in their torsos. Only one had been hit more than two times. McAfee's gaze went beyond the men to the tapestries that hung on the walls. It appeared that a couple of rounds might have gone through the men and pierced the rugs.

McAfee's scan continued to the floor. An idea occurred to him then, and he checked behind himself. When he was confident he couldn't find what he was looking for, he eyed Chambers, "No brass."

"I noticed that, too. Maybe the shooter took the time to pick up all expelled shell casings."

McAfee raised an eyebrow.

"It's a possibility," Chambers said, "and one that must be considered."

He took the time to contemplate it then. After a shooter killed five men, it would take a special type of control to delay fleeing to pick up expired casings.

"So, no brass…" Chambers prompted.

"Probably means a revolver was used."

Chambers motioned toward the bodies. "I've counted twelve rounds—maybe there are some I can't see, but let's assume twelve. Two rounds for each victim on the outside of the ring. The victim in the middle of the horseshoe appears to have gotten four."

"So two revolvers with six rounds in each." McAfee extended his arms—the notepad in one hand, his pen in the other—and mimed holding two guns. "He fired until he went dry."

"Or two shooters," Chambers said. He pointed his left hand.

McAfee lowered the sketchpad but kept his pen extended.

The two detectives stood silently next to each other. Both stared down the length of their own arm as they slowly moved toward the tan-skinned man in the middle of the U-shaped couch.

"Two shooters," McAfee said. "Maybe."

"Each shooter starts with the man closest to them, fires two rounds before moving on to the next guy. Bang-bang, bang-bang, boom-boom. Or perhaps, each shooter fired a single round into each victim until they got to the unlucky man in the middle, double-tapped him, and then shot the guys on the outside once more. Bang, bang, boom-boom, bang, bang. Either way, that's likely why the man in the middle was hit four times."

McAfee shrugged. "I think it's a leap to say two shooters, so let's put a pin in it. We'll come back to it later."

Chambers pulled a pair of blue latex gloves from his jacket pocket. He blew into one and inflated it like a small balloon before tugging it on. He repeated the action for the other. Chambers then reached around the hookah to pick up the wallet nearest the victim, who had been hit four times. It was a thick leather bifold. Chambers flipped it open and read the driver's license. "Ahmet Dogan."

"The homeowner," McAfee said. "Is that his wife inside?"

"She's the one who called it in." Chambers cocked his head as if thinking. When he recalled something, he looked to McAfee. "Pembe Dogan."

"You talked with her?"

"Briefly when I first arrived. She was upset, so I didn't get much from her."

"If she saw this scene, I understand."

Chambers fingered the wallet's contents. "She consented to a search of the entire premises, so we've covered our bases. I figured we'd talk with her after we get done here." He flashed the wallet to McAfee. "No cash, only credit cards, and a driver's license."

"All right."

"A question springs to mind—"

"Just one?"

Chambers didn't answer. Instead, he balanced the wallet at the edge of his notepad while he copied the driver's license information. When he finished, he looked up.

"Your question?" McAfee said.

"Right." Chambers flipped the bifold closed. "Was Ahmet shot multiple times because he was the odd man out or because he was the target?"

"Good question."

"Thank you." Chambers returned the wallet from where he picked it up. He straightened, reconsidered the wallet, then bent over and tweaked its position slightly.

"Doesn't look like any of the men were armed," McAfee said.

"Maybe we'll find guns underneath them when we move the bodies."

McAfee opened his sketchpad. He eyed the room before lightly drawing in the pieces of furniture. Afterward, he noted the bodies—they were barely a step above stick figures. It wasn't a fantastic representation of the scene, but it would help him later in recreating the moment for his report. The evidence technicians would come in soon and process the scene. That would include photographing and recording what they saw. However, McAfee needed to do everything he could to preserve his own perspective.

Chambers leaned over the table. His right hand waved back and forth while his fingers wriggled as if he were playing the piano.

"Conducting a séance?" McAfee asked.

"They cleaned out their pockets."

McAfee lowered his sketch pad and stepped forward. In front of every man was something that held their money. It was either a wallet, a money clip, or even a simple rubber band around credit cards. There were also car keys, packets of gum, condom packets, cigarette packs, and a vape pen.

"No cash," McAfee said, "but the killers left the credit cards behind."

"Not many people carry cash anymore. Maybe the killers were after something else." Chambers pointed at the body of the white man who sat next to Ahmet Dogan. He wore a black silk shirt with white stripes and black slacks. "He doesn't have any keys."

"Maybe the guy came with someone."

Chambers lifted an eyebrow. He paused for a moment as if calculating something. "That's a fair assumption, but where does he live? Doesn't he need a set of keys to get inside his home?" Chambers grabbed the money clip from in front of the man. He opened it and slid a driver's license from inside a collection of credit cards. "Alexei Sidorov. Huh."

"That mean something?"

"You've never heard the name?"

McAfee shook his head. "Why should I? Have you?"

"There was a Russian journalist by the same name. If I remember correctly, he was killed by an organized crime syndicate sometime in the early 2000s."

"I'm sure you do, but how would you know that?"

Chambers shrugged. "I read."

"I read, too." McAfee felt weirdly defensive by the other detective's observation.

"Maybe we read different things."

"Obviously." McAfee rolled his eyes before returning his attention to his sketchpad. He noted Sidorov's position on his drawing

When Chambers finished copying Sidorov's info into his notebook, he flipped through the cards in the man's money clip. "Visa, MasterCard, and Costco. Even a library card."

"So he's a reader, too," McAfee said.

Chamber snapped the clip into place. He carefully set the bundle back from where he got it. "If there was money, would Sidorov have taken the time to resecure the clip?"

For the next twenty minutes, the two detectives went through the personal items set on the table to identify the other three men. When they finished, McAfee said, "Let me run this back to make sure we got it right."

Chambers waited.

Had another detective been assigned the case with him, they might have argued to hurry McAfee along. They might even have contended that the crime scene technicians would more than adequately cover their asses with video and photographs. However, Tim Chambers was not like other detectives. He was known for his fastidious nature. This was a case where McAfee was happy to have been assigned to him.

McAfee pointed at the black male nearest them on the left. "Ricky Scherff. Forty-one."

Chambers consulted his notebook. "Confirmed."

"Next to him is DeAndre Fuller, forty-two." Fuller was also a black male.

Chambers nodded. "Correct."

The man in the middle of the U-shaped couch was next. "Ahmet Dogan. Fifty-one years." McAfee looked up from his notes. "He owns that gold Oldsmobile out front."

Chambers lifted an eyebrow.

"Sergeant Lee told me." McAfee's attention returned to his sketchpad. He pointed to the white male sitting next to Ahmet. "Sidorov—forty-nine. Sitting next to him is Hasim Arap—fifty-two."

Chambers closed his notebook. "Looks like we're on the same page. Ready for the technicians?"

McAfee closed his sketchpad. "You go ahead and get them started."

"Something wrong?"

"No."

"Are you sure?"

McAfee nodded. "I'm good."

Chambers didn't leave, though. He patiently waited for McAfee to say something.

Reluctantly, McAfee said, "Let's go."

"Excellent." Chambers moved toward the door.

***

Shane McAfee pulled his shoulders back and held his head high as he walked toward the large white van emblazoned with *Spokane County Sheriff Forensic Unit*. He slowed slightly and let Chambers lead the way.

Geri Utley stood next to the van while a group of five deputies gathered around her. She smiled politely as they laughed and joked. Geri was an attractive woman with long, blond hair that was now pulled back and hidden under a blue baseball hat. She wore a dark blue windbreaker and faded jeans. Before entering the home, she'd slip into a hazmat suit to reduce further contamination of the scene.

The remaining evidence technicians gathered amongst themselves at the back of the van and watched the flirting deputies with a mixture of hostility and mockery. They'd obviously seen this ritual before.

Chambers stepped through the group and said to Geri, "We're ready for your team."

She nodded before flicking her gaze over the detective's shoulder to McAfee. Her polite smile melted. "We'll get on it," she said flatly. Geri spun on her heel and walked toward the other technicians.

Chambers faced McAfee and stared questioningly at him.

"It's a long story," McAfee said.

"I see that. Care to elaborate?"

"No."

McAfee turned to search for Sergeant Lee. He found the man standing next to Lieutenant Dina Enzler. McAfee started in their direction, but Chambers grabbed his arm.

"Hold on," he said. "Where are you going?"

"To ask about the neighborhood canvassing." McAfee's gaze returned to the group of five deputies. Their attention remained on Geri even as they laughed amongst themselves. "There're a lot of guys standing around when they should be knocking on doors."

Chambers lowered his voice. "I've been thinking."

McAfee's gaze shifted to the other detective. "About?"

"What we saw in there."

"And?"

"Maybe it was a hit."

McAfee frowned. "You don't know that."

"I understand, but the evidence supports the theory."

He didn't want to argue with Chambers. Most detectives—cops, for that matter—could be stubborn when they believed something. Hell, they could be stubborn most of the time. Chambers was no different when it came to that trait. However, it seemed too early in an investigation to make such a bold claim. "We should talk with Ahmet's wife."

"I agree we should," Chambers said, "but right now, we both believe two shooters were involved—correct?"

McAfee looked away. He wasn't entirely convinced. It could still be one killer with two revolvers. Hell, the killer could have used an automatic and stopped to pick up the brass shell casings. The latter scenario was improbable, but that didn't make it impossible.

The laughing and leering continued from the nearby deputies, and it frustrated McAfee. He suspected there were things they could be doing to help the investigation.

And if he was wrong, then they should leave and quit muddying up his crime scene.

He returned his attention to Chambers, who watched him expectantly. "No brass on the floor likely means revolvers were used—I'll agree. But two shooters—I don't know."

"Due to the accuracy of the fired rounds—" Chambers tapped a single finger into his palm. "—and the position of the bodies, the victims were surprised at the shooters' arrival and the level of violence they brought."

"So you think the killers knew about The Shisha Room before tonight?"

"I do—one hundred percent. They weren't guests, or the room arrangement would have been different. There would have been more glasses on the coffee table. Understand?"

McAfee did.

"The killers arrived with violence as a mission or at least a consideration." Chambers pointed at the garage. "Those victims didn't have time to move when the shooting started. That's why I'm sticking to two shooters—at least."

"Now you're thinking that there's more?" McAfee asked.

"If those five men moved all at once, they could have overpowered one man. Or at least forced him to miss some shots. Or maybe one or more of them could have gotten away, but it doesn't look like anyone moved. It also doesn't look like any shots went awry. Perhaps I'm wrong. The techs will tell us soon enough."

McAfee remained silent. This was a side of Chambers he hadn't seen before. He thought the man to be meticulous, to hesitate about going out on a limb. Yet here he was, claiming this might be a hit and that the two shooters—or more—had some prior knowledge of The Shisha Room.

Chambers continued. "The victims rising to fight would be less likely with two shooters, especially considering how the room was laid out. The U-shaped couch and the table in the middle would slow their reaction time."

McAfee scratched his cheek and studied the other detective.

Chambers glanced around. His tone now took on a conspiratorial tone. "One shooter with two guns only works in the movies. Therefore, two shooters entered the room and controlled it from the onset."

"Why are you whispering?"

"I don't want our brainstorming to be overheard."

"You're brainstorming. I'm listening."

Chambers waved dismissively. "I don't want the others to think we're not unified."

McAfee didn't give a damn what the others thought. He showed that daily by maintaining his relationship with Emily. He believed Chambers to be like him—that he didn't care about the opinions of the department. The man was an odd duck. While most of the department was made up of alpha-male meat-eaters, Tim Chambers was the rarity—a quiet, thinking man who preferred books over guns.

"Screw them," McAfee said. "Who cares what they think?"

Chambers shook his head. "In most things, I would agree. But in a case of this magnitude, we need them to believe we're on top of this. They haven't seen what we have. If they start forming opinions without complete knowledge, they'll taint their efforts, drag their feet."

McAfee eyed the snickering deputies.

Chambers waggled a finger between himself and McAfee. "Only you and I matter at this moment. We need a unified front. The sergeant and the lieutenant will want to know what we think. We need to present a concise picture."

"Two killers," McAfee said.

"I need you to believe it. Don't let me bully you."

McAfee looked toward the garage. His thoughts drifted back to its door. There wasn't any forced entry. Perhaps Ahmet Dogan left it unlocked. Why wouldn't he? If the man constructed a hookah lounge for him and his friends to enjoy, he wouldn't secure it while they were inside.

"The shooters didn't force their way in," McAfee said. "Whoever they are, they just walked in."

Chambers nodded.

"It was a robbery," McAfee said emphatically, "since the killers made the victims empty their pockets."

"Okay, but that doesn't rule out the hit. The two aren't mutually exclusive."

"A robbery that turned into a mass killing? Or a hit with a robbery kicker?"

Chambers bobbled his head. "We still don't know if there was any cash taken. The only thing we suspect missing is Alexei Sidorov's keys."

"What if that was the killers' intent all along, and these killings were an accident."

"Five murders are accidental?"

McAfee waved off the question. "You know what I mean. Things went bad. For whatever reason, the killers originally came here to steal Sidorov's keys."

Chambers shook his head. "Or Sidorov's keys were only an opportunity, and murder was the real mission." He looked over McAfee's shoulder. "They're coming."

"Who?" McAfee turned to see the sergeant and lieutenant approaching.

"I'm going to talk with the wife." Chambers patted McAfee's shoulder. "Brief them on what we know."

"Wait." McAfee spun to say something further, but the other detective was already moving away.

"Where's he going?" Sergeant Lee asked.

McAfee turned around once more. "To interview the complainant."

Lieutenant Dina Enzler studied McAfee. She was in her late forties with short gray hair and a steely stare. "Give us something, Shane, before the press gets a whiff."

McAfee inhaled deeply. "It looks like it could be a robbery that went bad."

"But you're thinking something else."

Shane pursed his lips before speaking. "It might have been a hit."

Enzler furrowed her brow. "Like a mob assassination?"

"It's a possibility."

The lieutenant seemed perplexed. "It's the valley, for Christ's sake. Who was the target?"

McAfee shrugged. "We don't know. The homeowner, maybe. He was shot a couple more times than the others."

"What'd he ever do to anyone?" Enzler asked.

"Wait a minute," Sergeant Lee said. "You said it's a possibility. So you're not even sure?"

McAfee turned his palms upward. "What can I say, Irv?"

Lee rolled his eyes and then glanced toward the lieutenant. "You see what I'm dealing with here?"

She held up a hand. "Run it down, Shane. I know it's early in the process but give me what you've got."

Chapter 3

When Shane McAfee entered the house, he stopped at the edge of the living room.

Pembe Dogan sat on the edge of the couch with her head in her hands. She wore full-length cream-colored pajamas that were printed with little elephants. Her shoulder-length dark hair was tousled. "Who could do such a thing?" she asked through her long fingers. Her voice was thick with an accent.

Two burgundy wingback chairs sat across from the couch. A large multi-colored rug lay on the hardwood floor. Various portraits hung on the walls. They were vivid paintings of people that McAfee suspected were of Middle Eastern descent. No photographs hung on the walls, nor were any displayed on the end tables.

Detective Chambers stood near one of the wingback chairs. He held his spiral notebook and looked up when McAfee entered the room. Chambers didn't acknowledge him.

Deputy Serena Torres sat on the couch next to Pembe. McAfee caught her eye and motioned with his head. She stood and moved toward the edge of the living room.

"Does your husband have any enemies?" Chambers asked.

"No," Pembe said. Her fingers slid into her hair and balled into fists. "No, no, no!"

McAfee leaned toward the deputy's ear. He whispered, "Has a chaplain been called?"

Torres softly replied, "One responded, but the wife turned them away."

"Where was I?"

The deputy shrugged. "Probably inside the garage. She asked me to stay with her."

McAfee nodded. "Thank you."

He missed the question Chambers asked but heard Pembe's answer.

"My husband owns a bar."

Torres returned to her position on the couch. Pembe didn't look at her when she settled in.

Chambers held his pen over his notepad. "Which bar?"

"The Kedi." Pembe's hands released her hair and returned to holding her face.

McAfee glanced at Chambers. The other detective didn't look his way but shook his head as he jotted the establishment's name into his notebook. Neither man had heard of the bar.

"Where's it at?" Chambers asked.

"On Trent," Pembe said.

McAfee struggled to place the establishment. He'd have to research it when he returned to the department.

Chambers looked up from his notepad. "Did you know the men Ahmet was with?"

Pembe's fingers spread apart, and she glared at the detective. "I told the second policeman the same as the first." Her hands dropped into her lap. "And I will tell you the same—no, I do not know those men." She faced Torres. "Do you people even talk to each other?"

The deputy nodded. "Yes, ma'am. We do, but things are moving quickly."

Chambers consulted his notebook. "Were you asleep when you heard the shooting?"

"Of course I was asleep," Pembe said curtly. "I already told the first officer that."

Deputy Torres lightly touched Pembe's shoulder. "He's only trying to understand."

Pembe nodded several times. "Yes, I was sleeping. What else would I be doing? It was so late."

"But your husband was still awake."

The longer the deputy's hand remained on Pembe's shoulder, the more her expression softened. Finally, the woman inhaled deeply before letting the breath out in a long, slow exhale.

"Yes," Pembe said. "My husband was still awake."

"Did he do that sort of thing often?"

"What sort of thing?" Pembe's eyes narrowed, but her voice remained calm. "Get murdered?"

Torres didn't say anything, but she stiffened. Her hand remained on Pembe's shoulder.

Chambers averted his eyes by consulting his notepad. "No, ma'am. Did he stay out late in the garage smoking tobacco with his friends?"

"He stayed out late because that was his business. He would sometimes invite people to smoke after the bar closed. It is what he did."

"And you were okay with that?"

"I did not tell my husband what he could and could not do." Pembe stood and pointed at the garage. "And those men were not his friends."

Torres glanced at McAfee, but he shook his head and discreetly waved his hand. He wanted Pembe's emotions to run free. Some investigators preferred to have a victim calm and under control. McAfee would rather have them upset. Victims were less likely to hold back something important if they were irate and spewing their feelings.

Chambers asked, "How can you be sure those men weren't his friends?"

Pembe moved to the windows. Her finger tapped the glass. "I do not know those cars."

"Did you see anyone leaving the garage?"

"No." Pembe spun around. "No one was there except—"

The bodies, McAfee thought.

She covered her mouth and closed her eyes. Chambers considered his notes.

McAfee asked, "Did you see or hear a car drive away?"

Pembe opened her eyes. "No," she said softly.

"Are you sure?"

Anger flashed over Pembe's face. "Am I sure?"

McAfee didn't look away.

"No, Detective, I am not sure. Everything happened so fast. It was a blur. The bangs— And before you ask, I do not know how many there were or when I realized what they were. I do not think I even thought they were real at first. Then suddenly, I am at the garage door looking inside, and it is—" Pembe fought back the tears. "It is—"

McAfee's gaze slid to the other detective.

Chambers asked. "Did you step inside the garage?"

"Yes." Her lip trembled. "How do you think I knew my husband was dead?" She looked pleadingly at Torres. "I already told the others this. Why do these men not talk to each other?"

The deputy nodded knowingly. "They need to make sure they understand everything. This is important."

Chambers tapped his notepad. "Did any of the other men look familiar?"

It wasn't a stupid question. Pembe might have entered the garage, seen her husband had been murdered, then fled to the comfort and safety of her home. She might not have consciously paid attention to the other men. The mind would play tricks during critical incidents, especially if a person was not used to being in them.

Pembe cocked her head. "Are you asking if I stood there long enough to wonder who those other men were?" Her voice rose, and her face reddened. "No, Detective, I could not care for one moment about those other men. My husband was dead—*is* dead."

McAfee cleared his throat, and Pembe's attention shifted to him. "How long were you and your husband married?"

"Excuse me?" Her face pinched. "Why does that matter?"

"I'm wondering what kind of man your husband was."

Pembe eyed Deputy Torres, who stared impassively back at her. "My husband," she said as her gaze slowly returned to McAfee, "was a good provider." They were carefully chosen words. Before McAfee could ask his next question, Pembe offered, "We have been married for twenty-seven years. You asked that question, or did you forget?"

"I didn't forget." He pointed at one of the wingback chairs across from her. "May I sit?"

She nodded.

McAfee sat on the edge of the chair. He leaned forward and rested his elbows on his thighs. "Did you work at the bar?"

Pembe shook her head.

"I'm sorry. I forgot its name. What's it called?" McAfee remembered the bar's name, but he wanted her to answer a simple question so they could develop a back-and-forth rhythm.

"The Kedi. It means cat."

"Is that significant?" McAfee asked.

Pembe shrugged. "They are clean animals. Our parents, our ancestors, put a certain value on them."

"What value?"

The suspicion returned to her eyes. "We're Muslim if that's what you're asking."

McAfee glanced to Chambers, who motioned for him to continue. He eyed Pembe. "I wasn't asking, but since you brought it up—"

"I didn't."

"Have you had any trouble?"

"Because of our heritage?" She sniffed. "This is Spokane, Detective. We are Turkish. Do you know how many people have accused us of being terrorists?"

"I do not."

"Many, let me assure you. It's gotten less since the attack on our country, but those early days were scary."

He lifted an eyebrow after she uttered the words "our country."

"You're a U.S. citizen?" he asked.

"Why wouldn't I be?" She waved away any response McAfee could attempt. "Since 1999." Tears streamed down her cheeks now. "Both Ahmet and I came for a better life."

"Why did you pick here?"

"America?"

"Spokane Valley." They were technically in Millwood, but everyone referred to the area east of Spokane as the valley.

She angrily wiped her eyes. "Is this important?"

"We don't know what's important at this time."

Pembe studied her hands. "We did not start here. We began in Seattle." She looked up. "It was not to our liking."

"If you're Muslim—"

"I just told you we are." Her expression hardened.

McAfee paused. "What I'm asking is—"

She interrupted. "Why did my husband open a bar?"

He nodded.

Pembe's jaw tightened. "Are you a religious man?"

"No."

Her gaze flicked to Chambers, and he shook his head. When Pembe looked at Torres, she nodded. "Yes, ma'am."

"All religions have their laws," Pembe said. "Only the most ardent live within them."

"But Islam—"

Pembe dismissed McAfee's interruption. "You know nothing about our laws, Detective. Please do not try to pretend. Christians lie, cheat, and murder in violation of their laws, do they not?"

"Some do."

"And the Jews do as well."

"I guess."

"Do not guess. They do. They are like us—not perfect. Nobody is."

McAfee didn't want to get into a theological debate because he would lose. He cared as much about religion as he did politics. "Did Ahmet open the bar immediately after you moved here?"

Pembe's expression relaxed. "Not right away, no. He worked in many bars first. He learned how to bartend and manage the operations. We saved our money, and then he opened The Kedi."

"Did you help get the bar ready?"

She nodded. "But only until it opened. The business was his dream. Not mine."

"Where do you work?"

Pembe looked down at her hands again. "I do not work."

McAfee remained silent. It seemed as if Pembe wanted to say something further. Maybe she'd grown reluctant to talk after the interchange about her religion. Perhaps she held something back due to a personal conflict with her husband. Whatever it was, McAfee waited and studied her.

Chambers stood mum. Silence was an effective tool for an investigator. Often it would work on a suspect or victim and lead them to say something—anything—to fill the void.

Deputy Torres quickly grew uncomfortable with the quiet, though. She shifted her sitting position, which caused her leather duty belt to creak and the couch to ripple. McAfee's eyes met hers, and she stopped moving.

Finally, Pembe said, "Ahmet was a good provider. Will there be anything else?"

***

McAfee stepped onto the front steps and waited while Chambers pulled the door shut behind him. His gaze landed on the sheriff department's command van—a boxy RV that could just as easily be found at a campground. It was parked in the middle of the street, right behind the evidence techs. The command van's official purpose was to help coordinate efforts during critical incidents. In the eyes of line-level deputies, though, the vehicle was to make the administration comfortable while the real work was done outside.

Barricades stood at the opposite ends of Willow Road and were monitored by senior volunteers.

McAfee's attention dropped to the two cars parked in front of Ahmet Dogan's house. His gaze drifted to those vehicles parked in the driveway.

"What are you looking at?" Chambers asked.

"Let's figure out who owned which car."

"One of the deputies ran the plates, so it should go quickly." Chambers stepped by McAfee and started down the stairs. He motioned toward a young male deputy that McAfee knew only as Higbee. He couldn't remember the guy's first name.

While Chambers and Higbee chatted, McAfee approached the cars in the driveway. There were three of them.

The first was a white BMW 320is with spoked rims and shiny black tires. Next was a gray Mercedes 300SD. And the final car was a gold Oldsmobile Cutlass with golden rims and white-walled tires. All three cars appeared to be models from the 1980s. They seemed to be meticulously kept, and none had been modified in any way.

Chambers and Higbee approached.

Higbee looked like countless deputies in the department. Mildly handsome, broad-shouldered, and white. McAfee imagined that others might have lumped him and Chambers into that category as well.

The deputy consulted his notepad and pointed at the BMW. "The registered owner is DeAndre Fuller." His finger moved to the Mercedes. "Hasim Arap." He looked up. "And the Olds belongs to—"

"Ahmet Dogan," McAfee said.

Higbee nodded.

"Was the wife listed on the registration?" Chambers asked.

"Just the husband."

McAfee and Chambers exchanged a glance. It wasn't a cultural comment but rather a procedural acknowledgment. They wanted to search Ahmet's car, but without the wife listed, they would need to write a search warrant.

Chambers said to Higbee, "Do me a favor. Contact dispatch and ask them to check on the legal owner of the house."

The deputy nodded.

"Now, for the cars on the street." Chambers walked away.

Higbee hurried to keep up, and McAfee followed.

When the three of them made it to the road, the first car they encountered was the blue Saab 900.

"That belonged to Ricky Scherff," Higbee said.

"What about that one?" Chambers pointed to a late model Honda Accord that sat at the edge of the property. Compared to the four classic cars they just looked at, it seemed like an orange in a barrel of apples. Higbee motioned toward it. "That one is also registered to Ahmet Dogan."

Chambers eyed McAfee. "The daily driver?"

"Or the wife's car."

"She wasn't listed on the registration," Higbee said.

McAfee reconsidered the cars and the names that the deputy listed. "Alexei Sidorov's car is missing."

Chambers said, "That explains the keys."

"Assuming he drove," McAfee said. "But if he did—" He pointed to the area between Ricky Scherff's Saab and Ahmet Dogan's Honda. "—he might have parked there. Don't you think?"

"Sidorov?" Higbee asked.

"One of the victims in the garage." Chambers flipped open his notebook and quickly jotted something. He ripped out a page and handed it to Higbee. "That's Sidorov's information. Pull an AVR for him."

Higbee nodded and walked off to request an All Vehicles Registered report.

"Don't forget the legal owner of the house," Chambers called.

The deputy raised a hand in acknowledgment.

"What's the plan?" McAfee asked.

"We need warrants to search the cars. We should probably write one for the house, too."

McAfee nodded. "I want to see the bar—not a priority but sometime."

"We'll get a warrant for there, too." Chambers nodded as if thinking to himself. "Better safe than sorry. We should check with Pembe to see if anyone besides Ahmet has access to it. If there are employees, we need to notify them or post a deputy, so no one goes in before us."

"And we need to notify the families of the victims."

"We're going to need help." Chambers eyed the command vehicle.

"You do the talking on this one. You stiffed me the last time around. What was up with that, anyway?"

Chambers shook his head. "It was nothing." He pulled his shoulders back and defiantly lifted his chin—a man preparing to walk into the boxing ring. "I guess it's my turn."

***

Detective Tim Chambers knocked on the boxy RV's side door. McAfee stood just behind him. He was more than happy to let the other detective lead the conversation, but he still wanted to know what was going on in the man's life. He never knew Chambers to shy away from any discussion, let alone one with the brass.

Voices could be heard from inside the vehicle before the door popped open. Sergeant Lee stuck his bald head out. "Yeah?"

"We need additional resources," Chambers said flatly.

Lee's lip curled before calling over his shoulder. "Lieutenant." He pushed the door further open and stepped out of the RV.

Lieutenant Enzler appeared in the doorway with a cup of Starbucks coffee. McAfee wondered who had brought the drink to her. She raised an eyebrow in a questioning manner.

"They need more men," Lee said.

Enzler frowned at Lee's choice of words before turning her attention to Chambers.

Chambers seemed emboldened now. He glanced back at McAfee before saying, "We need help with the search warrants."

"Why can't one of you go back and write them?"

"I'd be happy to do that, ma'am, but we need warrants for the vehicles, the house, the garage, and Mr. Dogan's bar." Chambers ticked each item off on his fingers. "We're going to tie up a lot of deputies securing this scene until that's done. Plus—"

Enzler held up a hand to interrupt him. "I thought the homeowner consented to us searching the house and garage."

"She did," Chambers said.

"Well, ask her for consent to search her cars. That'll save a warrant, right?"

"The cars are only registered in the husband's name. We suspect that the house and business are recorded in that manner, too."

Enzler grunted her disapproval. She leaned a shoulder against the door's frame.

Washington was a community property state, but no one wanted to rely on that argument if a defense attorney moved to suppress evidence from an improper search.

Chambers continued. "It's in our best interest to create the extra paper."

"Just what we don't need," Sergeant Lee said, "a loophole some scumbag lawyer can squirm a client through."

The lieutenant's lips twisted as she thought. "And due to the different parties involved, one blanket warrant will not work."

"No, ma'am." Chambers shook his head. "Also, we want a unit to secure Alexei Sidorov's place of residence." He opened his notebook. McAfee looked over the detective's shoulder to watch him copy Sidorov's address to a new page.

"Who's this guy?" the lieutenant asked. "And how's he figure into it?"

"Sidorov is one of the victims and—"

Enzler interrupted Chambers. "You're not asking me to secure every victim's home, are you?"

"No, ma'am." Chambers ripped off the page from his notebook and handed it to Enzler. "We'll contact the victim's families when we break the scene. However, Sidorov's car keys are missing. We suspect his car was taken."

"Which likely means they have his house keys," McAfee said.

Sergeant Lee's eyes narrowed. "She knows what it means, McAfee."

Enzler cleared her throat. "I'll contact the DA's office and see if they can lend an attorney to help with the warrants. Maybe speed things along." She turned to the sergeant. "Get a deputy to secure Sidorov's home."

Lee frowned. "Yes, ma'am." He sounded disappointed.

Chambers said, "We also need the victims' histories run."

"You can't do that back at the station?" the sergeant asked.

"We're going to be on scene for some time." Chambers glanced back at McAfee before continuing. "We want to know if any of the victims had criminal backgrounds, gang affiliations, the usual. That'll give us a head start on a motive and where to start looking."

"Fine," Enzler said. She motioned toward Lee. "Assign someone to that task."

The sergeant's frown deepened. "Yes, ma'am."

Both McAfee and Chambers nodded their thanks.

Enzler turned and disappeared into the RV.

Sergeant Lee asked, "Anything else?"

"Something to eat would be nice," Chambers said, "since we've missed breakfast."

"Food," Lee muttered.

"And coffee would be great," Chambers added. He looked at McAfee. "You like coffee, don't you?"

"Love it." McAfee fought the urge to smile.

Lee angrily rubbed his mustache. When his thumb and forefinger cleared his mouth, it appeared like he had mashed his lips into a scowl. "Goddamned caterer is what I am." He climbed into the RV and yanked the door closed behind him. It banged but didn't secure. Lee reached out, grabbed the door again, and forcefully shut it.

McAfee smiled now.

"What?" Chambers asked.

"I like when you do the talking."

***

Twenty minutes later, McAfee walked along the shrubbery that lined the front of the house. His head was down, scanning the ground. He hoped to find something that the killers might have dropped or tossed. It was unlikely, but the moment he didn't search for something was the exact moment something *would* appear. He knew that was a simplistic way to look at things, but it suited his personality.

McAfee considered himself a grinder. He was never the smartest guy in school, and it seemed to be that way at the department, too. Tim Chambers could probably claim the title of smartest, but McAfee had tenacity. Grit, his high school football coach called it. He was willing to practice when others weren't. He was willing to gut out uncomfortable moments to reach a satisfying result.

Maybe that's why he put up with outside ridicule of his relationship with a younger woman. Many gave him grief over it, including his parents, her parents, his co-workers, and even the department's administration, albeit unofficially. The fact that her father was the mayor of Spokane Valley exacerbated matters.

He wondered why anyone cared so much. First, none of them was living his life. She was twenty-two, and he was thirty-five, soon to be thirty-six. If the two of them didn't have a problem with their ages, why should anyone else?

Second, the mayor was a position voted by the city council; it was a figurehead role. It wasn't like the strong mayoral form of government that Spokane had. And even if it was, screw them.

McAfee looked up when Chambers said, "Got the histories back on our victims."

He'd been so lost in his thoughts that he hadn't heard the other detective approach. Chambers shuffled several pieces of paper before flicking the stack with his middle finger. McAfee imagined another deputy calling in the names to dispatch and an operator faxing the results back to the command vehicle. It was one of the benefits of having the boxy RV on scene. There weren't many other advantages in McAfee's eyes.

"Hasim Arap had no contacts with law enforcement," Chambers said.

"None?"

"Why's that surprising?"

McAfee looked around. "We're at the scene of a multiple homicide at an after-hours joint. It's not exactly Joe Citizen behavior."

Chambers cocked his head. "This was Ahmet Dogan's hangout. It wasn't an after-hours joint."

"They came here after The Kedi closed. That's the definition of an after-hours joint."

Chambers crossed his arms. "This is a clubhouse. After-hours joints are public places."

"Tomato potato." McAfee spun his hand in a circle. "Get on with the histories."

"That's not how you say it." Chambers moved Hasim Arap's page to the back of the pile. He read from the next document. "Ahmet Dogan is listed multiple times as a—" He abruptly looked up. "It's tomato to-*mah*-to."

"Let it go." McAfee smiled. "Dogan is what?"

Chamber's attention returned to the document. "Ahmet is listed multiple times as a complainant, but those seem attached to his business. Mostly drunk and disorderly complaints."

"Right," McAfee said. "That would make sense. He can't cause trouble himself, or the liquor board would pull his license."

Chambers flipped to the next page. "DeAndre Fuller." He inhaled deeply and looked up. "I guess you could say potato po-*tah*-to."

McAfee shrugged. "I like the way I say it."

"But it's wrong."

"Who says?"

"Everybody. Everybody says you're wrong."

"Well, I think it's right so I'm sticking with it. Tell me about DeAndre."

Chambers cleared his throat. "DeAndre Fuller was a suspect in an assault case more than twenty years ago. No correlating arrest. He's had a handful of traffic citations, a couple of recent domestic disturbance calls where he was listed as the suspect."

McAfee leaned to look at the papers. "But no arrests?"

"No arrests in any of them. All verbal."

"Huh."

Chambers flipped to the final document. "And Ricky Scherff."

McAfee interrupted. "All this talk about tomatoes and potatoes is making me hungry. Is it too late to order a salad?"

He made the comment for two reasons. First, he *was* hungry. Second, tweaking Chambers was fun, and a multiple homicide scene could wear an investigator to a nub if they weren't careful.

"It's too late," Chambers said. "Food is already on the way. You're getting what you're getting. Ricky Scherff—"

"Although if I thought of them as to-*mah*-toes and po-*tah*-toes, I'd rather have clam chowder than a salad. Isn't that strange?"

Chambers waggled the papers in front of McAfee's face. "Ricky Scherff has a fairly clean record."

"Fairly?"

"Scherff was a poor driver." Chambers consulted the paper now. He paused as if he expected McAfee to interrupt him a third time. "Speeding, failing to come to a complete stop, that sort of thing. Nothing rising to criminal, though."

"All right."

Chambers looked at the last paper. "And finally, the winner, Alexei Sidorov." The detective consulted the documents once more. "Sidorov had a lengthy history of receiving stolen property. He was also a known associate of Gary Gaspar."

"I don't know who that is."

"I ran across him while I was in Property Crimes. A real piece of work."

McAfee motioned toward the papers. "Should we talk to this Gaspar?"

"No need. He's dead."

"Recently?"

"About ten years ago. Give or take a year."

McAfee looked toward the garage, then cocked his head. His eyes narrowed.

"What?" Chambers asked.

"Why'd you call the victims out that way?"

"What way?"

"By their race. First, the Middle Eastern guys, then the black guys, then the white guy. Why group them that way?"

Chambers blinked several times, then a nervous smile slowly emerged. "Are you screwing with me?"

"No."

Now, Chambers blanched. "I didn't mean for it to look that way."

McAfee shrugged. "Well, it did."

"It was a numbers thing."

"A numbers thing?"

"Two, two, one." Chambers swallowed and suddenly looked embarrassed. "It seemed better organized to do it that way." He looked away. "But I can see now how it appeared." A twisted smile appeared that did little to hide his uneasiness. "I wouldn't—"

"Yeah. I know."

Chambers folded the papers and walked away.

***

The food arrived shortly after ten. By then, the number of deputies on the crime scene had diminished considerably. Only a few were needed since the evidence team did most of the work.

Members of the press had assembled at the southern barricade. Cameras mounted to tripods pointed in their direction.

The current shift leaders sat inside the temperature-controlled RV along with an undersheriff. Sergeant Lee and Lieutenant Enzler were also in there, but McAfee expected them to depart the scene soon. Their shifts ended a while ago, so they were only collecting overtime pay now.

A delivery driver arrived with several boxes of sandwiches, bags of chips, and canned soft drinks. One of the volunteers—a slightly stooped man McAfee only knew as Delmont—carried the boxes and placed them on the trunk of a volunteer's car. Deputies and evidence technicians headed toward the fare.

McAfee waited for Geri Utley to get her sandwich before he walked over to the food box. Chambers went with him, and both men pulled a sandwich and a bag of potato chips from one of the boxes. They returned to McAfee's car and spread their wrappers on the hood.

A few minutes later, a second delivery driver arrived with a large white paper sack. The name on the bag was from The Max—a higher-end restaurant in Spokane Valley. The driver presented the bag to Delmont, who nodded his thanks.

"You seeing this?" McAfee asked.

Chambers opened his sandwich as Delmont headed for the command van. "What about it?"

"We're out here humping while they're in there sipping tea and getting better grub."

"What did you expect? It's what leaders have done through recorded time." Chambers pulled the sliced tomatoes from his sandwich and flipped them onto the wrapper.

"To-*mah*-to," McAfee said.

Chambers lifted his chin in the direction of the command van. "Those inside rise to a level of power then forget where they came from. It happens generation after generation. Don't be surprised that it's occurring again."

McAfee bit into his sandwich. Through a mouthful, he said, "I hate them."

"I'm sure the feeling is mutual."

The comment surprised McAfee.

Chambers lifted his sandwich in sort of a toast. "Don't worry. They don't like me any better."

McAfee despised being ostracized because of his choices, but he wasn't going to back off them. Chambers didn't make unpopular choices, but he walked to the beat of a different drummer. Knowing that the man might not be in the good graces of the administration made McAfee feel slightly better.

Nearby, the evidence technicians clustered together. They seemed to be a tight-knit group that got along well. Geri Utley stood among her team and smiled as she ate. She didn't look in the direction of the detectives.

"What's the deal with you and Geri?" Chambers asked.

McAfee glanced in her direction once more before biting into his sandwich. "I don't know you well enough."

Chambers exhaled heavily. "Yeah, all right." He turned his attention to his sandwich.

McAfee watched the other detective for a couple of seconds. He thought about asking Chambers why he wasn't curious about Emily, but he left it alone. Why prompt him to inquire if the guy didn't want to know about that relationship? Instead, McAfee asked, "What did you do to get on the wrong side of the administration?"

"I don't know you well enough."

McAfee studied his sandwich. "Yeah, all right," he said, parroting the other detective's earlier comment.

Deputy Higbee strode across the lawn. His brow was furrowed, and his face was red. His arms swung wide to avoid bumping equipment hanging around his waist. He looked like a gunfighter hurrying to stop a fight at the town's saloon. "Your radios are off."

Absently, McAfee touched the gray brick clipped to his belt. "And?"

"That Russian guy—"

"Sidorov," Chambers said.

"That's the one." Higbee snapped his fingers. "The address you gave us was bad. The man doesn't live there anymore."

"I apologize," Chambers said. "It was on his driver's license."

"What about a vehicle?" McAfee asked. "Did you find out if he owns one?"

"We did," Higbee said. "And it's a classic." He waved at the cars in the driveway. "Like those. An '82 Audi Quattro. What do you wanna bet that it looks as cherry?"

"Could these guys have been in some sort of car club?" McAfee asked.

Chambers shrugged. "Did a deputy check the address on the vehicle registration?"

Higbee rolled his eyes. "We're not incompetent, Detective. It was the same one he had on the driver's license. Doesn't matter, though. We found where he was living."

McAfee and Chambers exchanged glances.

"Score one for patrol." Higbee grinned. "Believe it or not, even we can find our asses every now and then."

"How'd they locate Sidorov's residence?" Chambers asked.

The deputy shrugged. "That I don't know, but if it was me, I'd have probably asked the guy who moved into the old residence. Or a former neighbor. Good ol' fashioned police work. Knock, knock, who's there?"

McAfee motioned his sandwich toward the command vehicle. "Did you tell the brass so they can get a warrant?"

Higbee's expression flattened.

"Yeah," McAfee said. "You're not incompetent. We get it."

The deputy motioned toward McAfee's hip. "Maybe you guys should turn on your radios."

McAfee took another bite. With a mouthful of food, he said, "Thanks for the advice, *Deputy*."

Higbee flicked his hand before walking toward another group of deputies—the conquering gunfighter returning to his posse to celebrate a verbal joust with the town's rebels. McAfee swallowed and then spat. He refrained from swearing.

Chambers said, "Finding Sidorov's home is something."

"It's something all right."

Sergeant Lee stepped out of the command vehicle. He wiped his mouth as if he'd just finished eating. His head swiveled about until he found the two detectives. He held several papers in his hand as he stalked to McAfee and Chambers. "Don't say I never did anything for you."

"You never did anything for me," McAfee said flatly.

Lee smacked the papers on the hood. "Search warrants, smart ass. You're welcome."

"Is the warrant for Sidorov's apartment in there?" Chambers asked.

"They're working on it," the sergeant said. "We just found out about it, but you'll have it soon enough." He glanced at McAfee. "Anything else?"

"Thank you for lunch." McAfee held up his sandwich and smiled broadly. "You outdid yourself."

"Asshole," Lee muttered. The sergeant stormed back toward the boxy van.

The detectives watched him go.

Chambers asked, "Why do you hate the man so much?"

"It's the mustache."

"If he shaved it off, would you like him more?"

McAfee squinted as Lee turned to look at him a final time. He shook his head before stepping into the RV. The door slammed shut.

"Nah," McAfee said. "You're probably right. It's the face under the mustache that I hate."

Chapter 4

It was nearly two in the afternoon when McAfee arrived at his desk. The sheriff's office shared the Public Safety Building along with the Spokane Police Department and Spokane Municipal Court. McAfee would have preferred to work in the valley away from the drama associated with being near so many commanders, the department's public information deputy, and the office of Internal Affairs. However, that would mean he had been assigned to the Spokane Valley Police Department.

Notwithstanding his current relationship with Emily, working for the SVPD came with its own drama.

He glanced across the office. Tim Chambers sat at his computer, and his fingers danced across the keyboard. The man seemed to be intently concentrating. Other investigators and deputies walked through the confined space. None bothered looking at either McAfee or Chambers. It was as if neither detective existed in the Major Crimes office.

McAfee tapped the space bar on his keyboard, which called his computer to life. When a login screen appeared, he entered his username and password. He ignored feeling ostracized and returned to his earlier thoughts.

The sheriff's office had a policing contract with the municipality of Spokane Valley. Every couple of years, the agreement came up for renegotiation, which created undue stress for all those involved. Deputies and detectives assigned to that area operated under the banner of a police department, but it was in title only—they were deputies in police uniforms. Or, as the men and women of the SCSO joked within the walls of their agency, they were wolves in sheep's clothing.

McAfee called up his internet browser, and Google's search bar greeted him. He entered *shisha* and pressed Enter.

More than half a million people lived in Spokane County. Fifty percent lived within Spokane's city limits. The city was 69.5 square miles, while the county was 1,781 square miles. But the law enforcement agencies assigned to their protection were roughly the same size.

Cops in Spokane tended to act like they were the toughest kid on the block, yet they almost always did their jobs with backup. And if they didn't respond with a second officer, they knew help was only a few precious moments away.

Deputies usually handled calls alone, so they did so smartly and efficiently. Back-up could often be five minutes away—maybe more—even when driving with lights and sirens activated. Critical incidents could go bad in seconds. A minute was a painfully long time. Five minutes was literally someone's lifetime.

It was the same way for county detectives. They rarely partnered up—there was too much distance to cover. They helped each other out on the initial crime scene or, if asked, but other than that, each detective handled their own cases.

The search engine produced several local businesses that advertised themselves as hookah lounges. McAfee scrolled down until he found the definition of *shisha* and clicked it.

Today was an anomaly concerning the usual partnership scheme. The sheer magnitude of this case—five dead men—demanded a second investigator. He'd worked with other detectives before. He wasn't a malcontent and liked Chambers but working with another investigator meant considering them before taking any action. McAfee didn't like that. During a case, he wanted to take the initiative. Motion felt good to him. It made things feel like a case progressed, even if it didn't. Some investigators argued against putting too much emphasis on tasks, but McAfee learned long ago that his attitude directed many of his results. If he felt poorly about a case, the likelihood of it suddenly breaking his way was slim. Yet, things often worked out if he kept pushing and stayed positive.

He didn't want to be at the department now. Instead, he wanted to go to Alexei Sidorov's Deer Park apartment. Afterward, he wanted to notify the next of kin. If there was still time in his day, he wanted to visit Ahmet's bar—The Kedi.

Paperwork and computer time could wait.

Tim Chambers, however, insisted they stop by the department so he could "clear his head and make some quick notes." Supposedly, fifteen minutes was all Chambers needed. McAfee told him to sit alone in his car for a while, but the other detective refused to hear that. They almost went their separate ways, but McAfee knew that would look bad. As Chambers pointed out earlier, the two detectives needed to show a united front in this investigation. It would be easier for McAfee to reel himself in than to push Chambers to be something he wasn't. Besides, it seemed both men could use all the friends they could get.

McAfee glanced at the other detective. Chambers furiously scribbled into his notebook, then looked up and touched his computer screen. The man had a notorious reputation as an oddball. Most in the department were considered doers, while Chambers was the rare thinker.

Ponderer might be a better word, McAfee thought.

Chambers abruptly stood and walked toward the hallway.

McAfee leaned toward his computer monitor and considered the definition of *shisha*. It was from the Persian word *shishe* and was literally translated as glass. Hookah. He returned to the previous search result to consider the three local businesses advertising themselves as hookah lounges.

Ahmet Dogan owned a bar yet hung out in his garage clubhouse that he called The Shisha Room. McAfee settled back in his chair and crossed his arms. Why would Ahmet do such a thing?

Was it because smoking was banned inside establishments? That happened before McAfee could legally drink, so he had no idea what it was like then. He was thankful for that. He wouldn't want to be around a bunch of smokers while he tried to enjoy himself. He'd visited other cities in the United States where smoking in bars was still allowed. He disliked that experience.

Behind him, a man cleared his throat. McAfee turned to see Undersheriff Rick Gleese.

"Got a bad one out in Millwood, huh?"

McAfee glanced down the hallway to see Chambers enter the men's room. Had he noticed the approaching undersheriff and took off? That didn't seem like the detective, but he avoided an earlier conversation with the sergeant and lieutenant. Yet, he did talk with them about getting help with the warrants. McAfee wondered what trouble Chambers might be facing.

His attention returned to the undersheriff.

Gleese looked like an overboiled potato—milky white and puffy. His neck bulged over his collar, and his belly strained against the buttons of his shirt. His colorful tie sat twisted on his gut. The undersheriff hadn't always looked that way. When McAfee first entered the department, Gleese was a fit and trim sergeant. But his move to administrative posts put him behind a desk. The extra pounds and facial sag soon followed.

The undersheriff oversaw the Investigative and Intelligence Division. McAfee was surprised he hadn't come out to the crime scene. Only the patrol undersheriff had made an appearance, and that was just brief enough to climb into the command van and grab some lunch.

"Got all the resources you need?" Gleese asked.

"Yeah."

"Sorry I didn't make it out there. The sheriff is out of town." Gleese glanced around. "Yeah. So I was needed back here in case anything else happened."

McAfee didn't know why the man was explaining this to him. Department scuttlebutt had it that Gleese was being groomed to take over for the sheriff when the big man quit. Maybe McAfee should rethink his assessment of the undersheriff. He was a climber. A man going places. He wasn't an overboiled potato; he was a stewed po-*tah*-to.

Gleese glanced around. His lips pursed as he surveyed the Major Crimes office. "Where's Chambers?"

"The restroom."

The undersheriff's gaze returned to him. "How's he been today?"

"Fine. Why?"

Gleese rolled down his lower lip and dismissively shook his head. "No reason. Making any headway on the case?"

"Just started."

"Uh-huh." Gleese stared down the hall.

McAfee looked in the same direction. No one was coming from that way. Was Gleese waiting for Chambers to return? The undersheriff's gaze dropped to McAfee.

"Something you want to ask, Sheriff?"

Gleese surveyed the office once more. He lowered his voice. "Rumor has it you had dinner with the Valley mayor last night."

McAfee didn't respond; the man hadn't asked a question.

Now, Gleese looked uncomfortable. The sheriff never looked this way when he asked personal questions. "Yeah," Gleese said. He cleared his throat. "So."

McAfee wasn't going to make it easy on the man. He waited for Gleese to ask his question.

The undersheriff nodded several times before working up the courage to look directly at McAfee again. "Well?"

"Sir?"

"Did the mayor mention the budget?"

"The topic never came up."

"Never?"

"We don't talk much about work. In fact, we don't talk much about anything."

Gleese looked nonchalantly around the office. A few seconds passed before he asked, "Why's that?"

"Why's what?"

The undersheriff pursed his lips. "Why didn't the topic come up?"

"The mayor's not exactly happy that I'm marrying his daughter."

Gleese's eyebrows lifted briefly before his entire body sagged. "You're not."

McAfee stared at him.

The undersheriff's mouth hung open. "Well, fuck."

"That's pretty much how the mayor responded to the whole thing."

Gleese puffed his cheeks. "Goddamn it, McAfee. Now, the mayor will be pissed at the department non-stop."

"The department isn't marrying her. I am."

"But you're one of us, you stupid—" Gleese bit off the word, then shook his head. "If he can't take his anger out on you, who's he going to take it out on? The department, that's who."

"Probably, sir."

"No probably about it."

McAfee shrugged. "Is there anything else?"

The undersheriff's cheeks reddened, and he woodenly said, "Let me know if you need any resources for the case."

McAfee turned toward his computer. "Tell the sheriff it won't be forever."

"The marriage?"

"The mayor."

"Huh?" The undersheriff leaned toward him.

"The mayor won't be in office forever."

Gleese straightened. "Oh, right. Like I'm gonna tell him *that*." He walked off.

Down the hall, the restroom door opened, and Chambers appeared. He rubbed his hands as if he'd just washed them. He nodded as he passed Gleese.

"Where the hell you been?" the undersheriff barked.

Chambers thumbed toward the restroom.

Gleese paused, lifted a hand in frustration, then grunted before continuing on his way.

When Chambers arrived at McAfee's desk, he asked, "What did Gleese want?"

"To check on us."

"That was nice of him."

McAfee leaned back in his chair. "Oh sure, it was. I noticed how you took off right before he arrived."

"Fortunate timing, I assure you." Chambers headed for his desk. "I'm ready when you are."

"So, you cleared your head?"

"You're a detective. I didn't think I needed to spell it out for you."

McAfee grabbed his notebook and stood. "It might have been helpful."

Chambers walked toward the exit. "Should we ride together now?"

***

The detectives were northbound on Division Street. Chambers was behind the wheel of his Chevy Impala. McAfee watched the scenery go by from the passenger seat. The police radio squawked with a deputy reporting a traffic stop in the town of Spangle.

"What's the deal with you and Geri?" Chambers asked.

McAfee eyed him.

"Don't tell me if you don't want." Chambers motioned at the thick traffic up ahead. "But we've got thirty minutes to kill."

McAfee leaned his head back against his seat. "Only if you tell me what's going on with you and the administration."

Chambers glanced at him but remained silent.

"You're ducking them today," McAfee said. "Maybe you've been ducking them for a while, and I haven't noticed, but it's apparent today."

Chambers gnawed on his lower lip. He checked both mirrors, changed lanes, then shrugged. "You first."

"Geri and I were an item."

"Is that so?"

"A while back."

"The story goes she doesn't date deputies."

McAfee rested his head against his seat back. "She doesn't date anyone affiliated with the job."

"No city cops either?"

"Anyone with a badge."

When they came to a red light, Chambers cast a sideways glance. "How did you rate?"

"I never asked."

"What makes you so special?"

McAfee turned his palms upward. "What can I say? It happened away from the department."

"I would imagine."

"Not like that." McAfee waved a hand. "I was at the grocery store. She was, too. We got to talking in the cereal aisle, and she asked if I wanted to grab a coffee. I thought it was an innocent invite, so I said yes."

"An innocent invite from a woman that looks like her?"

"It can happen," McAfee said.

"Not to me. Probably not to most men."

"Yeah, well, one thing led to another, and that's it."

Chambers grunted. "That's very cryptic."

"I don't kiss and tell."

The light changed, and the traffic moved. Chambers accelerated. "You two kept it very quiet."

"We didn't want tongues wagging."

"Very wise." Chambers checked the rearview mirror. "I take it that things didn't work out."

McAfee sighed. He glanced at Chambers and caught the other detective looking at him. "She wasn't over her previous boyfriend," he said.

"You were a rebound?"

"Don't make it sound so appealing."

Chambers smiled politely.

"Her feelings were jumbled." McAfee shrugged. "She suggested we take a break."

"Right after you started? And you didn't think that was a good idea?"

"Not really."

"Because you had feelings?"

McAfee rapped his knuckles against the door panel. "More than I should have."

"Did she go back to her old boyfriend?"

"You like picking old wounds, don't you?"

"You're not forthcoming with information. I've got to get to it somehow."

McAfee rapped his knuckles against the door panel some more. "She went back."

"Then you found a new girlfriend."

"You heard."

Chambers looked over his shoulder, signaled a lane change, and sped around a slow-moving delivery truck. As they passed, McAfee eyed the driver. The young man behind the wheel focused on the road, but he flipped the bird to the detectives.

"I try to ignore departmental gossip," Chambers said, "but it's pretty hard when it's concerning a detective and a mayor's daughter."

McAfee ignored the delivery truck driver and his act of silent defiance. He faced Chambers. "She's her own person."

"Of course she is. We all are. And I'm not judging. As the saying goes, the heart wants. So what happened?"

"With Geri?"

Chambers nodded.

"It didn't work out with the old boyfriend."

"How come?"

"I don't know. She never said."

Chambers chuckled. "She couldn't get over you. That's it."

McAfee smirked. "Nah. She got over me plenty to go back to him."

"But she wanted to get back together." Chambers banged the palm of his hand against the steering wheel. "But you'd moved on."

"No moss on this rolling stone."

"And now she's upset because you said you had feelings for her."

McAfee tapped the door panel. "Congratulations, now you know. It's your turn. What's up with you and the administration?"

Chambers checked the mirrors but didn't change lanes. Instead, he shifted in his seat.

"Cat got your tongue, Detective?" McAfee asked.

"I have my own relationship problems."

"With someone in the administration?"

Chambers rolled a hand off the steering wheel. "My girlfriend is—" He became silent.

"What?"

"Married."

McAfee stared at Chambers. The man continued to surprise. Tim Chambers seemed as likely to step out of bounds as an assembly line robot.

"Her husband filed a complaint with Internal Affairs."

"On what basis?"

"Conduct unbecoming."

McAfee looked forward. "Well, there you go."

The conduct unbecoming charge was a catch-all. Deputies could be charged with it for doing just about anything that made the badge or the department look bad. If the sheriff wanted to get rid of an employee, he could use the conduct unbecoming charge as a cudgel and beat the deputy into submission. However, if the administration wanted to protect the deputy from the charge, they could dismiss it as too vague. Or, as a third option, if those in power needed to teach a lesson, they could hang the conduct unbecoming charge over a deputy's head and threaten action until the affected employee responded accordingly.

Chambers said, "I tried to break it off."

"It didn't take?"

"No." Chambers lifted a hand as if to wave it about, but he dropped it back to the steering wheel. He briefly cocked his head before shaking it. The emotions that played out upon his face were like watching a movie of the man's life. After a few seconds, Chambers ran his fingers through his hair and repeated, "No."

"Then the husband found out and called Internal Affairs."

He nodded. "It shouldn't be anyone's business."

"What are you doing about it?"

"Trying to avoid the administration."

"You can't do that forever."

"It doesn't hurt to try."

McAfee knew it was a futile effort. He'd already attempted it.

***

Alexei Sidorov lived in a second-floor apartment in Deer Park, a bedroom community thirty minutes north of Spokane. The apartment building was painted white with brown trim and located northwest of the roundabout at H and Main Streets.

McAfee and Chambers stood on a small landing. Deputy Kelly Runke remained on the stairwell. Runke was a squat woman with short dark hair and intense eyes. Her patrol car was parked in a stall with a view of the apartment. She had been there for the past ninety minutes and watched the unit until the two detectives arrived.

The apartment manager waited on the sidewalk. He was an early fifties white male who wore a hooded sweatshirt, long gray shorts, and Nike Air Jordans. The detectives had caught him on the way to an afternoon basketball game. He held a manila file and a set of keys.

"And you saw no movement inside the apartment?" Chambers asked.

Runke hooked her thumbs into her duty belt. "That's right. I attempted contact upon arrival. No one has been here since. No movement in or around the apartment."

McAfee knocked on the door. "Sheriff's Department!" He eyed Chambers. "You looked for an additional phone number?"

"I did. Nothing. The guy didn't have a digital footprint."

"A ghost?"

Chambers shrugged. "Maybe the guy consciously stayed offline. It happens."

"Maybe, but it's weird." McAfee banged on the door again. "Sheriff's Department!"

"Why?" Chambers asked. "Because he wants his privacy? Because he doesn't want the internet snooping in his business?"

McAfee cocked his head. "Snooping in his business" didn't sound like the Chambers that McAfee thought he knew. The admission of a married girlfriend, a jealous husband, and an overzealous Internal Affairs investigation might change a guy's disposition. McAfee hoped he never found out. He looked down at the apartment manager. "Do you have an emergency contact for Sidorov?"

The manager shook his head. "He left it blank."

Chambers grunted his dissatisfaction. "Let's announce." He tucked his notebook away. "Spokane County Sheriff's Office," he said loudly. "We have a warrant."

McAfee looked around the apartment community. Several residents gathered in the parking lot to watch. Others stood on their balconies. Even more faces were pressed against windows. A group of lawn care workers huddled near one of their trucks. "We're getting a crowd."

"Let's give them a good show," Chambers said.

McAfee banged on the door with his fist.

Chambers shouted, "Spokane County Sheriff's Office! We have a warrant."

"Open it," McAfee said to the apartment manager.

McAfee and Chambers both removed their 9mm Glocks. Due to the position of the door, the two men could not take opposite sides of the entry. They had to line up on the left side of the door—McAfee stood in the first position.

Deputy Runke removed her weapon and lined up behind Chambers.

The apartment manager hurried up the stairs and unlocked the apartment. McAfee grabbed the man by the shoulder when the door popped slightly open and pulled him back. The detective pushed the door all the way open.

"Sheriff's Office," McAfee yelled. "We have a warrant, and we're coming in."

Even though Alexei Sidorov was dead, they treated the entry into his apartment cautiously. The man's keys and vehicle were missing. It was a reasonable assumption that the killers had visited Sidorov's apartment. If the killers had been inside when Deputy Runke arrived, they could still be there now.

McAfee entered the apartment with his gun level, and his arms pulled in tight to his chest. He felt Chambers behind him. He imagined Runke was in the tail position. The three moved methodically into the two-bedroom apartment.

They passed through the living room, by the kitchen, and down the hallway. McAfee cleared the first bedroom. Chambers checked the bathroom.

Runke entered the rear bedroom. "Clear," she announced.

The three of them returned to the living room. Nothing seemed out of place. The apartment appeared orderly and smelled of vanilla.

"Sidorov was a tidy man," Chambers said appreciatively.

McAfee looked at Runke. "You can wait outside if you want, but we still need to keep the apartment under observation."

"For how long?"

"A day?" He eyed Chambers. "What do you think?"

"No idea." Chambers looked to Runke. "But we'll get you some relief. You won't have to sit out there all afternoon."

"I'd appreciate that." She headed for the door.

"Oh, and Runke," McAfee said, "let the manager know he can take off. We'll lock up when we leave."

The deputy nodded and exited the apartment.

McAfee walked through the unit one more time. Everything seemed neatly put away. The bed in the first room was made. The second room was used as an office. Nothing was out on the desk. McAfee returned to the living room to find Chambers standing there with his hands on his hips. "What do you think?"

"About?" Chambers continued to scan the room.

"Doesn't look like the apartment was tossed."

"If someone did, they were very considerate."

McAfee walked over to the kitchen counter and flipped through a small stack of mail. It contained nothing but bills and advertisements.

"What's that say?" Chambers asked.

"That we beat the killers here."

Chambers faced McAfee. "Would they have taken the car if they only wanted to get into the apartment?"

McAfee looked up from the mail. "Meaning they could have taken the keys and driven away in another vehicle, the one that brought them to The Shisha Room?"

"Right. Maybe the killers never had any intention of coming here. If they wanted something of Sidorov's, it would be long gone."

McAfee shoved his hands into his pockets. "So they killed five men to steal a car?"

"I don't know. Maybe. It's an '82 Audi Quattro. How much is something like that worth?"

"No idea." McAfee shrugged. "It's not worth anyone's life. I'll tell you that much."

"Or maybe they knew exactly what they were after, entered the apartment, and took it. All without making a mess."

McAfee smirked. "Great. We don't know anything, is what you're saying."

Chapter 5

Ricky Scherff lived in a brown, tan California split on Bigelow Gulch Road with his girlfriend, Rebecca Anderson. "Becca" was in her late thirties with mocha-colored skin and long black hair. She wore a beige sweater and faded blue jeans. Her eyes brimmed with worry when she answered the door.

After McAfee introduced himself and Chambers, he asked, "May we come inside?"

"Oh God," she said and covered her mouth with both hands. The woman bent over and wailed, "Oh no!"

The detectives helped her to a couch, where she bowed her head and cried for several minutes. Eventually, they were able to get her to identify herself. "I knew something bad happened."

"Why's that?" McAfee asked.

"Because he didn't come home." Becca looked up. Tears streaked her face. "Ricky always comes home." She lowered her head and sobbed.

While she cried, McAfee looked around. Framed posters of Martin Luther King Jr., Cornel West, and Billie Holiday hung about the room. The words *Make a Difference* were painted on one wall in scripted handwriting. McAfee noticed a scent of cinnamon. He looked for its source but couldn't identify it.

Becca looked up. "What happened?"

"Ricky was murdered," McAfee said.

Her tearful gyrations stopped, and her face pinched. "Murdered? By whom?"

"We don't know. We're working on that."

"Ms. Anderson," Chambers said, "we need to ask you a couple of questions."

She nodded, then snuffled. Becca rubbed the back of her hand under her nose.

"Have you ever heard any of these names?" Chambers listed off the men killed with her boyfriend.

As each name was read, Becca shook her head. When Chambers said, "Ahmet Dogan," she nodded.

"Him. Yes, him, I know."

"How so?" Chambers asked.

Her eyes softened. "Ricky and I went to his bar a couple of times. Did something happen there? Did something happen with Ahmet, too?"

Chambers nodded. "All of those men were murdered along with Ricky. It happened at Ahmet's house."

Becca's brow furrowed. "In his hookah lounge?"

"You knew about that?"

"Sure. Ricky went there to smoke with Ahmet." Her gaze bounced between McAfee and Chambers. "Tobacco, not weed."

"It's okay," Chambers said. "Marijuana's legal."

"Yeah, but Ricky didn't smoke that stuff—only cigarettes."

It was then that McAfee realized that Becca's home didn't smell of stale smoke. Instead, the aroma of cinnamon seemed stronger now.

Some new emotion passed over Becca's face—regret. "I quit cigarettes years ago, so when we moved here, I didn't want any smoking inside. Ricky never argued about it—not once. And whenever he came home from Ahmet's lounge, he always showered." Tears welled in her eyes. "He was always so considerate."

"Were they in a car club?" Chambers asked. "All the men had nice vehicles."

"It's strange what guys bond over. Whenever I went to the bar with him, Ricky and Ahmet talked about cars."

Chambers consulted his notebook. "Did Ricky ever say anything about anyone wanting to hurt him or Ahmet?"

Becca shook her head. "Never. Ricky was about the sweetest man you'd ever want to meet, and Ahmet always seemed so nice."

***

"Ahmet was an asshole." Heather Fuller shook her head. "DeAndre should never have gotten hisself messed up with that man."

Heather was a tall woman in her early forties. Her mousy blond hair was pulled back into a messy bun. She wore an Oakland Raiders T-shirt and frayed jean shorts. Her leather flip-flops revealed chipped toenails.

They stood in the living room of Fuller's house. Posters of TuPac, Malcolm X, and Che Guevara were tacked to the walls. Much of the place was in disarray. Cardboard boxes were scattered about—some were full while others waited. Women's clothes were haphazardly tossed into the middle of the room. Heather had confirmed that the couple was at the beginning of a divorce.

"Why do you say that about Ahmet?" McAfee asked.

A rap song played softly in the background. Heather had turned it down after McAfee and Chambers entered the house.

"Whenever DeAndre came home from that lounge—" Heather tapped her temple. "—his head was so full of stupid ideas. Oh, I'm gonna be an entrepreneur this." She waggled her fingers to the left. "I'm gonna be an entrepreneur that." She waggled her fingers to the right. "Motherfucker, I said, you gotta get a job before you entrepreneur anything." She picked up a wad of clothes and slammed them into an empty cardboard box. "*Want*repreneur is what he was. I should have told him that."

"The others were entrepreneurs?" McAfee asked. He'd already read the names of the men killed along with DeAndre. Heather said she did not know any of them except Ahmet.

"Hell if I know." She straightened with a wad of panties in her hand. "DeAndre said they was, but he was a dreamer. Somebody showed up at that lounge with some success story and he'd come home with a new scheme." She smirked. "Son of a bitch never executed on one of them. Like I was ever surprised." She shook the handful of panties. "That's not true. I am surprised. You know why? Because I didn't think he was really with those guys. I thought for sure that most of the time he was bullshitting me about his side piece." She dunked the panties into a box.

Chambers raised an eyebrow.

"Oh, I know he had hisself more than one," Heather said. "DeAndre was like a cat in heat. How do you think I got with the stupid son of a bitch?" She snatched a few items of clothing, one at a time. When she had both hands full, she straightened and continued. "I was one of them, you know, and I made fun of that heifer I replaced. Shoulda known better." She slammed both handfuls into a box.

"Do you know anyone who would want to hurt DeAndre?" McAfee asked.

"Besides me?" Her head bounced to the side, and she flashed a challenging look.

Both detectives stared at her for several moments. When she didn't change her answer, McAfee said, "Seriously?"

"I am being serious. He's lucky I didn't do it." She bent and grabbed some more clothes. "Hell, I'm probably lucky I didn't kill the man, too."

***

Hasim Arap had lived in a Shadle Park neighborhood across from Loma Vista Park. The rancher needed a fresh coat of paint, and its lawn required tending. An early '70s two-door Datsun B210 hatchback sat in the driveway. It appeared to be in fantastic condition.

McAfee knocked on the front door. Chambers stood on the opposite side of the small landing.

While the detectives waited for the door to be answered, McAfee scanned the neighborhood. Most of this part of town was built post-World War II, and the homes were of similar construction—small ranchers on tiny lots. Many of the homes appeared to be in the same condition as Hasim's. With the nation's economy booming, McAfee was surprised that more of these homes hadn't been upgraded. They seemed prime for selling.

The front door opened to reveal an early twenties male. He was handsome and of Middle Eastern descent. He wore a Seattle SuperSonics throwback jersey, black jeans, and black tennis shoes. A heavy gold chain hung around his neck. His dark hair was cut short.

The detectives shifted their positions into the middle of the landing. McAfee introduced himself and Chambers. "Is Mrs. Arap here?" he asked.

"My mom's dead." It was said flatly and without remorse.

"And you are?"

The younger man glanced at Chambers before turning back to McAfee. "What's this about?"

"Are you related to Hasim Arap?"

"Yeah." A couple of beats passed before the man admitted, "I'm his son. Where's he at?"

"And you live here with him?"

"That's right." His brow furrowed, and he again looked at Chambers. "What's this about?"

McAfee said, "Hasim Arap was murdered this morning."

The young man's gaze snapped to McAfee. "What?"

"May we come in?"

Several seconds passed before the younger man stepped back. McAfee and Chambers followed him inside.

The house smelled like two grown men lived there. No sweet fragrances hung in the air, nor did the sharp bite of cleaning supplies. Instead, it had the distinct aroma of musk locked in a small space. Opening the doors and windows might help air it out, but McAfee had the distinct impression that the odor was forever trapped into the furniture and carpet fabric.

The living room was sparsely decorated. No pictures were on the walls. Two recliners faced a big-screen television, and a couple of small end-tables sat near the chairs. The younger man perched on the edge of one of the recliners. He stared off into the distance.

"What's your name?" McAfee asked.

"Omar. Omar Arap."

"Do you have any brothers or sisters?"

"Just me."

"Have you ever heard these names?" McAfee listed the men found in the garage with Hasim.

Omar shook his head upon hearing each name.

"Not even Ahmet Dogan?

"Why should I have heard of him?"

"It was his house they were discovered at."

Omar blinked. "All those men—they were murdered?"

McAfee nodded.

"The names are not familiar."

"Did your father have any enemies?"

"What kind of enemies would he have? He's a grocer. People like him."

McAfee asked for the business address and Omar provided one in the Garland district. "You work there?"

Omar shrugged. "Yeah."

"You don't seem excited about it."

"It's the family business. It's not exactly my dream job."

"Did your father own other businesses?"

"Rental properties, but that's it. The only thing we work is the grocery."

Chambers shifted his stance. "Is the Datsun in the driveway yours?"

"Yeah."

"Did you and your father work on cars?"

Omar shook his head. "My father did not. Others did that for him. He spent all his time at the store."

"But you both liked cars?"

"Yeah, of course, we liked cars." Omar shrugged a single shoulder. "Big deal."

"Was he in a car club?"

Omar cocked his head. "Huh?"

"Your father drove a Mercedes."

"He's got to be in a club for that?" Omar motioned toward the window. "You think I'm in a club because of mine?"

Chambers jotted something into his notepad.

"What are you writing down?" Omar asked.

"Your thoughts about a car club."

He lifted slightly from the chair. "For real?"

"You want to see?" Chambers turned his notepad so the kid could read what he'd written.

Omar settled back into his sitting position. "I'm good."

Chambers turned and eyed McAfee in a questioning manner. McAfee knew what he was asking, but he didn't have an answer. Something seemed off with Omar, but McAfee couldn't place it either. Perhaps it was grief that caused it. Mourning family members acted strangely at times. Yet maybe this was unrelated to sorrow.

Was Omar hiding something? It might be akin to the murders, or it could be completely irrelevant. McAfee had no idea. He turned his palm upward. It was a subtle signal for Chambers to continue.

"Where is it?" Omar asked.

Chambers looked up from his notepad. "Where is what?"

"My father's Mercedes."

"Still at the crime scene."

"Oh."

Both McAfee and Chambers stared at him for several seconds. Eventually, Omar said, "What?"

"You haven't asked where the crime scene is," Chambers said.

"You said it was at the one guy's house."

"Ahmet. Do you know where he lived?"

"How would I know that?"

McAfee entered the interview. "Where were you this morning?"

Omar's brow furrowed. "Huh?"

"You heard my question," McAfee said. "Where were you at three o'clock this morning?"

The younger man jumped to his feet. "You think I had something to do with this? That I could hurt my father?"

"Answer the question," Chambers said.

Omar's face pinched with anger as he pointed at McAfee. "You think I killed my father!"

McAfee leaned forward. "You're avoiding the question, Omar."

The younger man glanced between the two detectives. He rubbed his face with a single hand and then sat on the edge of the recliner. "I was with a woman."

"What woman?" Chambers asked.

"She's a friend. Whatever happened, she wasn't a part of it. Neither was I."

"Quit playing around," McAfee said. "Five people are dead, and right now, you're looking like you're involved."

Omar's expression relaxed slightly. "I had nothing to do with hurting anyone. Neither did she." He pulled a cell phone from his pocket. He dropped back into the recliner. "Lala Galoyan."

"What's with the games?" McAfee asked.

"It's not a game," Omar said. Then he muttered it again as he scrolled through his phone, "It's not a game."

"Why wouldn't you tell us about Lala?"

Omar looked up from his phone. Several seconds passed before he said, "She's Armenian."

"So?" McAfee asked.

"My father hates them." Omar's eyes lowered. "Like, racist hate."

Chambers cocked his head. "You were with her to upset your father?"

He held up the phone. "Do you want her information or not?"

"Yes," Chambers said. He held his pen at the ready.

Omar recited Lala's phone number. After Chambers wrote it down, he read it back. Omar tossed the phone onto the small table next to him.

"Where does she live?" Chambers asked.

"In the valley," Omar said, "I don't know the address. I just get there because I know how."

"What street is it on?"

"Pines. It's behind the 7-Eleven next to the freeway. Do you know the one?"

There were several apartment complexes near the convenience store, but Chambers didn't ask for further clarification. With a name like Lala Galoyan, they should easily find a listed address in the system.

"And she'll verify you were with her all night?" Chambers asked.

"If you're nice," Omar said, "she'll tell you what we did." His eyes slid to McAfee. "Him, probably not."

Chambers lifted an eyebrow. "Excuse me?"

"We're friends with benefits. She calls when her daddy is busy."

Chambers studied Omar now. The younger man defiantly watched him back.

"You get what I'm saying?" Omar asked.

McAfee disliked the younger Arap. There was something about the man that bothered him. Perhaps it was the fact that he didn't seem broken up about his father's murder. That wasn't evidence of involvement in the crime, but it was a red flag. He'd gotten unsettled when he was accused of the murder, but the actual death of his father hadn't bothered him. Then again, Heather Fuller wasn't broken up about her husband's murder either.

"What's going to happen to it?" Omar asked Chambers.

"Happen to what?"

"The Mercedes, my father's car."

The detectives briefly traded looks.

"Unless you guys have some reason to keep it, I want it."

"Any special reason why?" Chambers asked.

"What reason do I need to give except it belonged to my father? Isn't that enough?" Omar waved a hand about. "Look at how we live. My father didn't believe in spending money on much, but he loved that car."

"Like you do yours," Chambers said.

Omar shrugged. "Mine's an economy classic. His is a luxury. I could never own one like his while he controlled the purse strings."

"Why didn't you move out?" McAfee asked.

"You don't know shit about our lives."

The attitude didn't surprise McAfee, but the curse word did. There'd been plenty of opportunities for Omar to swear, but he chose now to do so. The expletive sounded odd.

Omar continued. "That's how we did things in our family. We worked. I stayed, and he paid what he thought was fair."

"You didn't think it was reasonable?" Chambers asked.

Omar glanced at McAfee but quickly returned to Chambers. "I didn't kill my father. We lived together. We worked together. He paid me terribly, but that was how I was raised. He said my reward would come when he was gone. Well, that's happened. So, can I get the car or not?"

Chambers inhaled deeply. "Does your father have a will?"

"It's with his attorney," Omar said. "I'm the only heir. Everything comes to me."

"Then it should be no problem."

A faint smile grew on Omar's face. He tried to fight it but failed miserably. The younger man bowed his head.

"Don't look so sad," McAfee said.

"Listen." Omar stood. "I got an alibi. Talk to Lala, and she'll tell you. I was with her until I opened the store today. Then my father never showed. I left one of the employees there so I could come here, get some food and take a break."

"Weren't you worried about your father?" Chambers asked.

Omar lifted his hands. "He never took a day off. *Ever*. I thought maybe he finally had it with the store and called out. He could do that but never did. Maybe he met a woman. Or maybe he went for a drive."

"Or maybe he died."

"You still think I killed my father? Not a chance. But am I busted up that he's dead?" Omar twisted his lips. "Nuh-huh. Not really. I get to live my life now." Omar tapped his fingertips against his chest. "I just inherited a store and some rental properties. I'm gonna sell those as fast as I can and get out of this miserable town."

Chambers closed his notebook. It seemed that he wanted to comment, a snide remark perhaps, but Chambers wasn't the type.

McAfee moved next to him. "You like cars, Omar?"

"What of it?"

"What's an '82 Audi Quattro worth?"

"Is that the one that looks like a Toyota Celica?" Omar snorted. "It's worth a kick in the tailpipe, is what it is."

***

Chambers lifted the cell phone to his ear. "What'd you think?"

The two detectives walked toward their car, which was parked down the block.

"Of Omar?" McAfee asked. "We should run him—"

Chambers lifted a finger. "Hi, Lala. This is Detective Tim Chambers with the Spokane County Sheriff's Office. When you have a moment, please call me." He provided his phone number and then hung up. "You were saying?"

"Let's run Omar through the system," McAfee said. He walked around to the passenger side of the car.

Chambers opened the driver-side door. "It's after five. How are you holding up?"

"I'm wiped. Should we call it?"

Both men dropped into their seats.

"Let's call it after we get back to the department," Chambers said. "The victims aren't going to get any deader, and we've got an Attempt to Locate out on Sidorov's car. If Lala calls me back—" Chambers's phone rang. "Well, there she is."

McAfee rested his head against the seat. "It was too much to hope that we'd get to go home."

***

Lala Galoyan crossed her arms and set her jaw. "What about him?"

McAfee turned his palms up. "He said you and he spent the night together."

She was a small, fit woman with olive-colored skin and brown eyes. Her long, dark hair swooped over her right shoulder down to her breast. She wore a white Lulu Lemon top and dark green leggings. Her feet were bare.

The three stood in the entryway of Lala's second-floor apartment in Spokane Valley. It was a large complex built near Pines and Interstate 90.

Lala's gaze flicked to Chambers, who stood shoulder-to-shoulder with McAfee. "Am I in trouble?"

McAfee shook his head. "This is about Omar. We need to verify his whereabouts this morning."

Lala glanced at McAfee when she asked, "Why?" but her attention returned to Chambers. Her gaze dropped to his left hand. A polite smile then appeared. "What'd he do?"

McAfee cleared his throat. "We just need to know if he was with you."

Lala opened her mouth to respond, but a truck with a loud muffler drove through the parking lot. She leaned out of the doorway to glare at the noisy offender. When it left the apartment complex, she straightened and settled her attention on Chambers once again. Her smile returned, but it was slightly broader this time.

McAfee didn't bother trying to lead the interview anymore. He glanced at Chambers, who nodded and asked, "Was Omar with you this morning?"

Lala looked at her feet, and her voice changed. She sounded like a girl scolded by her father. "It isn't serious."

"What time did he arrive?"

She lifted her eyes, but her head stayed bowed. "Do you really have to know?"

"We do. It's important."

Lala wriggled her toes. "He came over about ten."

"When did he leave?"

"Around six this morning, I guess. I don't know. He had to open the store."

Chambers eyed McAfee. "Anything else?"

"Thank you for your time, Ms. Galoyan," McAfee said.

She reached out to Chambers. "It was very nice to meet you, Detective."

Chambers shook her hand. "Thank you for your help."

"If you need anything else," Lala said. She didn't finish the thought but held his hand longer than was necessary.

***

Shane McAfee walked into Emily's apartment. They were long past the need to knock. He had called to tell her he was on his way, though.

"You're here!" she announced cheerfully from the other room. "Dinner's almost ready."

The smell of cooking meat and pasta drifted through the small unit.

He ambled toward the kitchen. The events of the day weighed on him. McAfee had stopped by his house to shower and change his clothes. He now wore a red T-shirt with a faded Pepsi logo, blue jeans, and tennis shoes. He had left his gun locked inside the glovebox of his truck. Emily still wasn't accustomed to the weapon being at her apartment.

"How was your day?" she asked without looking at him. When she faced him, her smile dropped. "You look tired." Emily came to him then and slipped her arms around his waist.

"I'm wiped," he said. "What're you making?"

"Spaghetti." She leaned back to get a better view of him. "The sauce is from a can. I kicked it up with some spices, but that's as good as it will get. You're not marrying me for my culinary skills."

He wasn't. And he didn't care about food. He wasn't picky. Combine those facts with his desire for a nap, and she could have served him a bowl of cold cereal for dinner.

"Why don't you sit down for a bit?" She kissed him on the nose. "Dinner will be ready in a few."

He nodded but didn't say anything. There'd been enough talking during the day.

McAfee lumbered over to the couch and dropped into it. He picked up the television remote but didn't use it. Instead, he closed his eyes.

Emily said something to him, but it sounded dreamy—as if she were floating away.

PART II

Chapter 6

The cell phone buzzed on the nightstand. He rolled over quickly to silence it and smacked the picture frame. It clattered onto its face.

"What are you doing?" she moaned.

Andrew Parker found his phone and quieted it. "Sorry," he whispered. "Go back to sleep."

It felt early—too early. He usually awoke at 4:30 a.m. to work out, but this morning it seemed wrong—as if his sleep cycle had been interrupted somehow. He felt foggy and tried to remember if he had eaten late in the evening or if he had caffeine or alcohol with dinner. The quick inventory of his previous night's activities proved negative. He lifted the phone to check the time and noticed that the screen was still bright. The alarm wasn't responsible for the buzzing; it was a call.

And it was only 3:42 a.m.

He swiped a thumb over the screen and answered, "Parker."

"Hey, Detective, this is Chuck in radio. I'm sorry to wake you."

"Huh, Chuck?"

"You're up on the rotation."

Parker's wife grunted. "Go in the other room." Brooke hugged her pillow tighter. Her voice was muffled as she spoke into it. "I gotta get up with the kids in a couple."

He sat upright as Chuck continued.

"There's a multiple in the Audubon neighborhood. A complainant called in after hearing gunshots."

Parker shuffled down the hall past the children's rooms. He was careful not to make any noise. He wore only a pair of nylon shorts. "How many dead?" he whispered.

"Three. There's one wounded, too."

He paused at the end of the hallway. "A survivor?"

"A woman," Chuck said. "She's on her way to Holy Family, but it's not sounding so good."

Parker continued into the kitchen, where he clicked on the light. He closed his eyes against the fluorescent brightness and pinched the bridge of his nose. "Have you notified Johnson?"

"Not yet, but he's my next call."

"Good." Parker found a pen. "Thanks for calling me first." His partner tended to be faster than him. Parker could use the head start. "What's the address?"

Chuck gave him an address on West Euclid, and Parker jotted it onto the back of an envelope he found sitting on the counter. A homicide in northwest Spokane wasn't out of the ordinary, but a multiple was rare—not like a unicorn sighting, but more like the Mariners making the playoffs.

"I'm on the way," Parker said. He ended the call.

Brooke staggered into the room. She rubbed her eyes with the palms of both hands. She still wore long pajamas even though the winter months had long passed.

"What are you doing up?" he asked. He pulled her to him and hugged her.

She wrapped her arms around his waist and buried her head into his chest. "I'll make you breakfast."

"You don't have to."

"I know I don't." She nuzzled her head under his chin before looking up. "But this isn't the gym. You're gonna be a while."

"Longer than usual," Parker said. "It's a multiple."

"How many?"

"Three."

Brooke repeatedly blinked as his words registered. "So I should pack a lunch, too?"

"If you don't mind."

She shooed him away. "All right. Go get ready."

***

Andrew Parker liked routine.

After a quicker-than-normal shower, he dried his short hair.

Parker didn't think he was crazy like the Adrian Monk character from that old television show. His appreciation for routine wasn't based on numbers, touching things, or anything psychological. It was a simple preference for managing his limited time—he'd learned to do so while in the Army.

He flipped the towel around. Like buffing the toe of a shoe, he rubbed the cloth over his shoulders, down his back, then his butt.

Every morning, he awoke at half past four to get to the gym by five. When he was single, he didn't work out in the morning. Instead, he trained in the evenings while attending college. It was a rebellious attitude he developed after separating from the military. In those days, he'd wake up leisurely, attend class, then spend a couple of hours at the gym before hitting the clubs. It was a routine—not a healthy one, but still a routine. A younger, single man can thrive in a life like that.

Parker set a foot on the bathroom counter and dried his leg.

When he joined the police department, he discovered that shift work was not built around a traditional eight-hour day. Instead, a patrol shift consists of almost eleven hours. Young officers work swing and graveyard shifts, or a hybrid combination known as power shift. When their weekends roll around, officers often switch back to a normal schedule to fit in with their families or regular society. That's a tough life for a person who likes routine.

Parker switched his other foot to the counter and dried that leg.

He'd been a decent patrol officer. If he had to rate himself, he'd say he was average. He had no illusions about where he fell into the pack. He never tried out for SWAT or the Tactical Team—team sports were never to Parker's liking. He wrestled in school and was average at it. He dabbled in boxing but wasn't light on his feet like the other guys. Parker discovered bodybuilding while in the Army and knew he had found the sport that God built him to participate in.

The military preached a team ethic, and Parker swallowed it for the four years he was enlisted. Sitting alone behind the steering wheel of a patrol car should have been to Parker's liking, but he couldn't wait to leave that assignment behind.

Parker smushed some paste onto his toothbrush. He usually took his time with his morning ritual, but today wouldn't afford that. He tried to keep to his routine this morning—only faster.

Many in the department underestimated Parker because of his time in the weight room. Plenty of meatheads wore the uniform, and he got lumped in with them. That pissed him off, but he refused to let the judgments of others hold him back. He studied hard to get out of the patrol car and behind a desk. He wanted the structure that a detective's life would provide.

After he and Brooke married and finally moved in together, Parker quickly realized that two-hour nightly workouts weren't conducive to their relationship. She appreciated his physique—she'd been honest when she said it was the initial thing that attracted her to him. Yet, she didn't work out—it didn't interest her.

Brooke's figure was full of pleasant curves unlike the hard, intense women at the gym. It was what had attracted Parker to her—he had admitted as much. He liked her shape and propensity to be all the things that Parker wasn't—undisciplined, reckless, and sexy.

Those early days were full of delightful confessions.

Parker spat the toothpaste out. He didn't rinse.

He switched to early morning workouts when he became a Property Crimes detective. It fit great into his new schedule and made Brooke happy. It even worked on his days off. With three girls now under the age of five, Parker needed to complete his workouts before they awoke, or it wasn't going to happen. The family made too many demands upon his time.

His morning routine wasn't perfect. Some days he worked out and came home to have breakfast with the girls. Other mornings he got to the gym late due to a long night before and missed eating with the children.

But he tried to adhere to the routine as best he could—for his family.

Parker dressed quickly. He considered a black suit but went with jeans and a plaid button-up shirt instead. It was a callout, and the department's dress requirements were eased in these moments.

Parker's promotion to Major Crimes put a serious crick into his daily routine. He wasn't called out every day, but it was often enough that it irked him. No Property Crimes detectives were ever called out in the middle of the night for a stolen lawn mower. Brooke commented how he'd become grumpy as a homicide investigator. She was right, but he couldn't back out of the job now.

He stood in front of the mirror and tucked his shirt into his jeans.

Major Crimes carried a certain status—it was the big time—the pros. There was no higher honor in any police department. Even SWAT grudgingly respected Major Crimes. At a crime scene, Major Crimes was the Father, Son, and Holy Ghost rolled into one—even the chief showed deference.

Parker checked his face. He appeared bloated this morning. That irritated him. It couldn't just be the lack of sleep. He remembered what he had eaten the previous evening—they'd had steak, but he hadn't applied any salt or sauce to it. Parker pinched the skin of his cheek. He didn't mutter the expletive he wanted because he never swore in the house—the kids might hear, and Brooke would disapprove.

Nobody ever stepped down from Major Crimes. They either promoted out of the role or retired. If he requested a move back to Property Crimes, Parker would be seen as a failure or a loser. Those were things he'd never let anyone think of him. He'd suck it up until the day he could escape the assignment on his terms.

Brooke came into the bedroom. She reached up and smoothed his shirt. "Your breakfast is ready, and lunch is packed. I made something for Jessie, too."

"You didn't have to."

She rolled her eyes. "Like Ashley is going to make him something."

Parker grabbed for his wife, but she pushed him away. She took two long strides and dove onto the bed. She swam toward her pillow, snuggled her face into it, and said, "Go catch the bad guys."

He lovingly admired her. "I always do," he whispered, then flicked out the light.

***

There was only one way to the West Euclid address. Parker had to take a meandering drive around Drumheller Springs Park, a twelve-acre wooded slope in the middle of north Spokane. Had he not known better, he might have considered it part of someone's backyard.

Parker looped in from Liberty Avenue down Ash Place before heading east onto Euclid. He pulled his Chevy Impala to the curb and parked. A single entry point into a neighborhood seemed troublesome for a multiple-victim murder. Once Parker saw the crime scene, maybe he would reconsider his initial impression.

He grabbed the portable radio from the passenger seat and climbed out of his car. It was still dark out, although the sky was beginning to lighten over the horizon. While he clipped the radio to his belt, he looked north into the park.

Drumheller Springs was mostly scrub brush with some clustering of Evergreen trees. Parker thought the city overestimated what should be deemed a park, especially since this was on an elevation change greater than a two-story apartment building. The park appeared menacing at night—or early morning as it was now—as if something might come lurking down from above to harm this neighborhood.

Parker's gaze drifted south to the patrol cars lining Euclid Avenue. Most of the vehicles sat quietly, but one had its flashers still activated. The officer must have been on autopilot upon arrival and switched the swirling blue and red lights to the bouncing yellow.

Lights in every home in the neighborhood burned brightly, yet no looky-loos had assembled. Maybe that was due to only a few residences existing on the south side of the street. Once the sun broke over the horizon, Parker knew that people would come from other neighborhoods to watch—they always did.

The radio squawked on his hip as a north-side patrol officer called for dispatch to check a name. Parker clicked off the portable.

"What are you waiting for?"

Parker glanced over his shoulder.

Jessie Johnson approached. He wore a light jacket, jeans, and brown shoes. Parker couldn't see the brand, but he imagined Johnson purchased them at Nordstrom. His partner was a clotheshorse. Johnson's athletic build was sculpted by his hours in the gym. While Parker went for bodybuilding, Johnson was into Cross Fit. In his left hand, he carried a sketchpad. In his right, he held a half-eaten sandwich.

"The hell are you eating?"

"Avocado and egg." Johnson bit into his sandwich.

Parker rolled his eyes. "Lean into the cliché."

Through a mouthful, Johnson said, "You're a millennial, too."

"I don't act like it."

"That's right. You don't." Johnson motioned with his sandwich. "You act like a boomer."

Parker snickered. "I act like the generation that made the boomers. What were they called?" He eyed his partner. "That's right, the greatest generation. You're welcome." Parker opened the trunk of his car.

"For what? You weren't *actually* part of that generation." Johnson shoved the last bit of the sandwich into his mouth. "Besides, you can't call yourself great."

"If not me, who?" Parker removed a pair of latex gloves and a pair of booties. He tucked a small flashlight into his back pocket. He grabbed his sketchpad, remembered that Johnson already carried one, and tossed it back to its resting place. Parker slammed the trunk closed. "Well?"

Johnson shrugged. "I forgot the question."

They walked toward a California split that sat midblock. Two patrol cars had their spotlights pointed at the front of the house. A yellow string of tape cut diagonally through the front yard; it was hung between two trees.

"This one sounds like a winner," Johnson said.

"We got a good one. That's for sure."

"I'm surprised they didn't jump us to hand it to the Glory Hounds. Or at least send the Old Dogs to work it with us."

Parker grit his teeth. "We've made our bones."

"But it's a multiple."

Parker ducked under the line of yellow tape. "We deserve to be here."

Sergeant Wesley Blackwell broke away from several officers standing in the middle of the road. He waved at the detectives as he hurried toward them. He now moved his arms as if he were running, but it was just a show to hide that he wasn't moving any faster than he usually did.

"Look at this fat ass," Parker muttered. He stopped walking so the sergeant would have to cover all the ground to get to them.

"He could use the extra steps." Johnson burped.

Parker curled his lip. "Gross."

"Sue me. I pounded a protein shake, too."

"You're not going to do that all morning are you?"

Johnson burped again.

Parker shook his head and focused on the three patrol officers in the street. They continued to talk and ignored Parker and Johnson.

When he neared, Sergeant Blackwell exhaled as if he'd just completed a 5k run. He wore an SPD baseball cap with an uncurled brim. His uniform shirt appeared bunched above a leather duty belt that hung below his belly and canted toward the weight of his gun. His pant legs were too long, as if he never bothered to have them properly hemmed. The sergeant would never win a foot race, not even one to the donut counter.

Blackwell put his hands on his hips and bent slightly forward. "We're glad you're here."

"What have we got?" Johnson asked.

The sergeant pushed himself upright and pointed at the house. "Three dead. One at Holy Family."

"Did someone ride with the survivor to the hospital?"

"Yes."

"Was the shooting related to a domestic?" Parker asked.

The sergeant shrugged. "We haven't been able to determine that."

"Have you identified the victims?"

"We have," Blackwell said. He reached behind himself to dig into his back pocket. It was an awkward motion for the man, and the sergeant's face pinched with exertion. When the notebook appeared, Blackwell flipped it open. He was about to read the names when Parker lifted his hand to interrupt him.

"Hold on," Parker said. "There are a lot of lights on in the neighborhood." He motioned up and down Euclid Avenue. "Have officers started contacting the residents?"

The sergeant glanced over his shoulder before saying, "Not yet."

Parker's face grew warm. "Why not?"

Blackwell looked to Johnson, then returned to Parker. "We're short-staffed. We've got units tied up securing the house. I figured we'd wait until you got here."

It sounded like administrative double-talk, and the warmth in Parker's face spread down his neck. He pointed at the three officers standing in the street. One of them now animatedly told a story while the other two laughed. "What about those guys? They aren't doing anything."

Blackwell didn't look back. Instead, he smiled nervously and scratched behind his ear. "They've been running call-to-call all night and—"

"Hey!" Parker yelled.

The three officers turned in his direction.

"Come here."

Blackwell eyed the detectives. "They're supposed to go back into service."

Parker frowned. Not only did the sergeant's disregard for personal care bother him, but the man's lack of command did as well. He'd seen this absence of leadership while in the Army. It never boded well for those platoons.

"Knocking on doors is more important than shagging calls."

Maybe Blackwell could have argued differently, but Parker knew he wouldn't. Certain leaders in the department could be bullied, and Sergeant Wes Blackwell was one of them. It didn't take a Major Crimes position to know that.

Blackwell didn't look at the approaching officers. "I already said they could go back," he said under his breath.

The three men neared. The one previously telling the story seemed the most irritated—probably because Parker had interrupted his stage time. All must have been new to the department because Parker hadn't seen them before. Their name tags were silver, which signified they had passed their first year. Parker didn't bother reading their names, though. He didn't care.

"Yeah?" the first officer asked.

Johnson put his hand on Parker's shoulder and spoke. He was better at defusing inter-department conflicts—at least, Parker thought so.

"I need you to check the neighborhood for witnesses," Johnson said. "See if anyone saw or heard anything that might be useful."

The first officer thumbed over his shoulder. "We're handling calls."

"That's what you were doing?"

"Yeah."

"Well," Johnson said, "from over here, it looked like you were handling your dick."

Parker grinned. So maybe Johnson wasn't better at avoiding disputes.

"Excuse me?" the officer asked.

"You heard me." Johnson pointed into the middle of the street. "You three were over there acting like a bunch of rookies. If you can't figure out what to do at a homicide scene, we'll tell you." He motioned down the street. "Go knock on some doors. Ask some questions. Do your jobs."

The first officer turned to the sergeant. "You going to let him speak to us that way?"

Blackwell's embarrassment was evident. "It's their crime scene. They're in charge."

"This is bullshit," the officer said to Johnson. "When dispatch starts crying about a screen full of calls, I'm gonna tell them to contact you."

Johnson's eyes narrowed. "You do that. And in case you forget, he's a sergeant, we're homicide detectives, and that means you're at the bottom of the goddamned hill." He pointed. "Start with that house over there."

The three officers briefly glared at Johnson before wandering off.

"Nicely played," Parker said.

Johnson nonchalantly shrugged. "They got the point."

"Maybe I should deal with the interpersonal stuff next time."

"You think you would have done it better?"

"Couldn't have done worse." Parker faced Sergeant Blackwell. "Let's see the bodies."

Chapter 7

Parker and Johnson followed Sergeant Blackwell around to the back of the house. As they rounded the corner, a beam of light illuminated them.

"Halt," a male voice ordered. "Who goes there?"

Parker lifted a hand to shield his eyes. "Rudy?"

"Who else, meathead?" The light dropped away. Senior Patrol Officer Kyle Rudinger stood in the middle of the backyard with a flashlight in one hand and a clipboard in the opposite. "I see they sent in the B-team."

Parker grabbed his crotch. "I got your B-team right here."

"Is that what you tell Brooke?" Rudinger laughed and moved closer. "What's up, broseph?"

Parker slipped under the yellow line of POLICE—DO NOT CROSS TAPE that signified the inner perimeter and crossed the lawn. He extended his hand, and Rudinger shook it. The two men had gone through the academy together. They'd been early friends in the department. However, their differences in career aspirations were quickly discovered. While Parker couldn't wait to leave patrol, Rudinger was destined to remain there until he retired.

"They got you keeping the log?" Parker asked.

"Every man takes a turn." Rudinger illuminated Johnson with the flashlight. "Hey, Jessie. How you been?"

"Good, man. You?"

"Hunting zombies. Going for the high score. Might just make it."

Jessie eyed Parker. "I'll get started inside."

Parker nodded and turned his attention back to his friend. "What's it like in there?"

"Three dead. Double taps in each." Rudinger entered some information on the clipboard. "The fourth is at the Family, but I doubt she'll make it. She looked bad. Took some rounds to the back."

Parker grabbed Rudinger's upper arm. "How are you?"

Rudinger grunted as he finished filling in the log. When he looked up, he said, "We should get the families together sometime and catch up."

"I'd like that. Maybe do a barbecue."

"Only if I can do the cooking. You'll make the plain chicken you like. Yuck. How many are you and Brooke up to now?"

"Three."

Rudinger grimaced. "Damn, buddy. You going for ten or something?"

Parker shrugged a single shoulder. "If she lets me."

"I'd accuse you of being Catholic if I didn't know how filthy you are." Rudinger motioned toward the house. "Good luck in there."

"Stay safe, man."

Parker turned and left his friend in the dark.

***

Three bodies slumped over a round card table—all white men. A fourth chair was empty and on its side. Car keys, cell phones, wallets, and other pocket detritus lay amid puddles of liquid from four tipped-over bottles of Bud Light. A couple of rounds had pierced the flimsy table.

There were two other card tables in the room surrounded by other white plastic chairs—they were undisturbed as if they hadn't been recently used.

Johnson stood near the bodies. He wore a pair of blue booties over his shoes, and his pencil danced across his sketchpad. Parker never brought a sketchpad whenever Johnson was present at a crime scene. The man's artistic skills were exceptional, while Parker's sketches looked like a five-year-old attempted to document a crime scene for a school project—the only thing missing was that they weren't drawn in crayon.

The room the detectives were in was an addition to the house. Even though a couple of soft-glow bulbs were lit, the room was poorly illuminated. Parker slowly waved his flashlight about to examine every nook and cranny better.

It might have originally been a sunroom. This room had southern exposure and would get plenty of light. Large windows ran the length of the back wall. It was still dark out, but Parker believed there weren't many trees to block the sun. Maybe that's why it only needed two soft-glow bulbs. It might be overly bright during the day and even a nuisance to be in the room.

The north wall was the former exterior of the house—its siding still showed. Four faded movie posters hung along this stretch—*Bull Durham*, *Major League*, *The Sandlot*, and *Field of Dreams*. They were unframed, and pushpins were stuck in each corner. Neon signs hung between them—Bud Light, Captain Morgan, and a vintage Hamm's.

A white refrigerator stood in the far corner. Parker illuminated it with his flashlight. Baseball-related magnetics clung to it. Many of the major league teams were represented. A magnet for the Spokane Indians was stuck to the side.

Two magnets caught Parker's eye, and he moved closer to inspect them. On the first, a naked woman lay with a catcher's mitt between her legs. The tagline "Put it in the Strike Zone" was emblazoned above her. The second magnet was of a naked man wearing a baseball hat and holding a bat above his shoulder. Its tagline was "Batter Up."

On top of the refrigerator was a block of light wood with the burned phrase "The Shortstop." A plastic trash container sat next to the appliance.

Parker's gaze continued to sweep the room as Johnson worked his sketch.

Insulation was neatly tucked between the exposed ceiling beams. A hanging fan remained silent. Parker paused on the fixture for a moment. There were no lights attached to it. He briefly wondered why and then decided it didn't matter.

The scuffed hardwood flooring held the tell-tale signs that members of the fire department had responded—dirty boot prints, opened bandage packages, discarded latex gloves, and a popped cap from an IV drip. The fire department's mission was critical, but every homicide investigator universally referred to them as the Evidence Eradication Unit.

Blood had pooled where the missing victim had fallen. There wasn't much gathered under the other victims due to them being killed in a sitting position.

Parker's attention returned to his partner. He didn't say anything, though. While Johnson's pencil jumped around the pad, he quietly waited. They had developed this routine, and it worked for them. Once Johnson got the basics down on paper, he'd let his partner know. Until then, Parker would remain silent and let the man do his thing.

He illuminated the walls behind the other bodies. It appeared that a round may have entered the wall behind one man. Either the bullet traveled through the victim, or the shooter missed their mark entirely. Parker hoped a slug got caught in a stud and didn't pass through the outer wall.

Sergeant Blackwell moved and bumped into a plastic chair at another table. It tipped over and clattered to the floor.

"Sorry," the sergeant muttered.

Parker scowled.

Blackwell lifted both hands in apology but didn't say anything further. Parker wanted to give the man credit for doing something—anything—right, but it was hard. At least he wore a pair of booties. Then again, Johnson might have given them to him.

The sergeant was an enigma. He was out-of-shape and slovenly, but he'd made it to sergeant—that meant he tested well. The department didn't have annual physical fitness tests like the military branches. If SPD did such a thing, Parker imagined a third of the department would either quit immediately or be placed on a performance improvement plan. Personally, he longed for such a thing.

Blackwell reached down and lifted the chair back to its original place. Parker's gaze remained on the floor, though. He quickly scanned the entirety of the room. There were no shell casings anywhere.

"If you build it," Johnson said as he continued to sketch, "they're supposed to come. Isn't that the promise?"

Parker glanced at his partner. "Say again."

"The movie," Blackwell answered for him. He pointed at the dull *Field of Dreams* poster. "It's a classic." The sergeant smiled. "One of my favorites."

Parker grunted. It was better than a snarky reply. He eyed Johnson. "You see the block of wood on the refrigerator?"

"What about it?"

"Maybe this is a clubhouse for a softball team." Parker pointed to the man on the left. The guy wore a baseball jersey with the name *Blair* written across his upper shoulders.

Johnson shrugged but didn't look up from his sketchpad. "Either that or it's a sex society."

Parker cocked his head. "You okay?"

"Shortstop is code for dry humping."

"Since when?"

Johnson looked up. "You're killing me, Smalls."

"What?"

"The movie," Blackwell interjected again. He pointed at another movie poster, but Parker waved him off.

"How is this a sex society?" Parker asked.

"You've been around the bases—right?"

"I got the kids to prove it, but I've never heard anything about shortstop. You're making that up."

Johnson clucked his tongue. "It's common knowledge." He looked to the sergeant, who seemed surprised to be included in the conversation.

Blackwell nodded enthusiastically, but Parker didn't believe he knew what Johnson was talking about.

"Listen," Johnson said, "first base is kissing, second base is hands in the pants, and third base is going down on each other."

"Okay." Parker elongated both syllables.

"There's gotta be something between second and third."

"Dry humping," Blackwell said.

Johnson pointed his pencil at the sergeant.

Parker motioned at the three dead men. "You think these guys came here to dry hump?"

"I'm keeping an open mind." Johnson stared at him with a flat expression. "You should, too."

"It's a baseball hangout, jagoff. Not some sex club."

Johnson chuckled. "Maybe they came here for a dry hump orgy." His face pinched. "Although there was only one girl, but maybe that was her thing." Johnson shrugged. "What would we call that—a bump train?" He looked to Blackwell. "What do you think? Could she get a rug burn doing that with three guys?"

Parker thought Johnson was a great partner—he wouldn't want to be paired up with anyone else in Major Crimes—but there were times that the guy irritated the hell out of him. This was one of them. They were standing in the middle of the biggest crime scene of their careers, and he wanted to make cracks about people screwing with their clothes on.

Johnson eyed him. "Ready to get started?"

"I'm waiting on you."

"I'm done." Johnson turned to the table. "Check out the keys."

Parker moved closer. "What about them?"

"There are three sets." The guy furthest from them only had a wallet and some gum. The keys for the missing woman were still there.

"Maybe he walked," Parker said.

"Yeah. Could be."

"Did you notice the brass?"

"You mean that there is none?" Johnson's gaze drifted to the floor. "What're you thinking? The shooter stopped to pick up the expended cartridges?"

"Pretty ballsy if you ask me. Maybe he used a revolver." Parker turned to Sergeant Blackwell. "Was anybody inside the main structure?"

"We cleared it."

Parker glanced at the door to the house. "Why wouldn't they drink inside there?"

Johnson pointed through the windows to the moon. "You probably can't see that from inside."

"And it was a nice night," Sergeant Blackwell said.

Parker admitted that the temperature felt comfortable for this time of year. It wasn't too cool. He could probably remove his windbreaker and still be warm enough in just his long-sleeved shirt and jeans.

He studied the table again. There were four beers and as many bottle caps. He looked at the trash bin next to the refrigerator. "Hey, Sarge. Check out that can and tell me how many beers are in there."

Blackwell popped open the receptacle and peered inside. "None. It's a new bag."

"What about the fridge?"

The sergeant yanked open the refrigerator door to expose a rack mostly full of Bud Light.

Parker waved for Blackwell to close the door. "They hadn't been here long. Looks like they were still on their first round."

"Then the shooter arrives," Johnson said. He continued to work on his sketch. "You think the killer was waiting for them? Or followed them here?"

Parker shrugged. "Maybe the victims just got off shift from somewhere. They could all work late in a warehouse or something."

"Dunno," Johnson said. "Maybe."

Parker rubbed his chin as he thought. Eventually, he looked over his shoulder to Blackwell. "You said you identified these guys?"

He nodded.

"How?"

"After my guys checked everyone's vitals, they contacted dispatch to start medics. While they waited, one of them went through the wallets and called in the names."

"Did your guys wear gloves?"

Blackwell blinked twice before saying, "The wallets were out."

"Maybe the killer checked their IDs, too."

The sergeant frowned, but he didn't look away. "They didn't know."

Typical, thought Parker. He waved toward the table. "Give us the rundown, so we don't have to disturb it anymore than necessary."

Blackwell awkwardly tugged his notebook from his pocket. Parker wondered why he put it away after struggling to get it out earlier—probably habit. Parker thought a lot about habits.

The sergeant flipped the notebook open with dramatic flair when he got it free. Parker half-expected him to lick the tip of his finger before flicking through the pages.

Blackwell pointed to the dead man on the left side of the table—the one with the white baseball jersey. His head lay with his face turned toward Parker. The cheek pressed against the table was so mushed that it made him look like a one-eyed man.

"That's Albert Blair," Blackwell said. "Thirty-seven. No history."

Johnson jotted the name onto the sketchpad. "Next."

The sergeant pointed to the man in the middle. He wore a red T-shirt and had light brown hair. "That's Jarrod Stone. Forty-two. Registered sex offender."

"For what?"

"Kiddie rape," Blackwell said.

Parker and Johnson both stared at him.

The sergeant cleared his throat, then consulted his notebook. "Third-degree rape of a child."

Parker moved so he could get a better look. Unfortunately, the man lay face down, and Parker didn't want to disturb the body until the crime scene technicians took their photographs and collected their evidence.

"Next," Johnson said.

Blackwell motioned to the last man. He wore a green tracksuit jacket and faded blue jeans. "Jeffrey Krill. Thirty-nine. The homeowner. No history."

Parker squatted to look at Krill. Like the first man, he'd landed on the side of his face. He was thin, and his cheek didn't compress his bottom eye closed. Krill stared unblinkingly back at Parker.

"And the woman at the hospital?" Parker asked.

"Lindee Dawson. Thirty-four. Rape victim about ten years ago."

Johnson pointed at each body and said their names, "Blair, Stone, Krill." For the empty chair, he muttered, "Dawson."

Parker studied the wallet of the missing woman. It was a simple leather billfold—something he'd imagine a man might carry. He lifted a single eyebrow. "She say anything?"

"She was unresponsive when the first officers arrived," Blackwell said. "She's lucky to be alive, although the medics didn't give her much chance at survival."

Parker and Johnson made eye contact.

"Robbery gone bad?" Johnson asked.

"Wallets and cell phones were left."

"Check the contents of the wallets."

Parker pulled a pair of latex gloves from his pocket and tugged them on. He opened the first wallet. "Credit cards but no cash."

"Who carries cash anymore?" Johnson asked.

"I do," Blackwell said from the corner of the room.

Parker moved to the remaining three wallets. Each was the same—no cash. "Could be a robbery," he said without much conviction.

"If they had cash to begin with," Johnson said. "I haven't carried cash in years."

"But one out of four had to," Parker said. "Right?"

Johnson shrugged. "If we're playing the odds, maybe."

Parker removed the gloves. As he did, he noticed the posters on the wall. He lifted his chin toward them. "You've watched them all?"

"You haven't?"

He hadn't seen any of them, but since he didn't participate in team sports, he never wanted to watch a movie about them. "You ever see a home bar like this?"

"Sure—my grandparents' basement. My grandfather built one for him and his war buddies after he had a falling out with the VFW. Cantankerous old bastard."

Parker resurveyed the scene. He squatted and let his gaze sweep back and forth over the room. He stood and looked at the exterior door. He twisted the knob and pulled it open.

In the backyard, Officer Rudinger turned. The beam of his flashlight crossed the lawn until it illuminated Parker. The light quickly snapped off. "Sorry, bud."

Parker waved, but he didn't respond. There was a different concern that he didn't want to lose track of. He glanced over his shoulder to Johnson. "If this was your home and you had a bar in it, would you invite just anybody over?"

Johnson motioned to the bodies. "You don't think these guys are friends?"

"That's not what I'm saying." Parker turned around. "I think they were friends or at least associates, but how did the killer know this hangout was here?"

"Maybe he followed them."

Blackwell spoke up. "I see what Parker's saying. Like had the killer been here before?"

Both detectives stared at the sergeant. He lifted his hands in mock surrender. "That's what you two are working out."

"The entrance is in the rear of the house," Parker said. "So, how did the killer know to get back here?"

Johnson eyed his partner. "If it's a hangout, then the killer's a friend, but if it's an after-hours joint...?" He let the question trail off.

"Like anybody could come here and drink?" Parker looked around. "This is sort of a dumpy place for people to come to willingly—isn't it?"

"I don't know," Johnson said. "You ever been in an after-hours joint?"

"I thought they were the stuff of legend."

"Maybe not. Maybe we're standing in one."

Parker smirked. "I think it's a clubhouse for a softball team. Maybe the killer heard about it after some game. Maybe he's mad that his team lost."

Johnson motioned with his pencil. "You think these guys got killed because of a game?"

"People have been killed for less."

"But softball?"

"We're going down a rabbit hole." Parker pointed at the door. "I'm wondering how the killer just walked up to this entrance." He now waved at the bodies. "Didn't they think it weird that someone else was here at this time of the morning? Or were they expecting the killer? Or were strangers welcomed?"

"And if they weren't welcomed, why didn't they try and do something about it?" Johnson handed his sketchpad to the sergeant. "Hey, help me check if these guys are carrying."

Parker moved toward Albert Blair. He carefully moved his hands around the body but did not find a weapon. "Nothing."

Johnson did the same thing with Krill. "Negative."

Parker shimmied around the table to Jarrod Stone and patted his hands over the body. "Same."

"So," Johnson said, "the killer enters the room—"

"The Shortstop," Sergeant Blackwell corrected. He absently pointed to the block of wood on top of the refrigerator.

Johnson frowned. "The killer enters The Dry Hump and shoots everyone. Why?"

Parker held his hand over Jarrod Stone's head. "To steal old boy's keys?"

"Seems like a lot of death to bogart a set. What was on them? House, car, maybe a key to a lockbox or something?" Johnson surveyed the room again. "What would the killer have done if the other tables were full?"

Parker eyed the two empty tables. If all the chairs had been occupied, that would have meant twelve people in the room. "If the killer was known, maybe he would have had a drink and waited until the rest of the team left."

"Or," Johnson said, "maybe he would have come back another night." Johnson turned toward Blackwell. "Hey, Sarge. Get on the horn to your officers and have them ask the neighbors how much activity this house had. Maybe we're not understanding what went on back here."

The sergeant nodded and reached for his microphone.

Parker added, "And have them ask if those neighbors ever filed a complaint."

Sergeant Blackwell paused. "It would have shown up on the house's history when we responded. There was nothing."

"You know how things are," Parker said. "Maybe they didn't complain to Crime Check."

The sergeant cocked his head. "Who, then?"

"If a neighbor filed a complaint, maybe they did so through a local COP shop, and an NRO got involved."

Neighborhood Resource Officers were assigned to geographical areas. Their workload consisted of those problems that fell between calls for service and cases assigned to detectives. They focused on drug houses, neighborhood nuisances, and problem individuals.

Spokane's Community Oriented Policing Services (COPS) program had offices sprinkled throughout various neighborhoods. An NRO was often assigned to those locations and worked fairly autonomously. If a neighbor had complained about this house to the NRO, perhaps someone was already working on it but never notified dispatch; therefore, it wasn't logged into the system.

Sergeant Blackwell nodded his understanding, then activated his microphone to call dispatch.

"Let's get out of here," Johnson said, "until the crime scene guys arrive and finish processing the scene."

Both men exited The Shortstop and removed their booties. They walked around the side of the house toward the street. Each was lost in his own thoughts.

Up ahead, several crime scene technicians milled about a boxy white van. The side of the vehicle was emblazoned with the logo *Spokane County Sheriff Forensic Unit.*

Johnson said, "We need a warrant for the house."

Parker stopped and looked toward the backyard. The murder occurred in the home's addition. Officers had searched the house upon their arrival for other victims and potential suspects. They did so under the auspices of officer safety.

That meant the detectives still had access to the house. It wouldn't take anything for Parker to quickly walk through the structure. However, if a critical piece of evidence was found, a defense attorney might be able to get it tossed as part of an illegal search. Parker would like to slam the door on any wiggle room a defense attorney might have.

"Yeah," he said. "Let's write it up."

Parker headed toward the crime scene technicians. Two of the patrol officers who were supposed to be out door knocking were back and trying to talk with Geri Utley. She seemed distracted. Perhaps she was tired. Whatever it was, the officers pressed with their patter, and her face registered discomfort. She didn't tell them to stop, though.

"You two," Parker said, "don't you have something to do?"

"Yeah," the nearest officer said. He casually turned to the detective and curled his lip. "Your mom."

The officer stood several inches taller than Parker and looked down at him. This wasn't the first wannabe bully that Parker had faced in his life. And it wasn't the first who thought he could intimidate Parker with his height.

Parker exaggeratedly leaned in and read the officer's silver name tag. "You got a problem, Henderson?"

Henderson glanced to Johnson, who stood about the same height. "I was talking to Geri."

"Not anymore," Parker said.

The officer glanced over his shoulder, but Geri had stepped into the evidence truck.

Parker eyed the second officer. "What about you?"

"There are some doors a block over." The officer lifted his hands in deference and spun without further comment. It was clear he understood that arguing with a homicide detective at an active investigation was a losing proposition.

But Henderson dug in for a fight. He crossed his arms, and his scowl deepened.

"What's your problem?" Parker asked.

"I see how it is."

"And how is that?"

"You guys show up, and everyone is supposed to kiss the ring. Well, not me."

Parker scoffed, and Johnson barked a laugh.

"Listen, slick-sleeve," Parker said, casually pointing out that the man had yet to pass his first three-year mark and earn a time-in-service strip. "The coffee grounds in my trash can have been in the department longer than you."

"Probably worth more than you, too," Johnson added.

Henderson's face reddened. "You can't talk to me like that. I'll go to my guild rep."

Parker thrust a finger into the officer's chest. He felt the steel plate in Henderson's Kevlar vest. "I'll talk to you any way I want. This is *my* crime scene, not yours." Parker's voice rose. "You either stop acting like a frat boy while you're out here and follow my directions, or I'll let your chain of command know about your inability to do your job. No guild rep will protect you from dicking the dog at a homicide scene. Do you understand?"

Henderson's scowl eased. He glanced uncomfortably at Johnson.

"Now," Parker said, "take a hike."

The officer seemed to consider a response but ended up only nodding twice. He quietly slipped between the two detectives and walked off.

Johnson lifted an eyebrow. "Dicking the dog?"

Parker shrugged. "It made the point."

Geri stepped from the van and joined the detectives. "Thank you."

"Why didn't you tell them to get lost?" Parker asked.

Her lips twisted into a frown. "I try to be nice, but they take that as an invitation."

Johnson waved off the departing officer. "He hasn't got the memo that you don't date cops."

"That's why they try so hard," Parker said. "You don't fall prey to the CDI factor."

Geri cocked her head in a questioning manner.

"Chicks Dig It. They're used to a certain amount of attention from the female half of our species due to the badge."

"You should develop a new policy," Johnson said. "Shut those ding-dongs down before they get any momentum. Cut them off at the knees. Be a bitch."

She smiled wanly. "I don't know. That's not me."

Parker studied Geri. She wore a nylon jacket, blue jeans, and boots. She was an attractive woman, but something was off in her eyes today—she looked exhausted.

"You doing okay?" he asked.

"We caught another multiple in the valley yesterday. We were out there most of the day. Then we spent the evening at the property room logging everything in." She shrugged. "That's how it goes, though, I guess. How bad is this one?"

"Messy."

Johnson looked toward the back of the house. "Three bodies in an attached room." He shrugged a single shoulder. "Looks like it might have been a clubhouse. Whatever it was, it's a hokey setup."

Geri stiffened.

"What?" Parker asked.

"That's what we were on yesterday, although everyone kept referring to it as an after-hours joint." She quickly filled them in on the details of five deaths at a hookah lounge. "McAfee and Chambers are running with it."

"They get any leads on their murders?" Parker asked.

"I don't think so," Geri said. "At least not while they were out there. Maybe they developed something later in the day."

Parker flexed his jaw. Maybe the two incidents weren't related. Perhaps it was a giant coincidence. But he didn't believe in coincidence, especially when he thought after-hours joints were alcohol-infused myths.

"They were looking for a car," Geri said as she reached back into the evidence van.

"What kind?" Parker said.

***

Parker and Johnson checked the vehicles parked along Euclid Avenue. Both sides of the street were lined with them even though Drumheller Springs sat to the north. They found a couple of abandoned vehicles with flattened tires, busted windows, and dusty bodies.

"What's an '82 Quattro look like?" Johnson asked.

"How would I know?" Parker said. "Look for the Audi logo."

"I guess all those cars from that decade should look the same."

That stopped Parker. He watched his partner walk away. Eventually, Johnson realized he was alone, and he turned around.

"What's that supposed to mean?" Parker asked. "They should look the same?"

"Dated," Johnson said. "Old. Don't overthink it."

Parker reconsidered the cars. "We need to figure out who drives what."

"You mean which cars belonged to our victims?"

"Exactly." Parker headed back toward the scene.

Sergeant Blackwell stood on the sidewalk in front of Jeffrey Krill's home. His hands were on his hips, and he was frowning. His face relaxed when Parker sidled up next to him. Johnson stood nearby.

"All good?" Parker asked Blackwell.

"Just thinking."

"We need an officer to search the immediate area for an '82 Audi Quattro."

"What for?"

"There was a multiple in the county yesterday," Parker said. "It has some similarities to this case. An Audi was stolen from one of the victims."

Blackwell rolled his lip down. "I didn't read about that in the Hot Sheet."

"Me either."

The Crime Analysis team accumulated information from within the department and neighboring agencies that might be useful and put it together in a daily packet called the Hot Sheet. The CA team worked on spotting trends that officers and detectives could quickly respond to.

"The murders probably didn't make it onto yesterday's sheet," Parker said, "due to the time of day, the scene broke down. I bet they'll be in today's sheet. From what Geri told us, there weren't any witnesses, and it sounds like there were no early suspects."

Blackwell looked toward the Krill home. "Sounds familiar."

"So this Audi—"

"You think the killer stole that car and drove it here?"

Parker shrugged. "I've got no idea—"

"Why would they do that?" The sergeant furrowed his brow. "It's sort of an easily recognizable car."

"I've got no idea why they'd do it, Sarge, but can you get an officer to check the surrounding neighborhoods? There's only one way in here." Parker motioned along Euclid Avenue. "And there's no Audi here."

Blackwell surveyed the street. "Maybe they drove it away."

Parker stared at him.

"Yeah. All right. We'll look for it." The sergeant grabbed his shoulder microphone and announced his call sign.

Parker turned to his partner. "One of us should go to the hospital while the other runs the crime scene here."

Johnson said, "You go."

"No, that's cool. If you want—"

"Not me, buddy." Johnson patted Parker's shoulder. "I sat around the last time."

"Come to my car." Parker started walking.

Johnson hurried alongside. "What's up?"

"Brooke made you lunch."

"Why'd she do that?"

Parker smiled at his partner. "Why do you think?"

Johnson appeared defensive. "Ashley worked a double yesterday."

"I didn't say anything." Parker reached into his car and pulled out a brown paper bag. He handed it to his partner. "Brooke worries about everyone. You know how she is."

"Ashley will kill me if she finds out another woman made my lunch. You know how she is."

"Don't tell her. Say the volunteers brought sandwiches for everyone." Parker dropped into the driver's seat. "Gotta go."

Chapter 8

Parker left his car in a Police Vehicles Only zone and headed toward Holy Family Hospital. He walked past an ambulance parked near the emergency room entrance.

A large metal detector sat in the building's entryway. Anyone entering the lobby would need to proceed through the contraption. A security guard watched Parker with bored eyes. He was a heavy-set white man in his early fifties with a flat-top haircut and a jowly face. He rested on the edge of a metal stool. His right elbow leaned on the butt of his gun. Parker imagined the man had retired from a career in law enforcement from another agency and started the security gig as a way to supplement his income.

Parker stepped to the side of the machine and introduced himself.

With some effort, the guard slipped from the edge of the stool. It looked painful for the man to stand. With all that weight on those knees and hips, Parker could understand why. The guard motioned Parker around the metal detector. "You here for the shooting victim?"

"Lindee Dawson?"

"If that's her name. They already got her in surgery. She wasn't looking so good when she came in."

"She say anything?"

"Not that I heard. The cop who rode with her took off once they wheeled her in." The guard pointed back outside. "But that's her ride out there. Maybe you can talk to the medics who brought her in."

Parker spun on his heel.

No one was behind the steering wheel of the ambulance, so Parker headed toward the back of the vehicle. Both doors were opened. Two medics were inside—a man and a woman. They appeared to be cleaning up after delivering Lindee. Parker caught a piece of their conversation.

"*God made man*," the guy sang out of tune, "*but a monkey was the glue.*"

"Devo," the woman said. "Right? But I don't think that's how it goes."

"Close enough. You impress the hell outta me. You really do. I didn't think you'd get that one."

Parker knocked on one of the doors. "Excuse me."

They both looked in his direction.

The man was in his late thirties and pale. The woman was roughly the same age, but she was a dark-skinned Latina. She appeared embarrassed at the interruption.

Parker showed his badge. "You picked up Lindee Dawson, the shooting victim on Euclid?"

Both medics moved toward the rear of the ambulance. Parker stepped back and allowed them to hop down. The woman's name tag identified her as Rodriguez. The man's tag showed him to be Smith.

"We picked her up," Rodriquez said. "Yeah. She was messed up six ways to Sunday. Shot twice in the back." She had a slight accent. It wasn't Hispanic, but rather from back east. Maybe Jersey or New York.

"You're sure?" Parker asked.

"We cut her shirt off," the woman said. "Hard to miss seeing them after that."

"You check for exit wounds?"

Rodriquez playfully smirked. "This ain't our first rodeo, Detective."

It had been a dumb question, Parker knew. He should have framed it differently. Smith chuckled at Parker's gaffe. Maybe he was laughing at the woman's comment. Either way, Parker's face and ears warmed.

When Smith noticed Parker watching him, the man's grin faded, and he cleared his throat. "Two entry wounds near the spine." He reached an arm around his back. "Then a couple of exits—" Smith tapped himself on the lower sternum with his other arm.

"Got it," Parker said.

Smith shrugged. "Not sure how one of them didn't blow her heart out, but she was wheezing bad when we found her, so at least one caught a lung."

Parker thought about the placement of the bodies at the Euclid house. Lindee sat with her back to the killer. She'd been shot at close range, and the rounds had passed through her to lodge into the table.

Rodriguez asked, "Ever hear a sucking chest wound?"

He had while on patrol. It was a sound he wouldn't likely forget.

The security guard appeared around the opened rear door of the ambulance. "Yo, Detective?"

Parker turned toward him.

"She didn't make it. Thought you should know."

"Great," Parker said sarcastically. "Thanks."

The guard nodded once and ambled away.

"Another one bites the dust," Rodriguez muttered.

"Queen," Smith said. "From their album, *The Game*."

Rodriquez seemed surprised by her partner's statement. "I wasn't playing," she whispered.

Parker studied the medics.

"It's a game," the female medic said with an embarrassed shrug. "To pass the time."

"Did the victim say anything about a shooter?"

"We don't normally ask those types of questions," Smith said. "We just try to keep them alive."

Rodriquez eyed her partner. "What about the cat?"

Smith's head bobbled. "She was out of her mind."

"A cat?" Parker asked.

"*The* cat," Rodriquez corrected. "That's all she said. It was like she was worried about it." Rodriguez held out her hand and dramatically said, "The cat. *The cat.*"

Parker pulled his notebook from his pocket and wrote the phrase into it. He wouldn't likely forget it, but he wanted it recorded, just in case. "What'd you do with her shirt after you cut it off?"

"It's with the staff inside," Rodriquez said. "Standard procedure."

Parker made another entry into his notebook.

If he was able to locate Lindee Dawson's killer, her clothes would become a significant piece of evidence. He'd have to document the chain of custody—how she was transported from the crime scene, who cut the shirt and why they did it, who received the shirt at the hospital, and when he recovered it.

"Can I get your full names for my report?" Parker asked.

After he got the information he needed, Parker thanked the medics and returned to the hospital's lobby.

The guard slid off his stool again. It looked no easier than the time before. "What can I help you with, Detective?"

"I need the victim's clothes."

***

Shortly after ten, Parker returned to the Euclid crime scene. As he pulled up, he noticed Jessie Johnson sitting on the hood of his patrol car. A small brown sack sat next to him.

Parker stopped his vehicle, grabbed his lunch, and joined his partner. He didn't sit on the hood though. Instead, he leaned over the front end.

"Evidence team is still inside," Johnson said. "How was the Family?"

"The girl is dead."

Johnson grunted and took another bite of his sandwich. He lifted it and said, "Tell Brooke thank you, by the way."

Parker reached into his brown paper bag and pulled out a sandwich. He tried to avoid eating bread, but when Brooke made his lunch, he didn't complain. He appreciated her efforts, especially on callout days. There had been other callouts when he didn't get anything to eat. Suffering through the additional calories would be the least of his worries today.

"Patrol identified three of the victims' cars," Johnson said. He motioned toward the street. "I'll show you after this." He stuffed the last bit of food into his mouth.

Parker bit into his sandwich. He wished he had something to drink. He'd forgotten to grab a water bottle when he left the house in the morning.

Johnson swallowed. "Jarrod Stone's car is missing."

While Parker chewed, he asked, "We're still going with the assumption that he drove?"

"What assumption?" Johnson brushed the crumbs from his hands. "Stone's missing keys means the killer stole his car. He had to have keys to get into his house or apartment, right? People don't just leave their home unlocked even if they walk."

"Unless they're homeless."

Johnson cast a sideway glance. "Why are you arguing?"

"Where did he live?"

"About half a mile north."

Parker opened a palm. "So he could have walked."

"He would have had his keys."

"Not if he left them at home."

"And left the house unlocked." Johnson's face pinched with frustration.

"Maybe Stone lived with someone."

"Maybe he did, but he'd still have keys."

Parker considered his sandwich. "What if he and that Lindee chick shacked up together."

"You think she carried the keys?"

"What if?"

"That's very modern of them."

Parker shrugged. "It's a modern world." He took another bite of his sandwich.

Johnson watched Parker eat. "I'm going with my assumption."

"Assume all you want." He swallowed before continuing. "But let's get proof before we run too far down that rabbit hole."

"You and your rabbit holes. The sergeant is running an AVR for Stone."

A thought occurred to Parker, and he looked around. "How come we don't have a command van out here? Since when doesn't a multiple homicide rate an administrative circle jerk? With the lieutenant in school, I'd figure at least Ackerman would be out here." Lieutenant George Brand was assigned to Major Crimes while Captain Gary Ackerman oversaw the entire Investigations Division.

Usually, both men would make an appearance on a case of this magnitude. So would Chief Dillon, for that matter.

At the moment, Brand was attending a leadership school back east. He'd been gone for a week and was expected to be gone for three more. The pleasure of his absence was one thing the otherwise splintered Major Crimes team universally agreed upon.

"I asked Blackwell the same thing," Johnson said. "Supposedly, the chief and most of the command staff went to Olympia yesterday afternoon to be in front of the governor this morning. You know, as a show of support against that use-of-force bill." Johnson mimed tossing off. "I guess it's a mass protest by the leadership of all police departments across the state."

"Who's in charge then?"

"Loose Lips."

Lieutenant Lorraine Lipsitz was a day shift lieutenant. The moniker was a reference to her willingness to share too much information with her team. Parker worked with her when she was a sergeant and liked her. She seemed capable of holding the department together for twenty-four hours. Beyond that, he wasn't too sure.

He eyed Johnson. "You want to flip for the warrant?"

"No need. Higgins and Nash are writing it for us."

Parker lowered his sandwich. "How'd that happen?"

Johnson shrugged. "I guess you playing nice with Nash paid dividends. The lieutenant asked them to help, and they jumped right in. If she would have asked the Glory Hounds, on the other hand—"

"I got it," Parker said. Neither he nor Johnson needed to say anything further. They wouldn't have gotten any enthusiastic support if their supervisor had asked those detectives.

Besides Parker and Johnson, there were two other teams in Major Crimes.

Dallas Nash and Glenn Higgins were the Old Dogs. They'd been around the longest and were quieter types who seemed to fly under the radar. Initially, Parker disliked them, especially Nash. They weren't the type of detectives to lend a hand to the new guys. Parker expected some sort of mentoring when he joined Major Crimes. Instead, he and Johnson were thrown into the pool's deep end and handed an anvil.

But the Old Dogs were nothing compared to the Glory Hounds—Quinn Delaney and Marci Burkett. They were the department's golden children. Parker admitted that they were decent enough detectives, but they weren't any better than him and Johnson, and they certainly weren't better than the Old Dogs. They weren't any improvement over the investigators before them, although Parker only knew the previous teams by reputation. He wondered if the Glory Hounds' on-high status was because Burkett was part of the equation—that the department elevated them to show some sort of gender equality. Whatever it was, she rubbed Parker the wrong way, and the fact that Delaney played patsy to her irritated him.

Sergeant Blackwell hurried over in his mock-running manner. His face pinched with frustration. "Aren't either of you wearing a radio?"

Parker reflexively touched his. "Mine's off."

"Mine's in the car," Johnson said.

"For shit's sake," Blackwell said. "This is a crime scene."

Parker's eyebrows rose. The sergeant wasn't the type to get riled up or to curse. He looked past Blackwell's shoulder. "Is something happening?" It didn't look that way.

"Dispatch is calling for you."

"Thank you for letting us know, Sarge." Parker clicked on his radio.

"I'm not your goddamn assistant."

"Is everything okay?"

Blackwell's head bobbled. "Yes, it's fine." His tone was sharp, and the man must have realized it because he repeated, "It's fine," but more softly. "I'm sorry. I'm taking some flak from the guys."

"Because of us?"

"They don't like the way you talk to them."

Parker remembered what it was like to be a patrol officer. He also remembered what it was like to be an enlisted man in the Army. Yet, neither of those versions of himself was responsible for finding the killer of four people. "If they have a problem, tell them to sack up and talk with us."

Blackwell smirked. "That'll go over well."

Parker considered his sandwich. "Tell them to nut up. They're cops, not girl scouts. If they can't handle the real world, tell them to go work in the Parks Department."

Johnson shook his head before eyeing Blackwell. "What'd radio want?"

The sergeant faced him. "An officer found your car."

"My car?"

The sergeant motioned toward Parker. "His car. Whatever. That Audi."

***

Parker dropped into the passenger seat of Johnson's Chevy Impala. Due to Euclid Avenue dead-ending into Drumheller Springs Park, there was only one way in or out. Johnson pulled his car into a nearby driveway, quickly reversed out of it, then drove from the neighborhood.

According to dispatch, the Audi Quattro was located near the corner of Belt Street and Dalton Avenue. Dalton was a block north of Euclid Avenue. The detectives took less than two minutes to loop around the park.

A patrol vehicle sat behind the red Audi. Its emergency lights were silent. There was no reason for the wigwags to flash. The classic car wasn't going anywhere now, and there was no other traffic on this side street.

Johnson stopped his Chevy nose-to-nose with the Audi.

Parker slipped from the passenger seat. "We're walking distance to the crime scene." He didn't bother to look at the Audi. Instead, he headed toward the park.

"Where you going?" Johnson called.

"I'll be back."

Johnson laughed. "All right, Terminator. Good luck."

Parker found a walking path and followed it down to Euclid Avenue. It took several minutes, but he soon popped out in front of the crime scene. Sergeant Blackwell noticed him and then looked in the direction that he and Johnson had driven off several minutes prior. Parker walked back into Drumheller Springs. This time he kept his head down like a bloodhound searching for a scent.

When Parker returned to asphalt, he looked up. Johnson held his cell phone to his ear and nodded while he spoke.

"Yeah, yeah," Johnson said. "We'll hold on to it until you get here." He hung up.

"Who was that?"

"McAfee. He's a couple hours out."

Parker nodded. "What's he want us to do with the car?"

"Sit on it until they can see it in relation to our crime scene."

Parker eyed the uniformed officer. "Sorry, man. You're waiting for the County's investigator."

"Everything rolls downhill." The officer headed toward his patrol car.

Parker faced Drumheller Springs.

Johnson stood next to him. "What are you thinking?"

"The killer parks the car here and then walks in. Come with me." Parker led the way back into Drumheller Springs. "I'm wondering why the guy stole the Audi to drive it to a second crime scene."

"Maybe he didn't have a car."

"If that's the case, steal a different car. I mean, steal one today." Parker looked over his shoulder at his partner. "Driving the car from the previous murder scene is reckless."

"Bordering on stupid."

"No bordering about it." Parker stopped walking. He glanced around the wide-open area. The sun was up now, but he tried to imagine it in the cover of night. "Is walking through this park reckless and stupid?"

Johnson glanced around. "I think it shows planning. He knew where the house was."

"So, he knew where to dump the car."

"Maybe he wasn't going to dump the car. Maybe the original plan was to return to the vehicle and drive it out."

"So the Audi was taken from the other murder scene not out of opportunity but out of need?"

Johnson shrugged. "What do I know? I'm guessing right now."

Parker started walking again. "So we've got a killer who identified a target, acquired transportation to it, and stole different transportation out."

"You think he's trained? Maybe military?"

"Or he's played a lot of video games. Maybe he watched some war movies and is living out a fantasy. The guy could have read a lot of books, for all we know. It's not like this information isn't readily available."

The detectives left the park and stepped onto Euclid Avenue.

"Over here," Johnson said. He led his partner to a black Mitsubishi Lancer parked curbside in front of the crime scene. "This one is owned by Jeffrey Krill, the homeowner."

Sitting behind it was an older red Kia Sorento. Johnson pointed at it. "That's owned by Lindee Dawson."

Across the street was a red Tesla Model 3. "And that one belongs to Albert Blair."

"One of these things is not like the other," Parker said.

Sergeant Blackwell approached. He carried several papers. "Your warrants arrived." He handed them to Johnson. "And dispatch called about that AVR on Jeffrey Krill. You're looking for a 2012 blue Ford Fusion. I've already put an Attempt to Locate on it."

Parker nodded. "Thanks, Sarge. We appreciate that." He headed toward the back of the house.

Johnson walked alongside him. "Did the killer pick the two vehicles at random?"

"Let's say he did," Parker said. "Would it matter what he drove? He's not hauling anything—right?"

"I don't think so. But we're saying that the killer arrived at McAfee's crime scene, murdered some folks, and decided to steal an old Audi?"

Parker stopped walking. "That doesn't make sense."

"What doesn't?"

"How did the killer get to the first crime scene? Did he steal a car and abandon it there just like he did with the Audi?"

"Maybe his car broke down, so he was forced to steal one."

The two men stared at each other. "Then that means it could still be in the neighborhood."

Johnson shook his head. "But they hit Jeffrey Krill's house the next night by using a stolen car. It doesn't seem smart. And it definitely doesn't make sense."

"Why not?" Parker asked. "Who's going to report it stolen? At least for a couple of hours? The dead guy won't."

"At some point, someone will," Johnson said. "We would. So why still drive it?" He pointed in the direction of the Audi. "Some patrol officer could have stopped him at any time. Even if the uniform didn't know about the murder or the car, maybe the guy failed to signal, ran a stop sign, or for a thousand other reasons."

"Maybe the killer was driving around in it as some sort of thrill."

Johnson's jaw tightened. "Like getting off on the fact that the cops hadn't found him yet?"

"And if he does get stopped—" Parker's expression flattened.

"It'll be a shootout."

The two detectives headed back for Sergeant Blackwell. Parker didn't even have to ask if Johnson thought the same thing he did. He wanted to ensure that Blackwell had included an armed and dangerous modifier on the Attempt to Locate the blue Ford Fusion. He should have since the car was stolen from a murder scene, but an ounce of prevention might save an officer's life.

Parker also wanted the sergeant to request additional help to search Drumheller Springs Park. Perhaps the killer dropped something when he fled the scene.

Chapter 9

Parker walked around the back of the house. Geri Utley and several forensic techs moved about the addition. They wore hazmat suits as they carried out their duties. Small yellow cards with large black numbers were placed about the room.

The three bodies were gone. Parker wondered how long ago they'd been removed. On the table were four small brown paper bags. They'd been placed according to where the victims had been seated. The keys, cell phones, and other pocket detritus from the victims were now inside the sacks.

"Geri," Parker said.

She turned his way. A digital camera with a zoom lens hung around her neck.

"We've got search warrants for the entire house and the cars. Throw us the homeowner's keys, and we'll go in the front door."

Geri pulled the suit's headpiece away and exposed her blond hair. She motioned toward the back door. "Cut through there. We're done."

Parker motioned toward the bags. "Don't log those yet. We'll need to get into the cars after we walk the house."

She nodded. "We'll wait until you tell us."

The two detectives passed through The Shortstop and into Jeffery Krill's home.

Parker didn't know anything yet about the homeowner's life. Did Krill have a roommate or a significant other who wasn't home? Sergeant Blackwell's officers already did a health and safety search of the house, so Parker didn't expect to find another body.

The house was nicely kept and decorated in a more fashionable way than the clubhouse outside. If that was shabby chic, then the home itself was merely stylish. There were hardwood floors throughout—colorful rugs lay strategically about. In the living room was a small leather couch.

"That's from IKEA," Johnson said. When Parker faced him, he continued. "What? Ashley and I went last month. She wanted the same one. Don't tell me you and Brooke have never been."

"We haven't."

"Whatever."

A black and white photo on the wall caught Parker's eye. It was an artistic nude—the shoulders to buttocks view of a white male.

"Don't stare too hard," Johnson said as he headed toward the hallway.

Parker glanced around the living room once more. He was looking for books or magazines, but he didn't find anything. He gave up and headed toward the hallway. There were three rooms off the corridor—one bathroom and three small bedrooms.

"The guy's a musician," Johnson said. He left the first room and went to the second.

Parker poked his head into the room that his partner had just left. It was set-up as a small music room. Several guitars sat in stands. A small stool was near an amplifier. On the walls were photographs of guitars and autographed pictures of musicians Parker didn't know.

The room seemed too clean for someone playing professionally. It appeared to be set up for someone to practice in occasionally. Or to show off to others.

He turned and went to the next room. Johnson was still there. This room felt more lived in. There was a yoga mat on the floor. A variety of exercise bands and foam-covered weights were stored in a corner. Parker knelt to touch a series of scuff marks on the floor.

"Find something?" Johnson asked.

"Jump rope."

"Makes those marks?"

"He probably used a cable rope that's frayed." Parker found the skip rope, located the worn portion, and showed it to Johnson. "You haven't seen this at your gym?"

"We have good equipment."

Parker smirked. "Fancy pants."

The two men moved into the final bedroom. Like the rest of the house, the room was well-kept. Several pictures of Jeffrey Krill were on his dresser. He was with a group of men in each of them. On the wall were a couple of black and white prints like the one in the living room—naked men shown from the neck down.

"I was hoping to find some next of kin info," Parker said, "but this doesn't look promising."

"Let's check his phone," Johnson said.

They returned to the house's back addition. Geri Utley was the only tech in the room. She collected the yellow number cards and stacked them on top of each other.

Parker pointed at the small bags on the table. "Which one belongs to Jeffrey Krill?"

Geri tapped the nearest. "What are you looking for?"

"His phone."

She reached into the bag and pulled it out.

Parker didn't want to put another pair of latex gloves on, so he said, "Power it on," to Geri.

When it came to life, she said, "Lock screen."

"Try one, two, three, four," Johnson said.

"Won't work with my gloves," she said.

Parker tapped his knuckle across the four digits. The screen remained locked. "Never mind."

Geri dropped it into the bag.

"What do we know about the homeowner?" Parker waved his hand at the movie posters.

"He's gay," Johnson said. "And he likes baseball."

"And he's dead," Geri said.

"There's that," Parker agreed.

He pulled his cell phone from his pocket and started the Facebook app. He'd usually do this from the computer in his office, but he felt slightly frustrated by the lack of information they'd gotten on the homeowner so far. His own Facebook page came up—he had one that he kept under the false identity of Mark Kaminski. It was the character Arnold Schwarzenegger played in *Raw Deal*. Many cops had fake names on social media even though most kept their accounts private. It only took one friend to allow the wrong person access to their page, and they would know a lot about Parker's life. Oversharing on social media was like waving a red flag to an enraged bull.

"What are you doing?" Johnson asked.

Parker ignored his partner and entered "Jeffrey Krill" into the search bar.

Geri asked, "You need me for anything further?"

"Hold on," Parker muttered.

"What's he doing?" Geri asked.

"Playing Candy Crush," Johnson said.

Parker clucked his tongue. "Shut up."

Several results for Jeffrey Krill popped up on Parker's phone. He selected one that he was sure was the victim of the homicide. There were only a couple of entries.

Johnson said, "Wait. You're playing Pokémon Go, aren't you?"

Geri chuckled.

The most recent Facebook post was from a couple of years ago, and it showed a photograph of Krill standing in front of The Baseline, a rundown bar on Monroe Street less than a mile away. The announcement underneath read *Here she is—my new home! Follow me here.*

Johnson moved closer. "Got a Squirtle?"

Parker looked up at his partner. Even Geri studied Johnson with surprised curiosity.

"What?" Johnson looked embarrassed. "I got nieces, and they play the game. That's how I know."

"And Candy Crush?"

"Ashley plays it sometimes," Johnson asserted.

Geri rolled her eyes. "Are you going to tell me why I'm still here?"

"Hold on," Parker said. He returned his attention to the phone.

He located the business page for the bar. It was filled with photographs of food, beer, and customers enjoying the atmosphere. "I think," Parker muttered before looking up, "this guy either owns or works at The Baseline."

Parker found a photograph of Krill in the bar smiling with a couple of guys wearing baseball jerseys. "Look." He spun the phone, so Johnson and Geri could see.

They both leaned in.

"When did The Baseline turn into a gay bar?" Johnson asked.

Geri sighed. "It's not."

"How do you know?"

"I've been," she said. "It's a baseball bar."

"Whatever." Johnson checked out the photos on Parker's phone. "It looks like a dick ranch."

Parker stared at his partner. "What's your problem?"

"Nothing." Johnson tried to look contrite. "I'm just saying."

"Gay guys like baseball, too," Parker said.

Geri groaned. "Last chance. What did you want from me?"

Parker eyed her. "When you log Krill's phone into property, let the IT guys know about it. I want them to bypass his security after you check the phone for prints."

"You could have told me that without making me wait."

Parker shrugged. "Yeah, I guess." He dropped his phone into his pocket. "C'mon, Squirtle. Let's go catch a Pokémon."

***

Parker pulled to the curb on West Point Road and exited his car. Johnson's Chevy Impala tucked in behind him. A second later, his partner left the car and studied the home listed as Albert Blair's address.

It must have been on half an acre of land, the shape of which reminded Parker of a bowling alley. The residence sat midway on the property. It was a larger structure with two peaked roofs and an attached garage. The home was painted in several shades of brown.

Behind the property was a cliff that dropped to the Spokane River. Parker coveted the homes in this neighborhood. For years, he had wanted to live on this street instead of the South Hill. However, with rapidly rising home prices, it was unlikely he would be able to do such a thing.

Johnson approached. "This explains the Tesla."

The neighborhood was quiet. It always seemed to be that way, which was part of Parker's obsession with it. There were only a handful of homes along this street, and they likely had some of the best views in the city. He'd never been inside any of the houses to confirm his suspicion, so this notification held a bit of fascination for him.

The detectives walked up the driveway. No cars were parked outside. There were no windows in the attached garage for them to peek through.

"I've been thinking," Parker said, "why steal the Fusion instead of the Tesla?"

Johnson shrugged. "Maybe the killer isn't a fan of the electric car."

Parker knocked on the front door. Inside, a large dog barked.

"But it's a Tesla," Parker said.

"It would stand out compared to a Ford."

"He stole an Audi Quatrro to begin with. Not exactly low profile."

Johnson shrugged. "The guy's a killer. Maybe he doesn't think like a rational human being."

Both men tried to peer through nearby windows. Curtains blocked Parker's view. "Anything?" he asked.

"No," Johnson said.

Parker knocked harder this time. This sent the barking dog into a frenzy. Still, no one came to the door.

"What do you think a guy like Blair does to earn a house like this?"

"No idea."

"Pull out your phone, Facebook. Look it up."

Parker grabbed his crotch. "Look this up, Squirtle."

"You got an itch down there or something? That's twice today that you've done that."

Parker stuck his hand in Johnson's face, and his partner batted it away.

"Better keep that jock itch away from Brooke," Johnson said. "You don't want her catching anything." He stepped off the porch and headed back toward their cars.

Reluctantly, Parker followed. He didn't want to leave, though. He really wanted to see the view from Albert Blair's house. Unfortunately, he'd have to complete another search warrant to do so.

***

Jarrod Stone's listed address was in a home behind the Garland Post Office. It was located about half a mile from where he was killed. Two cars were parked along the curb.

Compared to Albert Blair's home, Stone's residence was exceptionally modest. It was a two-bedroom affair with a well-kept lawn.

After Johnson knocked, a scrawny older man opened the door but remained behind the screen. He appeared to be in his early sixties. He wore a tank top and a pair of nylon shorts. His salt and pepper hair was mussed. He rubbed one eye with the top of his fist. "Yes?"

"Hi, I'm Detective Johnson. This is Detective Parker. We're with the Spokane Police Department."

The older man blinked several times. When he focused, suspicion filled his eyes. "What's this about?"

"You live here?"

He hesitated before answering. "This is my home, yes."

"What's your name?"

The man looked from Johnson to Parker, then back to Johnson again. "What's this about?" When the detectives didn't answer, the man said, "Carl Stone."

Johnson glanced at Parker before asking, "You're related to Jarrod?"

"He's my son." Carl straightened, and his face hardened. "You gonna tell me what the hell is going on, or you two gonna play that lousy cop game where you hold all your cards back until someone confesses to something they didn't do?"

"Your son was murdered this morning," Johnson said.

The color drained from Carl's face.

"May we come in?" Johnson asked.

The elder Stone pushed the screen door open and stepped back. "What happened?"

Johnson led the way into the house.

Parker followed his partner into the living room. His gaze swept over a tattered couch, a worn recliner, and a homemade entertainment center. *Judge Judy* ran silently on a flat-screen television. On the coffee table was a copy of *The Inlander*, the local free newspaper. A bag of Doritos spilled out next to it.

A blanket lay crumpled on the couch. It appeared that the detectives had interrupted Carl Stone's sleep. It was nearly ten in the morning now.

Johnson removed the notebook from his back pocket. "Do you know anyone who would want to hurt your son?"

Carl snorted. "Take your pick."

Parker stopped his visual search of the room and concentrated on the father.

The older man appeared to be fully awake now. He crossed his arms and stared defiantly at Johnson.

"Can you elaborate on that?"

"Sure," Carl said. "You bastards railroaded my son twenty-three years ago and ruined his life. What did you expect was going to happen?"

Johnson remained calm and held his pen above his notepad.

Carl shook his head. "She was fifteen, for crying out loud. She knew what she was doing. Even told the court as much. But you all had to go and side with her father and the judge just because my boy was nineteen." The man's face reddened. "Had the whole incident happened six months later, none of this would have ever stuck. Explain that to me. Can you?"

Jarrod Stone had been convicted of Rape of a Child in the Third Degree. It was a narrow crime for victims aged fourteen and fifteen only, with perpetrators at least four years older than them. The age of consent in Washington State was sixteen. If Carl was right and the girl turned sixteen years old some months later, his son would not have been in trouble. But the law was the law, and the cops didn't write them; they only enforced them.

"Because of that conviction," Carl continued, "my boy had trouble getting a decent job, never could find a real apartment. All due to that girl's lousy father. And you cops helped him! People who didn't know Jarrod would find out he lived in this neighborhood and come here." Carl's face pinched, and he waved his arms. "They called him a monster for being a boy in love with a girl. They were in high school, for Christ's sake." Carl dropped his arms and woefully shook his head. "Why did they do that to him?"

"He wasn't gay?" Parker asked.

Carl's face pinched. "The hell is wrong with you? You tell me he's murdered, and then you accuse him of being a homo? It's not enough to ruin his life. Now you want to slander his name, too?"

"Mr. Stone," Johnson said calmly. "My partner and I are here today to find who murdered your son. He was with several others." Johnson listed off their names. "Do you know of them?"

"Oh hell. *Jeffrey.*" Carl looked at Parker. "That's why you asked if he was gay. He got killed, too?"

The detectives nodded.

Carl held his head and slowly spun around. When he stopped turning, the elder Stone motioned to the south. "Jeffrey works at that bar—the baseball one they hang out at."

"The Baseline," Johnson said.

"That's it. Jeffrey's good people. I'm sorry about the homo crack."

Johnson nodded. "Back to my earlier question, who do you think might want to hurt your son?"

Remorse crossed Carl's face. "I don't know," he muttered. "Probably no one. I was just popping off. Thinking about all those sons of bitches over the years who said mean stuff to him." He sat on the edge of the coffee table. The newspaper crinkled underneath him.

"Does your son drive a Ford Fusion?"

Carl nodded.

"Did he drive it yesterday?"

The elder Stone looked up. "What are you asking?"

"We believe it was taken from the crime scene. We want to confirm that someone didn't borrow it or that it's not in a repair shop."

Carl glanced at Parker. "He left home with it yesterday." His gaze returned to Johnson. "You're saying some maniac killed my son and his friends to take his car?"

"We don't know that was why they were murdered."

"It's a dented Ford. Why would anyone want to take that piece of trash?"

Parker moved over to Johnson. "Does the cat mean anything to you?"

"The cat?" Carl asked.

Johnson eyed Parker.

"We don't have cats," Carl said. "Never have. Jarrod was allergic to the damn things, and I hate the miserable bastards."

***

Parker pulled into the parking lot of Jacob's Java at Sixth Avenue and Washington Street. The drive-thru coffee stand was still active at that time of day. There was a walk-up window. Several high school students waited patiently to be served.

Lindee Dawson lived with a roommate, Rainey Young. Parker and Johnson learned this by talking with the apartment community manager where Lindee had lived. The manager was the one who told them about Rainey.

Johnson parked his car next to him.

Parker climbed out of his car and swung the driver's door closed. He felt sluggish now. The lack of a morning workout was already getting to him, and it was barely noon. His sleep schedule had only been thrown off by one hour, but the lack of a workout bothered him more. Perhaps it was psychological.

He headed toward the coffee stand.

Johnson hurried up next to him. "You all right?"

"It feels like we've been handed a turd."

"What do you mean?"

Parker stopped. "This case is a loser."

"We just started."

"Some rando walks into a home club and kills four people before stealing a car. You think we're solving this?"

"Why not?"

"Some patrol cop is going to bust the killer while driving that stupid Fusion. They're going to get credit—not us."

"It's a team win."

"Screw the team." Parker continued toward the building. He bypassed the waiting line of high school students and walked toward the window.

"Hey," a girl whined. "No cuts."

"It's the cops," someone whispered.

The barista at the window eyed Parker and Johnson. "Can I help you?"

Parker pointed at his badge. "We need to speak with Rainey."

The barista looked over her shoulder. "Rainey. The cops are here for you."

A tall blond woman leaned away from one of the drive-thru windows and looked at Parker. He motioned her toward his car. She nodded.

The detectives walked away.

"So you were saying?" Johnson said.

"About?"

"Screwing the team."

Parker cast a sideways glance. "I don't want to do all this work for some other schlub to get the bip."

"It's our case. We'll get the bip."

"I want to make the actual arrest." When they made it to his car, Parker leaned against the trunk. "I want the credit."

"What about McAfee?"

"What about him?"

"Maybe our cases are related. What if he arrests the guy?"

Parker crossed his arms, and his lips twisted. "Thanks for that."

"I'm just saying."

"Why can't we arrest the guy?"

Johnson shrugged. "Nothing's saying we can't."

Rainey exited the little structure and crossed the parking lot. She was in her mid-twenties. She wore a long-sleeved T-shirt that hugged her form. Her dark blue yoga pants and running shoes hinted at an athletic lifestyle. When she neared the detectives, Rainey crossed her arms. "Yes?"

Parker introduced himself, then Johnson. He softened his expression and relaxed his posture. "Are you Lindee Dawson's roommate?"

"That's right."

"I'm sorry to tell you this, but she was murdered this morning."

Rainey blinked several times before the realization hit her. Tears welled in her eyes, and she covered her mouth with both hands.

"Three other men were killed at the same time," Parker said. "Albert Blair, Jarrod Stone, and Jeffrey Krill. Do you know those names?"

She nodded, but she didn't speak. Rainey closed her eyes, yet the tears still rolled down her cheeks.

Parker glanced at Johnson before saying, "I'm sorry."

"Yeah," Johnson added. He reached for the younger woman but stopped short of touching her arm.

"Jeffrey," Rainey said. "He owned the bar where she hung out on her days off." She wiped her eyes. "The other guys she talked about."

"They were at Jeffrey's house," Parker said. "He had a bar in the addition."

"The Shortstop." Rainey nodded. "Lindee told me about it."

"Did you ever go there?"

"No. Lindee was a bartender, and we worked opposite schedules." Rainey fought back a wave of new tears. When they passed, she said, "She often hung out with Jeffrey until she knew I was up and getting ready for work. She didn't want to wake me."

Parker asked, "Where did she work?"

"At Mootsy's. That's where she met Jeffrey. They used to work together until he moved to The Baseline."

"How did you two meet?" Parker was thinking about their age difference. Rainey was roughly ten years younger than her roommate.

"Lindee was friends with my sister, Debra. They met while working at another bar a few years ago. Debra and I were living together until she moved to Boise with some guy. Lindee moved in. She needed a place, and I needed a roommate." Rainey lowered her head and snuffled.

"Do you know anyone who would want to hurt Lindee?"

Rainey shook her head. "She had a controlling ex-girlfriend once, but she died in a car accident. Happened right after she moved in with me. Didn't bust her up or anything, and I never met that person. Other than her, though, I don't know anyone who would want to hurt

Lindee. She was the best person I knew; besides my sister, I mean."

"What about Jeffrey?" Parker asked. "Did Lindee ever mention anyone wanting to hurt him?"

Rainey shook her head again. "I'm sorry I can't be of more help. I wish I could tell you who to go after."

Parker's face softened further. "You're doing fine."

"I can't believe this happened."

"Do you know how to get in contact with her family?"

"I never met any of them, but I can look through her stuff. If I find a number—"

Parker handed Rainey his business card. "Call me. We'll let them know. You don't have to do that."

Rainey stared at the card.

"One last thing," Parker said. "Did Lindee own a cat?"

Rainey's eyes widened. "The kitten," she said and covered her mouth. "Lindee just got it. She hadn't even named the silly thing. She was waiting for the right name to come to her."

Parker smiled softly.

Rainey dropped her hand. "Did she say something about it?"

"She did." He nodded a couple of times for no other reason than to buy him time to think of another question. When he couldn't come up with one, he said, "Thank you for your time."

"Do you think it's okay if I keep the kitten?"

Parker eyed Johnson, then nodded. "I'm sure it'll be fine."

When the barista walked away, Parker's face hardened. "Son of a bitch."

"Relax, man. We'll solve it."

Parker angrily slapped his hands together. "I thought we had something with that cat thing."

"Yeah? Well, I thought we might have been dealing with an anti-gay thing, but Jarrod Stone wasn't. So what are we dealing with?"

Parker rubbed his face as the frustration built. "Goddamn, this case."

Chapter 10

Parker was northbound on Monroe Street when his cell phone buzzed. He checked the caller ID screen—Dispatch.

He answered it, "Parker."

"Hey, Andy. This is Annie." Parker hated when people called him Andy. He didn't correct her, though. It was an old habit. Dispatchers controlled his world when he was on patrol, and he earned a healthy respect for them. They could either make his life easier or harder. She said, "You're needed back on Euclid."

Parker changed lanes. In the rearview mirror, he noticed Johnson changing lanes behind him.

"What for?" Parker asked.

"Detective McAfee is on scene."

"Tell him he can tow the car."

"He already has."

"And he hasn't left?"

"Guess not," Annie said. "Sounds like he's walking the scene."

"Why?"

"How would I know? All he said is he wants to talk with you. That's why I'm calling."

"Fine," Parker said. "Let him know we're on the way."

"Will do," Annie said. "I'll make sure to do it with all your enthusiasm."

She hung up.

Parker dialed Johnson. Using the rearview mirror, he watched his partner answer.

"What's up?" Johnson asked.

"Dispatch called. McAfee is on scene."

"That's good, right?"

Parker curled his lip. "He's traipsing around."

"So? We've already been there. It's not like it's a fresh scene or anything."

"But we don't need another cook in the kitchen." He slowed for a car making a left turn.

Johnson said, "Maybe he can give us some feedback."

"What are you talking about?"

"You know—as how it relates to his case. If things are similar. That sort of thing."

"We don't need his input." Parker looked at his partner in the rearview mirror. "I'll tell you what he's gunning for. He's going to try and lay claim to our case."

"He can't do that. There's no jurisdiction."

"The city is in the county. McAfee will play that card and say his suspect isn't respecting borders, so he should take over."

Johnson shook his head. "He's not going to say that."

"You watch. I'm telling you. Just wait and see."

"He won't."

***

"We should take over," Detective Shane McAfee said.

It had been more than a year since the last time that Parker had chatted with McAfee, and he was immediately reminded why he hated the guy.

McAfee was a tall man with a ruggedly handsome face and a charcoal gray suit that fit like it had been tailored. His broad shoulders and trim waist revealed an allegiance to a workout regimen. Not bodybuilding like Parker, though. Maybe he did CrossFit like Johnson or that high-intensity, interval-training nonsense that was so trendy with women. The guy brimmed with confidence, and it irritated Parker.

Standing with McAfee was Detective Tim Chambers. He was an equally tall man. He was also good-looking but in the way smart women liked—with dark, brooding eyes. His waist was soft, and his suit looked like it came off a rack like Parker's. His slow, thoughtful nod supported McAfee's demand. "This crime clearly links to ours," Chambers said.

Parker sneered before casting a sideways glance at his partner. "Did I tell you?"

Johnson motioned for Parker to calm down.

The four men stood in the middle of Euclid Avenue. Parker didn't like the optics. He and Johnson were in jeans and windbreakers, while McAfee and Chambers appeared ready for a day of litigation.

A suit was a psychological advantage. It represented order in a moment of chaos. It also showed the bad guys and other officers that "the man" had arrived. Parker hated suits, though. Due to his physique, they never fit right, even when tailored. That's why he took every advantage of a callout to dress down. There was no need to show up looking like a banker, especially when he thought he looked better dressed casually.

But McAfee and Chambers hadn't been called out today, meaning Parker felt the psychological imbalance's effect. It was one more thing to be pissed about.

Motion to the north caught Parker's attention. A group of volunteers walked through Drumheller Springs. All heads were bowed as they slowly walked in a line.

"But we can definitely use your help," McAfee said.

Parker's attention snapped back to the county detective. "Our *help*?" He tried to step forward, but Johnson grabbed his shoulder to hold him back. "You can use my foot up your ass."

McAfee's expression remained flat. He pointed at the crime scene. "You want to keep this dog?"

"We're halfway to cracking this thing," Parker said. "We'll probably have it done before day's end."

"Is that so?" McAfee asked. He seemed to be stifling a grin as he glanced at Chambers. "We must be doing things wrong."

Chambers didn't seem to find any humor at the moment. "I suggest we work together, Detective." He eyed Johnson. "*Detectives.*"

Parker held up his hand. He wasn't interested in hearing any pacification nonsense from Chambers. "Listen, McAfee."

"Chambers has a point," Johnson said. "Maybe we—"

Now, McAfee held a hand up to stop Johnson. "If we want this case, we're taking it. No two ways about it."

Parker lifted his chin. "Why don't you go back to the valley and—"

McAfee leaned over Parker and stared down his nose at him. "And what?"

Parker widened his shoulders and puffed his chest like a cobra opening its hood. "Tell those paste-eating window-lickers you report to that we're not giving up our case."

McAfee's nose almost touched Parker's. "You can't stop it from happening."

Parker and McAfee glared at each other.

"Turf wars aside," Chambers said, "we heard they took a car from one of your victims."

"A Ford Fusion," Johnson said.

McAfee and Parker didn't move. They continued to glare at one another.

"It got us wondering," Johnson said, "why they're stealing vehicles from the crime scene."

Chambers nodded. "We thought they wanted the Audi for a specific reason."

Parker broke his stare with McAfee to look at Chambers. "Obviously not if they dumped it."

"They could have still taken it for a specific reason," Chambers said, "then discarded it when it no longer served a purpose."

McAfee stepped back and reconsidered the house. "Stealing the Ford does put things into a different perspective, though." He eyed Johnson. "Want to walk us through the crime scene?"

Parker crossed his arms. "We heard you already walked it."

"You got bad information," McAfee said. "We waited. That's the proper etiquette."

Maybe Parker had misjudged the man. Still. "We're not giving up this case," he said.

McAfee motioned toward the house. "Show us what you got."

Parker frowned. Now Johnson and he had to work a multiple homicide case and swim in political waters to keep it.

Being a Major Crimes detective sucked. No one ever tried to take a case from him when he was in Property Crimes.

He didn't bother to force a smile. "Follow me."

***

"Killers?" Parker said. He eyed Johnson, who stared at McAfee.

The four men stood in The Shortstop. Parker and Johnson had just finished detailing what they saw and laid out their theory of what occurred when McAfee corrected them.

"You were just referring to them as 'they' out front," McAfee said.

"I thought we were talking about the singular they."

McAfee, Chambers, and Johnson all stared at him.

Parker's neck warmed. "You know, like in sort of an asexual way."

"As in a generic third-person pronoun," Chambers said.

"That's it," Parker said. "Just like that."

McAfee smirked. "Whatever. It's killers—plural. It's the only thing that makes sense." He and Chambers moved to the table where the four victims had been murdered. Each man mimed shooting a gun. "Besides, two shooters allow better control of a room. A single gunman could be overpowered."

"Or would have trouble hitting all three," Chambers added.

Parker looked to Johnson. "We were kicking around that idea."

Johnson raised an eyebrow.

"But we were on the fence."

"Now you can get off it." McAfee held up two fingers. "Multiple killers."

"Maybe," Parker said.

He didn't know why he was holding to the belief of a single killer. Two certainly made more sense, and he was surprised that he and Johnson hadn't latched on to it earlier. But it pissed him off that it was McAfee who pointed out the notion.

It didn't help that he was tired and hungry. His blood sugar felt off, and he wanted to eat. Combine that with the frustration caused by a couple of overly eager county detectives, and getting angry was a natural conclusion. He should eat something soon. Parker kept a protein bar in his glove box for moments like this.

Chambers tapped the chair where Lindee Dawson had sat. "Did the woman say anything on her way to the hospital?"

Parker shrugged. "She tried to tell the medics about her cat."

McAfee glanced at Chambers which set Parker on edge. "What?" Parker asked, annoyed.

McAfee said, "It's another link to our case."

Chambers turned a palm upward. "One of our victims owned a bar called The Kedi. It's Turkish for cat."

Parker frowned. "You're reaching. The woman owned a kitten, and she was worried about it. She referred to it as her baby."

"Maybe she knew about The Kedi," McAfee said. "It's something we've got to check out."

"Whatever." Parker stepped out of the addition.

McAfee leaned out of the doorway. "C'mon, man. Don't be like that."

Parker headed around the side of the house. Footsteps followed him.

"Hey," McAfee called. "Work with us here. We're trying to solve a murder."

"Yeah?" Parker glanced over his shoulder but didn't stop for the man. "We're trying to solve four."

"Wow, only four? We're trying to solve five, so I guess we win."

"Petty doesn't look good on you, McAfee."

"Hey, asshole." McAfee grabbed Parker's arm and yanked him to stop walking.

Parker spun quickly and shoved the county detective. His face warmed, and his body tingled with electricity. "Don't touch me."

"Tough guy, huh? Those beauty muscles don't intimidate me."

Parker clenched his fists and leaned forward. His eyes narrowed. "Walk away, McAfee."

"Ease up on the steroids, buddy."

He'd heard that joke for years. He tried not to let it bother him but in moments like this—with the blood pounding in his ears—all he wanted to do was smash a guy like McAfee in the face.

Johnson ran up. "What the hell is going on?"

"Nothing," Parker said through clenched teeth.

"Yeah," McAfee said. "Nothing. I'll be seeing you, Parker."

McAfee continued toward his car.

"Where's his partner?" Parker asked.

"Still in the house. Want to wait for him?"

"No, you talk to Columbo. I'm done. See you back at the station."

***

It was nearly seven when Parker pulled into his driveway. He parked his Chevy and lingered behind the steering wheel. Before going inside, he reflected on his day for a couple of moments. It had started okay. Not the phone call, but the arrival at the homicide scene went as well as expected. Parker was happy with how he and Johnson took control of things.

He even alerted Crime Analysis before they finished their day. They hurried a blurb out about the crime scene. A more detailed write-up would follow in a day or two, but Parker was pleased that he got something out to the patrol teams today.

The day also ended well—he'd been able to get a fair amount of notes transferred into a report. He'd have a head start for tomorrow.

Yet there were many moments during the day that he wasn't happy about.

He was disappointed in losing his temper with the younger, arrogant patrol officers. Parker knew he needed to be better than that—for many reasons, the least of which was he wanted to be respected by the men in uniform.

And Parker was embarrassed about his actions with Detective McAfee. He felt the other man was out of line, but that didn't allow Parker to react that way. He should have come up with a better solution. Giving his case to McAfee was out of the question, but Parker felt he could have handled the moment more logically.

He had developed this ritual—pausing and reflecting before he went inside—after he got married. He didn't want to bring the job inside to Brooke. It became more important when the girls came along. It became essential after he joined Major Crimes.

Parker only had a short drive from the department to home, so decompressing was never fully achieved inside the car.

Brooke never saw Parker's temper. He would die if the girls ever did. Therefore, these quiet moments behind the steering wheel were of extreme importance.

He wasn't a spiritual man, but his parents raised him in a religious home. Parker still felt the pull to pray every now and then. He put his hands on the steering wheel and bowed his head.

"Help me be better," he said. He didn't specify in which area he meant. He figured God would know which one he was asking about.

When he looked up, he stared at his garage door.

A hookah lounge inside a garage. Who would do such a thing?

PART III

Chapter 11

James Morgan snorted awake.

He repeatedly blinked before lifting his head to look down the length of his body. The television illuminated the living room, but the sound was off. When had he turned the volume down?

A commercial now played—something with that *Magnum P.I.* actor. Reverse mortgages, Morgan thought. He grunted and dropped his head back to its resting place. He'd probably turned the sound off for a similar reason but couldn't for the life of him remember why.

The right side of his face felt wet, and Morgan wiped the drool from it. He checked his watch—shortly after eleven p.m. He needed to get up—to get moving—but he lay there and stared at the ceiling. Shadows cast by the television danced across the white paint.

Several moments passed before Morgan heard a long-ago voice in his head *Move it, maggot.* He did that occasionally—harkened back to those days of boot camp and his drill instructor. It mostly happened in moments when he delayed doing something necessary.

Morgan gripped the armrests of the recliner and pulled himself upright. The footrest snapped down, and he hopped into a standing position. The sudden change in height threw off his equilibrium, and he swayed. Goddamn age, he thought.

He forced his eyes wide. Maybe he shouldn't have taken a nap. Morgan would have powered through a long night like this in his younger years. But now he knew to take advantage of the downtime, although it felt like he might have trouble reorienting himself to reality. He repeatedly blinked, squeezing his eyes tightly shut before opening them.

Morgan grabbed his cell phone from the nearby end table—no calls or texts. That was good, but the boys would contact him soon enough if he didn't get a move on.

He was alone tonight. Morgan was by himself every night now. The last steady girlfriend he had left a couple of weeks back. His relationship with Alyssa lasted almost nine months—a record for him.

She tolerated his game of push and pull longer than he could have imagined. He was sorry that it ended now, but Morgan didn't try to stop it because that was the endgame he wanted—a woman who was replaceable. He didn't want them to stick around too long. That led to commitments of money, time, and feelings. Morgan didn't want to provide any of those items—especially the last one.

He lazily yawned, then grimaced.

Move it, maggot.

Morgan angrily rubbed his hands over his face as if trying to start a fire. When he finished, he groaned and ran his fingers through his hair.

Taking a nap was the wrong choice. He should have stayed awake. Drank coffee or something.

Morgan shuffled into the bathroom and started the shower. He needed to wake up.

His team was hunting killers tonight.

***

Morgan pulled his Dodge Daytona Charger into the rear lot of Mulligan's on Monroe. The engine's throaty roar protested being put away so soon. He liked the car even though it was starting to show its years, but he wasn't willing to ask the department for a trade-up. Many who lived life in the criminal underworld knew the Charger. He suspected a lot of it had to do with the sound of its eight-cylinder Hemi engine. Morgan wasn't sneaking up on anyone with the car, but that was the point.

He was the great white shark in this ocean; everyone else was just swimming to survive.

Morgan climbed out of the car and slammed the door. There was no need to be quiet. Besides, he wanted people to know when he was around. There was a time and place for secrecy, and this wasn't one of them.

Music pounded from inside Mulligan's—some classic rock song he had heard more than enough while in the Marine Corps. He crossed the parking lot, yanked open the door, and entered. The aroma of stale beer and fried food invaded his nostrils.

It wasn't his first time to Mulligan's. Morgan was familiar with the dump. It was hard to do the job and not be acquainted with the dive bars along streets with names like Monroe, Market, and Sprague. Besides, Mulligan's was within walking distance from the Public Safety Campus. There had been plenty of nights over his early years on the department that one patrol team or another had wanted to meet there for an after-shift beer. Morgan went along for unit camaraderie and not because he enjoyed drinking in establishments like this.

Morgan spotted two men sitting at a high table. The long-haired white guy discreetly waved. The black man barely acknowledged his entrance. Morgan headed in their direction.

Mulligan's had a reputation built around a lie. The locals bought into the fabrication until it became truth and spawned a myth. That illusion earned it a write-up in the local newspaper when a reporter did her best to expose the constructed legend. However, no one cared that the once golf-themed bar was celebrating false brushes with greatness.

The bartender lifted his chin as Morgan walked by. "How you doing?"

Morgan nodded but didn't bother answering.

A framed photograph hung on the wall behind the bar. Morgan knew its story.

Sometime in the early eighties, the former owner of Mulligan's proudly displayed a picture of him and David Bowie taken at some meet-and-greet event in Los Angeles. The photograph was cropped so tightly on the two that it was hard to tell where it was really taken. In a moment of hubris, the bar owner told a slightly drunk patron that the picture was taken inside Mulligan's after Bowie's Spokane concert.

The problem was Bowie never played the city, and the slightly drunk patron was part of the scheduling team for the old Spokane Coliseum—known affectionately around town as the Boone Street Barn.

When the owner's fib was discovered, the bar's loyal patrons didn't care. Instead, they embraced the lie. Soon, framed pictures of customers standing with celebrities in hard-to-discern locales arrived. Each came with its own story, and the bar owner hung those on the walls—hubris be damned. One photograph became two. Those grew into a handful which multiplied into so many they eventually covered every wall. After the bar was featured in the *Spokesman-Review*, real musicians and other celebrities began visiting Mulligan's while on tour. They had their pictures taken with the staff. Those photographs were developed, framed, and hung.

It was hard to tell where the lies stopped and the truth started.

Morgan slid onto a stool between the two men. He eyed the skinny white man on his left. Officer Adrian Thorn's long, dark hair was greasy, and he hadn't shaved in days. He wore a ratty gray flannel button-up shirt with its sleeves cut off. It hung open over a black T-shirt that read *I Heart Single Moms.*

"You look like a stat-five," Morgan said.

"Then it's working." Thorn pulled his nearly empty glass of beer to him. "You don't want me ready for prayer group."

Morgan glanced at the man on his right.

Officer Jeremiah Strange wore a white and blue Steelheads jersey. A thick gold chain hung around his neck while a heavy gold watch dangled around his left wrist. His typically unkempt afro had been pulled back into tight cornrows. His gaze lay dully on Morgan. "Hmm?" he said dreamily.

"You all right?"

"As always."

Strange lazily dragged his finger around the rim of a glass tumbler. A clear liquid, ice cubes, and lime wedge were inside. "Just us three?" he asked.

Morgan nodded.

The Criminal Task Force was running at less than full capacity tonight. Nayla Senai, the other detective on the team, was on vacation. Courtney Earley, the team's third officer, had been temporarily detailed to the Special Investigations Unit for a case involving the local motorcycle gang. And the team's sergeant, Ken Bynum, was at home since his work hours closely mirrored those of the department's administration. Morgan liked Bynum just fine, but things always seemed to run smoother when he did what he did best—stayed behind a desk.

The bartender walked over. He was a broad-chested man with arms that strained against a faded green T-shirt. His red hair was cut short in a military manner. He also had an intense demeanor which was probably made worse by his thick-rimmed glasses. Recruits called them RPGs while in the Corps—Rape Prevention Glasses. For various reasons, Morgan no longer found humor in that term.

"Get you something?" the bartender asked.

"Where'd you serve?" Morgan asked.

The bartender stared at him.

"Nothing for now."

"What about you guys?" The bartender motioned with his left hand. A steel and wood wedding ring was on the appropriate finger.

Thorn lifted his nearly empty glass. "Another, yeah."

Strange reluctantly said, "If I have to."

The bartender walked away.

Morgan lowered his voice. "Are we working, or are we on a date?"

Thorn leaned closer. "Non-alcoholic."

"Tonic and lime," Strange whispered. "Dave knows the score. Chill out."

Morgan surveyed the bar. There were eight other patrons inside—he counted. Two men were drinking alone—one in his seventies at the bar, the other in his twenties at a small table. A group of four women sat at a high table. A couple snuggled in a booth. There were twelve empty chairs—Morgan counted those as well.

"How's this for business?" Morgan asked. "Normal or what?"

"Slow," Thorn said.

"Any reason why?"

"It's not Friday," Strange said. "Only the college kids and the professionals drink every night."

"To the professionals." Thorn held his empty glass across the table, and Strange clinked it with his.

Dave returned with three drinks. "I brought you what Doc is having." The bartender slid a glass tumbler in front of Morgan. "Can't have you sitting there without something."

Morgan pulled the drink to himself. "I hear you're the one we got to thank for tonight."

"Doc got me worried after he called." Dave glanced around the bar. Morgan suspected the man was checking for eavesdroppers. He returned his attention to the table. "But maybe I'm wrong."

Morgan frowned. He leaned back in his chair and glanced at both officers. The music overhead hid his words, but it didn't disguise his frustration. "If this guy doesn't believe his own intel, why are we here?"

Strange raised a hand. "Relax, man. This is our scene, and we know Dave. We believe his story. He's just—" The officer considered the bartender. "—feeling apprehensive with three cops in his joint."

Dave shrugged. He didn't seem apprehensive.

Thorn nodded toward the bartender. "Dave'll walk you through it, Morgan. Then you'll understand why we wanted you to come out."

"It's not jumping off here," Morgan said. "Doesn't fit the M.O."

Strange shook his head. "We wanted to get a vibe of the place."

"I got the vibe. I've been here before."

"That's not what I'm saying." Strange waved a dismissive hand. "*We* wanted to see who came in, who came out."

"The hokey-pokey," Thorn said.

Strange winked, and a squeak emanated from the side of his mouth.

Thorn lifted his glass but paused before sipping. "We thought it important to know if maybe these guys came in before they hit an establishment. We've been here a couple hours already."

"Drinking your non-alcoholic drinks?" Morgan asked.

"Acting the part." Thorn sipped and set his glass down.

"All right," Morgan said. "I'm here now. Convince me I'm not missing my beauty rest for a wild goose chase."

Strange motioned to Dave. "You got the floor, big dog."

The bartender looked around again. He made eye contact with the older man at the bar. "Need something, Lloyd?" The customer slowly shook his head before dropping his attention to his beer. Dave refocused on Morgan. "These killings are about our after-hours scene."

Morgan uncrossed his arms and put the palms of his hands on the table's edge. "This isn't Vegas, and Spokane doesn't have an after-hours scene."

Dave furrowed his brow. "You an expert on what's going on in the dark?"

"I think I am."

Strange turned his head so he could whisper into Morgan's ear. "Hear the guy out, boss."

Morgan slightly lowered his head as a way of apology. "The detectives who responded to the murder today said it was a clubhouse—a home bar. I think I got an idea of what we're talking about. People have done it for years. Probably since the first home was built. That's not exactly a scene, is it?"

"The kind of places you're talking about are for citizens—for their friends to come visit." Dave ruefully smiled. "What I'm talking about a civilian couldn't find."

"These places are for the cool kids," Strange said. He ran his finger around the lip of his glass tumbler. "Under-the-radar. Hush-hush."

Morgan read the briefing that Crime Analysis had rushed out before the end of their day. The Hotheads had stated that a homicide occurred in a home bar and that it was seemingly linked to a multiple killing in a homemade hookah lounge in the valley. Nobody mentioned an after-hours scene. The whole thing seemed implausible to the detective. If something like that was occurring in his city, he'd know about it.

Wouldn't he?

Secret bars would only come to light if they caused trouble and were reported to law enforcement. If any of the usual suspects Morgan dealt with—gangs or frequent criminal contacts—weren't involved, he likely wouldn't know about them. It was entirely plausible that this bartender was telling the truth. There might be an after-hours scene, and Morgan wouldn't know anything about it. He grunted. The idea of not knowing something like that bothered the detective.

Dave waited patiently. It seemed as if he were a professional listener. Maybe it was a skill he'd developed behind the counter. He watched Morgan and waited for him to respond.

"All right," Morgan said finally. "School me."

"These joints we're talking about are ours."

"Ours who?"

Dave smirked, then apologetically nodded. "Yeah, you wouldn't know. Sorry. Bartenders. These after-hours joints belong to the bartenders." His head bobbled. "Except for Ahmet's. He started his when slinging drinks."

Thorn furrowed his brow and looked at his partner.

"The hookah lounge," Strange said.

"Right." Thorn nodded. "Right."

"Why's that?" Morgan asked. "Why would a bartender start one of these joints?"

"For a variety of reasons, I guess." Dave extended his arms and motioned to both ends of Mulligan's. "But first and foremost, this isn't my place. Never has been and never will be."

"And that pisses you off?"

"Not really. That's the game, but these people are *my* people. They don't know the owners. The lazy broads who bought this place? They no longer come in. Not even to say hello to the folks who are letting them spend easy days on the lake. But everyone knows me. Well, and the off-night guy, but he's weak and replaceable. Mulligan's is me, but it's not *mine*. Understand?"

Morgan nodded.

Dave glanced around before hunching to lean his forearms on the table. Thorn and Strange bent in as well. Morgan remained where he was.

"Look it," Dave said. "You know the liquor board rules?"

Morgan absently spun his glass. "Mostly."

"I can't drink while on duty—not even a shot. Customers want to buy me one, and I gotta say no. Am I gonna get pissed at that? No. I'm a professional. Even if it is total bullshit, but that's the law."

"It's a stupid one," Thorn muttered.

Morgan eyed him.

"What?" Thorn said defensively. "I can't have an opinion?"

Outside, a car honked a moment before a noisy semi drove down Monroe Street and drowned out the music. The old man at the bar groaned loudly and pointed at the front window. "Asshole!"

"Cool it, Lloyd," Dave called out.

The old man waved apologetically and returned to his beer.

Morgan thumbed toward Strange. "Doc says you have one of these after-hours joints."

Dave nodded. "Adrian and Doc have spent many a night tiptoeing with me."

"Is that so?" Morgan slowly turned to consider his officers. "They didn't tell me that."

"The Tiptoe Lounge," Adrian whispered. "Dave doesn't normally invite cops."

Morgan studied the bartender. "Why's that?"

"Should be self-evident."

"Then how'd these two end up there?"

"They invited themselves." Dave shrugged. "Not much I could do about that."

Thorn seemed embarrassed when he faced Morgan. "We were in Dave's neighborhood one morning and saw some guys walk in the back. We thought maybe it was a drug house or something. We wanted to find out what was what."

"Proactive policing," Strange said. "But when we realized it was harmless, we decided we found ourselves a new hangout."

"Everything turned out all right," Dave said.

Thorn waggled his drink. "It's not open to the public. Only Dave's select friends and customers can come."

"And nosy cops," Strange added with a chuckle.

"Big deal," Morgan said. "Our grandparents did this in the sixties with their swanky home bars."

"Not like this," Strange said. "Think of this like Prohibition."

Thorn tapped the edge of the table. "The speakeasy. That's good." He grinned. "I like it. Makes it even cooler."

"You charge your friends?" Morgan asked Dave.

"Most of them aren't my friends." He eyed Thorn and Strange. "Present company excluded."

"Of course," Strange said.

Thorn waved off the comment. "Think nothing of it."

Dave's attention returned to Morgan. "But yeah, I charge. I gotta pay for the liquor somehow. The visitors at The Tiptoe don't want the party to end at two just because liquor control says it has to. Hell, look at Vegas. That party goes all night long down there." A man and a woman entered Mulligan's. "Excuse me." Dave walked away to help the new arrivals.

Morgan asked, "How good is this guy's intel?"

"Legit," Thorn said. "We've known Dave for a while. He's the real deal."

Strange leaned over. "He's got this network of bartenders and staff across the city. They talk to each other. It's a whole underground thing. Totally crazy."

Thorn dropped his head so low it almost touched the table. Some of his hair lay in a small puddle of condensation as he looked up at Morgan. "Everybody confesses their sins at a bar. If not to a bartender, then to their buddies. It's like alcohol gives absolution."

"I'll drink to that." Strange crossed himself, kissed his fingers, then drank his tonic. "Blech."

Thorn sat upright and lifted his hand into the air as if he were being sworn into the department again. "To God, Morgan. I had this girl once who poured drinks for a living." He glanced around before lowering his voice further. "The confessions she heard you wouldn't believe. Straight bonkers."

"Like what?"

"Cheating spouses, drugs, embezzlement." Thorn ticked them off on his fingers. "A robbery once."

"Why didn't we do something about that?"

"I wasn't a cop then."

Morgan harrumphed. He wasn't happy he did that. It was something he'd only recently noticed himself doing. Another sign of age, perhaps. "How come I've never heard you guys mention Dave?"

Strange snorted. "Do you share your personal life with us?"

He didn't, but an after-hours lounge seemed the sort of thing he would have expected his guys to have told him about. Morgan wondered what other things they were keeping secret. "Has Dave ever given you any good intel?"

"Nothing we could use," Strange said. "We'd let you know if he had, but the man is connected. Trust us. He's always telling us who's beefing who."

"And who's bedding who," Thorn said.

Strange snapped his fingers. "Those stories are the best. Like that one about the chick from The Gaslamp."

Thorn laughed and covered his mouth. He noticed Morgan wasn't laughing. Thorn coughed, then cleared his throat. "You should hear them."

"I'll pass."

Dave returned to their table but didn't cut into the conversation.

Morgan waggled a hand at Strange. "So, Doc called you about the murders because the victim was a bartender at The Baseline."

"That's right. We talked for a few minutes, and he mentioned that there was another murder in the valley at an after-hours hookah lounge. That's when I put the pieces together." He mournfully shook his head. "I knew both guys."

"What are your thoughts?"

"About why someone murdered all those people?" Dave shrugged. "Hell, I don't know for sure."

"These guys said you had a theory, so lay it on me."

The bartender looked around before leaning in. He lowered his voice. "This thing started earlier than you know."

"How's that?"

"A couple other joints were robbed."

"A couple—" Morgan glanced at Thorn and Strange. "How many of these places are there?"

Dave straightened. Something must have occurred to him because his eyes widened. "I got no idea."

"Don't give me that," Morgan said, "These two jackals were just bragging about how connected you are, and now you act like you don't know shit."

"Hey, guy." Dave took a half-step back and lifted his hands in defense. "Don't get hard with me."

Morgan waved him back to the table. "We're not looking to bust these joints. We want to stop further killings."

"Listen to him, Dave," Strange said.

Thorn reached out to the bartender and pulled him back to the table. "Morgan won't screw you over. Trust us."

Dave reluctantly nodded. "Yeah, all right." He glanced around before speaking. "In Spokane County, I personally know of three others besides mine, and the two already mentioned."

"So six?" Morgan said.

"And one more in Coeur d'Alene."

"No way. I don't believe it."

"Then I don't know what to tell you." Dave's face reddened. "I'm not the one in trouble. You need my help more than I need you."

"You got one of these clubs. Maybe you're worried someone's going to show up at your door, so you spin a story to get us to come over and hang out for a night."

"I don't care if you come or not. I'll close it down till I'm sure it's safe. Big whoop." Dave's head bounced from side to side. It was apparent he wasn't afraid of an altercation with the detective. Being in the bar business, he'd probably dealt with more than his share of cops. "What happens then?" Dave asked. "Nothing, I'll bet. I'm willing to take my chances."

Morgan rubbed his chin. He didn't mean to stir up the man. He'd been forthcoming with information so far, and he wanted to keep it coming. "Six, huh? Seven if we count Coeur d'Alene."

"You sound surprised," Dave said. "Why? You think that's a lot?"

"I do."

Dave once more looked around the bar. Maybe he was searching for customers in need. Not seeing any, he leaned on the table again. "We're half a million people in this county. Add in Kootenai County, and we gotta be close to three-quarters of a million. Seven joints for the after-hours crowd doesn't seem like much."

"Speakeasies," Morgan said.

Thorn extended his fist across the table, and Strange bumped it with his.

"That's right." Dave nodded. "I'm sure there are more I don't know about. Maybe a lot more. I can't know them all. Hell, I shouldn't know them all. That's the game."

"Have you been to any of them besides yours?"

"A couple. I went to The Shortstop because that's just around the way. It's for a different crowd than mine."

"How so?"

"Baseball fans are odd. They're all into stats and numbers. I don't go drinking to attend math class."

Morgan liked baseball. He never worried about the numbers side of the game. He figured that was just an excuse for someone not to enjoy the sport.

"Anyway," Dave continued, "The Shortstop was janky—totally done on the cheap. Plastic patio chairs. Folding card tables. They only had beer from a fridge, and everyone threw their cash onto the table."

"The honor system?" Morgan said.

"Almost. Which is so out of character for Jeffrey because at The Baseline, he's the most uptight guy behind a bar. It's like he ran his home joint opposite of how he acted at work. That's completely different than how I run mine. I operate like a legit establishment."

"Do these after-hours joints operate regularly? Like every night from two until six or something?"

Dave shook his head. "That's why they're special. They're infrequent. They're secret. You gotta be invited."

Strange leaned over. "You gotta be one of the cool kids."

Morgan eyed Strange. "Did you know about these other clubs?"

"Had no idea."

"It's the first rule," Thorn said. "Nobody talks about fight club."

Morgan rolled his eyes.

"We don't advertise," Dave said, "and we don't tell on other clubs." He glanced around. "Listen. I gotta start cleaning. Are you guys coming? Otherwise, I'm not doing it."

"I'm still not sold," Morgan said. "You haven't told me why you think these guys are hitting your place next."

"Then let's go to The Tiptoe, and I'll fill you in. I've got something for you there."

Morgan inhaled deeply. He puffed out his cheeks as he expelled the breath. "Fine."

Dave pushed back from the table. "Last call," he shouted.

Lloyd threw his hands into the air. "You gotta be kidding me!"

Chapter 12

Dave Elmendorf's home sat mid-block on Carlisle Avenue, about half a mile northeast of Mulligan's. The house was a large two-story Craftsman that rode the west property line. It had a full-width porch and large windows. It stuck out among its smaller neighbors—an eclectic mix of brick and wood ranchers.

A row of overgrown arborvitae trees guarded the east property line. The west neighbor had a six-foot cedar fence around its property line. It gave Dave a nice lane of privacy.

An alley ran the length of the block. A small garage squatted at the south edge of the property line. "Maggie parks back there," Dave had said upon their arrival. "I always leave my car on the street."

Morgan and Dave stood outside the rear of the home. Adrian Thorn and Jeremiah Strange sat in their cars at opposite ends of the block. They disagreed with Morgan's decision for them not to go inside, but that was the privilege of rank.

A sedan pulled through the alley. Its headlights were off. Morgan put his hand on his gun. He couldn't determine the make of the car as it slowed further.

"They won't stay," Dave whispered. "There are rules to The Tiptoe."

The vehicle passed by without stopping. It didn't speed away, either. It quietly left the neighborhood.

Dave descended several stairs to an exterior entrance to his basement. He unlocked the door, reached inside, and turned on the lights to the room.

"When the light is on," Dave whispered, "The Tiptoe is open." He flicked another switch, and the bare bulb on the rear of the house burned a bright blue. "If folks don't see that, they keep going. Blue means things are safe, but they still can't make noise. No disturbances. Doing so will get them banned for life."

"Have you had to do that?" Morgan asked. "Ban a customer?"

"A couple times."

"You think one of them might be causing this trouble?"

"If it was just my joint, sure. But the trouble happened elsewhere." Dave waved Morgan down the steps. "Come inside."

The Tiptoe Lounge hid underneath Dave's house. While most basements are filled with the detritus of life from the main floor, The Tiptoe was expertly built-out as a bar.

Everything was professionally finished. A rack of liquor lined the east wall and was fronted by a dark bar. Four barstools sat in front of it. Three tall tables with three chairs a piece stood equally spaced apart. Two egress windows were installed, but the vinyl blinds were pulled down on them.

A bathroom was even available, although a sign hung on the door—*#1 Only. We can hear you!*

Dave stepped behind the bar. "Want something to drink?"

"I'm good. Why don't you lay out this theory of yours before any customers arrive?"

"I made a list." Dave reached under the bar and pulled out a notepad. "There aren't any addresses, so you're not going to know what to do with it." He plopped the pad onto the counter. "Those are the joints I know."

On the ruled paper was a list of seven names. Besides the three Morgan knew, there were also The Down Low, Hillyard's Rathskeller, Hooligan's Hideaway, and Sneak's Tattle Tale.

Morgan looked up. "These are all after-hours joints?"

Dave tapped the notepad. "Someone busted into The Down Low a couple weeks back. Waved some guns around. Demanded their money. Then took off. Scared the woman who ran the club so bad she shut the joint down just like that." Dave blew air through his barely parted lips. "Pfft. Hasn't been open since that night. She said she was done with the scene."

"Why didn't she call the police?"

"And do what? Report an illegal bar? She'd lose her server's permit and never work in the industry again. No. She knew the rules of this game, and the first one is you don't talk."

"What about the people inside The Down Low?"

Dave smirked. "Citizens who drink at speakeasies at three in the morning don't call the cops."

Morgan reconsidered the list. "What about the others?"

"A few days after the robbery at The Down Low, someone hit the Rathskeller."

"Same thing—robbery?"

"From what it sounds like." Dave shrugged. "Then the same thing played out at Hooligan's Hideaway."

"Three robberies, and no one reports anything?" Morgan clicked his teeth. "Sounds like a fairy tale."

"Do you know how much I can clear in a night here? On a good one, five hundred, maybe six. That's pure profit, all for slinging drinks in my basement for a few hours. People tip like crazy, and they overpay, so they have somewhere to drink in private. These other joints—" Dave pointed at the list. "—they aren't as nice as mine, and I don't know how much they make, but it's off the books and tax-free. Nobody wants to give that up."

"But they were robbed."

"Many of us have been robbed in the bars we work at. We get paid a minimum wage that the government dips its dirty fingers into. Yeah, we make tips, but we're dealing with drunks, shootings, you name it. The people in my joint are by invite only."

"Nobody you talked to knew about any of these other incidents?"

Dave appeared frustrated. "I didn't know about any of this until Doc called. That's when I reached out to a guy I know, and we put the pieces together."

"Just the two of you?"

"The guy I called is a collector of information. He filled in a lot of missing pieces." Dave shook his head. "Adrian wasn't wrong when he said nobody talks about fight club. The people who are involved in this scene keep it secret. They don't want to lose a good thing. Maybe it's more than the money. It's sort of cool to do this." He leaned his butt against the back bar and crossed his arms. "The whole point of this scene is to do *our* thing with *our* customers. We want to keep the law out of our business."

"The wild west," Morgan said.

"Me having you here right now violates the whole principle."

"But people are dead."

Dave pushed his tongue underneath his lower lip. "That's how I'm squaring this with myself."

"Did you make the others aware of what's going on?"

"Not about the robberies because I only found that out as I went along, but I informed them of what happened at

The Shisha and The Shortstop. Most had never heard of those clubs."

Morgan waved his hand over the notepad. "Do the others know about each other? Like the way you do?"

"I doubt it. Like I said, some didn't know either Ahmet or Jeffrey."

"But you knew."

"I knew what to listen for and to ask about."

"How did the killers find out about them?"

"That's a good question."

Morgan scratched his chin. Something about the list caught his eye, and he leaned in to study it. "You put them alphabetically."

"It didn't start that way. That's how I categorized it after I made my initial notes—it's a habit I picked up so I wouldn't miss anything while ordering. Anyway, that's when I noticed the pattern."

"You think the killers are running through this list alphabetically? That's mighty kind of them."

Dave shrugged. "I could be wrong, but those are the only joints I know. There are probably more. If there are, then my theory falls apart."

Morgan pointed at Sneak's Tattle Tale. "Wouldn't this one be next?"

"Sneak's is in Coeur d'Alene."

"I should get units out there."

"It'll be a waste of time. Sneak's is closed. After I told him about the murders, he decided to take a vacation. He's already driving south to see his mother in Kansas. Or was it Kentucky? One of those K states."

"I want to talk with these people." Morgan tapped the paper. "I need their names and numbers."

"That'll be up to them."

Morgan knew he could press the man by threatening him with a charge of Interfering in a Police Investigation. But Dave had just provided a lead that Detectives Parker and Johnson didn't have. If the CTF could crack these after-hours murders, it would look good for the team and allow him to rub the noses of the Hotheads in it. Morgan would play nice with this bartender until doing such a thing no longer proved profitable.

"Call them," Morgan said, "but let them know we're coming one way or another. We need to get some conversations started in the morning."

"All right."

Morgan studied Dave as the man prepped for the arrival of customers. "Why are you doing this?"

"Doing what?"

"Opening."

Dave straightened. "I should stop living and be afraid of what might happen? That's what bullies want. That's what terrorists want. I'm not letting any crap like that dictate my life. Also…" He reached under the counter and pulled out a Colt 1911.

Morgan reached for his gun.

"They walk in here," Dave said as he pointed the gun toward the door, "I'm not going down without a fight."

"Put it away."

The bartender set the gun under the counter. "And that's another thing I can't do at Mulligan's. Guns are illegal inside a bar."

"While I'm here, that stays under there."

"While you're here," Dave said, but he never finished the thought. He had returned to prepping for customers.

***

Morgan spun his glass of tonic water. "Elmendorf," he said.

"That's right." Dave hurriedly mixed a variety of drinks.

The three tables were now occupied. No one sat at the bar except Morgan.

Soft jazz music played from two small speakers hanging from the walls. Morgan had expected rock music like he heard at Mulligan's. This was a nice change of pace. Even though he didn't care for music, he almost enjoyed this.

Dave looked up from a glass tumbler. "You got an issue with my name?"

"There was a serial killer with the same."

"I know who you're thinking of. He was *from* Elmendorf. Not *an* Elmendorf."

It seemed like a guy with the last name would know if that was right, so Morgan didn't bother challenging it. He lowered his hand to the radio clipped to his belt and pressed the transmit button. "Status check."

"Huh?" Dave looked up. When he realized Morgan wasn't talking to him, the bartender muttered, "Never mind."

Thorn transmitted, *"Bored as hell."*

"Copy that," Strange added. *"Times two."*

A small earpiece was in Morgan's right ear, the furthest from the door. A wire ran down his neck and underneath his leather coat. It was too warm for the jacket, but sitting in a bar with his radio out in the open would ruin any hope of discretion.

"How do we even know these guys are coming here?" Thorn asked.

"This was your idea," Morgan said softly.

"*We should be inside*," Strange argued.

"*Yeah, boss*," Thorn said. "*I'm with Doc.*"

Morgan didn't reply. There was no reason to add further fuel to their fire.

The three men spoke via Channel 4, which was reserved for car-to-car communications. Officers moved to this channel to have private conversations or to conduct special operations. They dropped the formality required on the main channels and didn't worry about other officers initiating traffic stops.

"You mentioned a variety of reasons," Morgan said.

Dave looked up again. "Talking to me?"

Morgan nodded.

"When did I say that?" Dave asked.

"Back at Mulligan's. You said that there were a variety of reasons why you and the others do this." Morgan lazily thumbed at the room behind him.

"Ah, I did." Dave nodded. "Be right back." He scooped up the drinks and walked them over to a table of women. One woman handed him a single bill. She squeezed his ass as he walked away before laughing with her friends.

When Dave returned, Morgan asked, "Your wife doesn't have a problem with that?"

"Maggie's not home." He motioned to the dim neon *Quiet!* sign. "That's on when she's here. Things get loose when she's at the hospital." He pulled a leather pouch from underneath the counter and tucked a fifty-dollar bill into a row of others.

"She a nurse?" Morgan asked.

"Trauma." Dave zipped the leather pouch and tossed it under the bar. It wasn't lost on Morgan that Dave didn't make change. "Maybe you two have met."

One of the women at the far table laughed loudly. Morgan glanced over his shoulder. "Is it always this way?"

"Busy? Yes. Noisy? Only when Maggie is gone."

"These folks weren't at the bar."

Dave shrugged. "But they have been." He smiled and lifted his chin to the men sitting at the table closest to them. "I don't allow people I don't know."

"But guests are okay?"

"Sure. Most of them become regulars."

Morgan shifted on his stool. "You think these people know about the murders?"

"How would they? But the energy does seem off tonight. Can't you feel it? There's a nervousness—like we're dancing on the edge of oblivion."

The statement seemed melodramatic, but Morgan didn't know Dave that well. He'd also gone beyond being afraid of moments like this. "Does your wife know what happened at The Shortstop?"

"What do *you* think?" Dave grabbed a dingy rag and wiped the bar where he had mixed the drinks. "She busts my balls for just having this joint. If she thought I could be in danger—"

"Maybe you are."

The bartender stopped swirling the rag and frowned. It was clear he didn't like the subject of his wife's disapproval. "You asked something about reasons—why we do this?" He motioned toward the customers. "Let me ask you something. Do you think we're hurting anyone? And don't give me that old song and dance about it being the law. I want to know if we're hurting anyone."

Morgan looked over his shoulder. There were nine others in the bar. The furthest table was filled with four women in their early fifties. The middle table was a man and two women in their thirties. The closest group was three older black men that Morgan guessed to be pushing seventy.

All the patrons drank and talked amongst themselves. Only the black men paid Morgan any attention, and he suspected it was because they knew he was a cop.

It wasn't overly boisterous inside The Tiptoe, so the neighborhood shouldn't have any complaints. According to Dave, the only person who would even be bothered was working a shift at the hospital.

"The state has all sorts of arbitrary rules," Dave said. "Who can serve alcohol, where it can be served, when a bar can open, when it can close. Blah blah blah. Then they charge a bar owner for the state's continued overlord-ing of those same rules, courtesy of the liquor board. It's a nice racket if you ask me."

"Oppression," Morgan said. "That's your reason for opening this joint?"

"I didn't say that, but that could be why someone else got into this. As for me, I didn't want the party to end. I told you that back at Mulligan's." He poured himself a shot of Old Grand-Dad and lifted it toward Morgan. "May we never go to hell but always be on our way."

Morgan grunted.

Dave kicked the glass back and grimaced as the liquor slid down his throat. "I could lose my license for just doing such a thing while on the clock, in case you didn't know."

Morgan knew. "You could also lose your license for doing this. Running an unlicensed establishment is a crime, in case *you* didn't know."

"You mean they'll take away my server's permit? Oh, boy." He feigned being scared. "Besides, who's going to tell? These folks?" Dave waved his hand like a salesman proudly displaying a showroom of new cars.

Morgan didn't bother looking. He knew none of the customers inside the basement would spill.

"I've done other things before tending bar, and I can do them again. Hell, I can dig ditches if need be, but whatever I do, I can always have The Tiptoe."

Morgan was beginning to see the allure of running an after-hours bar.

A new jazz song started. It was something Morgan remembered hearing from somewhere before. A movie, perhaps. Or maybe it was in a doctor's office. Whatever it was, the song was pleasant and unoffensive.

"So, those other reasons?" Morgan asked.

Dave knocked his knuckles against the countertop. "Beyond oppression and continued partying, there's money. Take Ahmet, for example. He owned The Shisha Room—basically, a hookah lounge. You know what I'm talking about? Anyway, he started that while still working downtown. He did it to raise extra money so he could open his own place. People would go to The Shisha after drinking, and Ahmet would charge them a cover to hang out and smoke."

"People can smoke anywhere."

"Not in commercial establishments—not anymore and not back when Ahmet started The Shisha."

"But it's smoking." Morgan couldn't see the appeal of that.

"There's something special about hanging out with your friends in a public place. Man, it doesn't even need to be your friends. Just being in a public place is the deal. Why else do people go out when they can save money and drink at home? Why do you go out?"

Morgan shrugged.

"Ahmet's customers even brought their own tobacco and alcohol yet paid to be there. Think about that. Crazy, huh? I guess it had this vibe—like a tobacco commune. Is that the right word?"

Morgan had no idea. "Did you go there?"

Dave shook his head. "I don't smoke. I would have been a square peg in a round hole. Ahmet said that I could have just hung out, but cigarette smoke bugs the hell out of me. Maggie, too. No one is allowed to smoke in here because of it. Ahmet was super chill, though. He came here a couple of times. He opened a little bar over on Trent called The Kedi. Ever been?"

"No. Why'd he keep his hookah lounge after he opened that?"

"It's a different circle," Dave said. He leaned in and lowered his voice further. "Any Joe off the street can get service at Mulligan's, but you gotta be someone to come in here. Get it? It may not be much, but some folks take this place very serious. Look it… the rich have the Spokane Club, the soccer moms have the PTA, and the holy rollers have—well, I don't exactly know what they have, but you get my drift. People like exclusive clubs."

Morgan knew that to be true. Even the officers of the SPD used to have a private club. It was inside a building that the police guild leased. Morgan only heard about it because it closed years before he came on the department. A Field Training Officer drove him by the empty building one evening and wistfully spoke of wild nights away from the public's prying eyes. If the cops behaved that way, why would Morgan expect the rest of society to act differently?

Dave straightened. "I'm sure you know this, being a cop and all, but the Wasted Souls have had their clubhouse out in the open for decades, yet no one complains about that. What do you think they're doing in there—reading the bible?"

Morgan turned his tumbler. "No one complains about the Souls because they're a private club."

"So is this."

"It's not the same."

"Why not?" Dave turned his palms upward, and his voice rose with indignation. "The Souls have a bar set up. They allow smoking. Hell, they even got a stripper pole."

One of the women from the far table must have heard Dave because she lifted her arms and shook her breasts. "Woo-woo!" she hollered. Her friends laughed and clapped. The drunk woman slipped from her chair and shimmied around. She grabbed the bottom of her shirt as if to lift it.

"Not tonight, Kay." Dave's voice was full of authority.

She stopped immediately and looked toward the bar.

Dave slightly cocked his head toward Morgan.

Everyone looked in the detective's direction. All the women, including Kay, appeared distraught that the interloper interrupted their fun. The young couple watched with open suspicion. But the expressions of the three older black men didn't change—they'd been playing poker in the game of life for too long to let their feelings be known.

Morgan didn't turn away from any of them, though. His gaze slowly swept over each table until everyone looked away. He might have swum into a new part of the ocean, but Morgan was still the great white shark. There wasn't another predator in the basement with whom he needed to concern himself.

Kay returned to her seat, and everyone went back to their drinks. Murmurs of conversation began.

Dave lowered his voice. "Sorry about that. Things sometimes get—" He paused as he searched for the word.

"Loose."

"Exactly. I figured tonight wasn't a good one for letting things roll that way." Dave grabbed the rag and wiped the already clean counter. "Back to the Souls. Everybody knows they're violating the liquor laws, but the control board doesn't give a damn. Why not? Because they're afraid of them—that's why."

"Have you been inside?"

Dave feigned innocence. "Not me."

"Just speculating, huh?"

"As far as you know." He swirled his rag as if buffing a car. "Everybody's got their clubs, Detective. Besides us bartenders and the Wasted Souls, who else has them? There's a whole 'nother world, right under your nose, that you don't know about."

Before Morgan could ask a follow-up question, the earpiece squelched.

"*Hey, boss,*" Strange transmitted. "*A dented Ford Fusion is rolling through the neighborhood.*"

Chapter 13

Morgan slid off his stool. "You got the plate?"

There was a pause from Strange. Morgan's gaze swept over the bar.

The women at the far table laughed. The young couple held hands and whispered to each other. The older black men watched Morgan with curiosity. Dave stopped wiping the counter to study the detective.

Morgan stiffened as several seconds passed without a reply. "Well?"

"*It's a match,*" Strange transmitted. "*I'm eastbound on Carlisle.*"

"*I'm rolling your way, Doc,*" Thorn said.

"How many are in the car?" Morgan asked.

"*One.*"

The brief that Detectives Parker and Johnson blasted through the department earlier in the day mentioned that they suspected two or more killers were involved in the murders. Maybe the Hotheads got it wrong, Morgan thought. Perhaps there was only one shooter. He didn't like any of the detectives in Major Crimes, especially the Hotheads, but he figured to give them the benefit of the doubt. The safety of his guys and the customers of The Tiptoe Lounge depended on it.

"There's supposed to be at least two," Morgan said. "Switch to channel one and get units in the area before you call the stop."

"*Copy,*" Strange said.

Morgan flipped his radio to channel one in time to hear a male dispatcher say, "*Nora Eighty-three, go ahead.*"

"I'm at Carlisle and Adams behind a blue Ford Fusion." Strange read the license plate. *"This is the vehicle Detective Parker has an ATL on. Just following for now. Start units in my direction. No lights or sirens. I don't want to spook him."*

"Nora Eighty-three, the vehicle is confirmed as the Attempt to Locate," the dispatcher said. *"Channel is restricted."*

Morgan imagined the dispatcher also notifying south units on Channel 3 about Strange's impending traffic stop.

"Morgan," Strange said, observing the earlier relaxed protocol since the channel was restricted for them. *"The car's looping the block. I think he's heading back your way."*

Why would the driver do that? Morgan wondered. Was he checking to see if The Tiptoe was operational so he could come back later? Or had the killers separated? Was the man behind the wheel the getaway driver, and the actual shooter was on his way to the club right now?

Morgan moved toward the door and removed his gun. He looked through the window but couldn't see anything but his own reflection. Morgan should turn out the light, but if a killer was out there, they'd realize something went wrong and turn the other direction. He would have lost the element of surprise.

The Tiptoe Lounge suddenly became quiet. The only sound was the soft jazz song.

Morgan glanced back. All eyes were on him. "Grab your gun," he said to Dave, "and get these folks upstairs."

The bartender's eyes widened. "If Maggie finds out that people were in the house—"

"They're running," Strange said. His usually relaxed voice barely revealed any strain. *"We're coming past you,*

Morgan. I can't wait for the other units. Nora-83, a traffic stop."

Outside, a siren pierced the night.

Thorn said, *"I'm behind you, Doc."*

"Now," Morgan shouted to Dave.

"Upstairs!" The bartender reached under the counter for his gun. "Let's go!"

The customers noisily clambered up the steps to the main floor.

Morgan looked through the window once more. Seeing his reflection again, he knew there was no option but to turn off the light. He flicked the switches next to the door and the room went black.

He left The Tiptoe Lounge, locked the door behind him, and entered the darkness of the basement stairwell.

Police sirens pierced the night. It sounded as if they were coming from all directions, but Morgan knew the arriving cops would flow toward Jeremiah Strange's pursuit.

Morgan ascended the stairs and fought the instinct to turn in the direction he thought the chase might be headed. Instead, he brought his gun up to eye level and scanned the backyard.

He'd pushed away his doubt of a second killer; Morgan fully believed one to be out here. Perhaps there was only one suspect, and that man was behind the steering wheel of the Ford Fusion. But Morgan had been trained by the Marine Corps to be alert for diversionary tactics.

Morgan hunched, brought his gun closer to his chest, and continued to scan. He saw nothing in the darkness at the back of the house.

Strange's voice entered his ear. *"Nora-83, we're northbound on Madison now."*

"Eighty-three," the dispatcher said. *"Advise of speed and conditions."*

Morgan cocked his head slightly and side-stepped away from the top of the stairs. He kept his back to the house, and his gun pointed toward the dark alley. Morgan slowly stepped around the corner of the house. He now pointed his gun at the front yard and moved in that direction.

The large arborvitae trees lining the side of the property were a bonus for hiding the entrance into The Tiptoe Lounge, but it was a fatal funnel for anyone in a situation like this.

"Roads are clear," Strange said. *"Speed is seventy."*

Morgan was three steps along the side of the house when a shot rang out, and a bullet whizzed by. He dove to the ground as two more rounds were fired. He bellyflopped and expelled a large whoosh of air.

The dispatcher spoke calmly into Morgan's ear, *"The sergeant is monitoring."*

Morgan pulled himself into the prone shooting position—on his stomach, elbows tucked in, with his gun pointed toward Carlisle Street. His mind whirred—where had the shot come from?

"Start a K9," Strange said.

"No K9 is currently on," the dispatcher replied.

Morgan reached for his radio and discovered it had popped loose from his belt. He located the wire that led from the earpiece and yanked it. The hard plastic brick bounced against his hip.

A thought occurred to Morgan, and he abandoned the radio. He violently rolled over to his back. The radio whipped underneath him and pressed angrily between his shoulders. Morgan lifted his head and pointed the gun down the length of his body. No scanning for threats was necessary.

At the end of the yard, near the edge of the alley, stood a figure—a man. Morgan couldn't describe him in greater detail due to the darkness, but he had seen the clothing before. The figure wore cammies—the combat utility uniform. The Army and the Air Force called them something different, but Morgan was certain the man wore a camouflage uniform. He'd seen plenty of them in the dark.

"Drop the gun!" Morgan shouted. He couldn't see a weapon, but it seemed a prudent order since several rounds had just been fired. "Get on the ground!"

The man turned and ran behind the garage.

Morgan couldn't shoot. Perhaps the figure was a scared citizen—a looky-loo—who happened upon The Tiptoe Lounge at the wrong time. Maybe the camouflaged shadow was unarmed and just out for a late-night stroll. The detective felt all of that was untrue, but he instinctively knew how far he could push at any moment. If Morgan was wrong, killing an unarmed citizen would be impossible to defend.

He flopped about, trying to free the radio from his body weight. When Morgan grabbed it, he activated the mic.

"Ida-77," he said, interrupting Strange's pursuit. Morgan rose to a knee. "Shots fired."

The dispatcher calmly said, *"Ida-seventy-seven. Go ahead."*

Morgan trotted toward the alley. "Backyard of the target house. Three shots. Suspect is on foot westbound through the alley. Dark clothing, possible camouflage."

"Terminate pursuit," the dispatcher announced. *"Sergeant advises terminate pursuit and set a perimeter around Ida-seventy-seven's location."*

Morgan sprinted into the darkness now. The suspect was no longer in the alley.

The detective exited onto Jefferson Street, then looked north and south. Sirens headed toward his location.

Morgan held his gun in the ready position but spun around, desperately trying to locate the runner.

"Shit," he muttered.

***

Morgan stood in the middle of Carlisle Street with Jeremiah Strange and Adrian Thorn nearby. The three men watched as a rookie strung a line of yellow POLICE—DO NOT CROSS tape around Dave Elmendorf's backyard.

The bartender waited near a sergeant's patrol car along with the patrons from The Tiptoe Lounge. Dave seemed extremely worried. However, his customers appeared to have the time of their lives. Many held onto glasses as if the party had only relocated outside after it had moved upstairs.

"Who'd they call?" Thorn asked.

Morgan turned to him. "The Hotheads. It's their case."

"How much time before they arrive?" Strange asked.

"They're not exactly the types to be out late partying."

Thorn faced Strange. "That sounds like a swipe at us."

Strange shrugged. "When the glass slipper fits."

"Let's talk with Dave," Morgan said.

He walked away without waiting for any more banter. Thorn and Strange dropped in behind him.

Dave noticed the three men heading in his direction. He moved away from his customers. When he neared the officers, he motioned toward the commotion on Carlisle Street. "Maggie's gonna kill me."

"Tell her it was a drive-by," Strange said, "that it had nothing to do with the bar."

Thorn nodded. "We'll help you sell it to her if you want."

Morgan sliced a hand in front of his throat, signaling the two officers to stop talking. "Listen," he said, "a couple of detectives are going to show up soon and take over this investigation."

The bartender furrowed his brow. "Aren't you a detective?"

"They're with Major Crimes, and they're the ones investigating The Shortstop murders."

"The Shisha, too?" Dave asked.

Morgan nodded.

"Don't get too excited," Thorn said. "They're a couple of douchebags."

Morgan glared at him. He was beginning to wonder if the man had really been consuming alcohol earlier.

Thorn tried to appear innocent. "I'm only saying what we all think."

It was *exactly* what Morgan thought about the Hotheads. However, he didn't want to disparage the Major Crimes detectives to a citizen publicly. Morgan could talk poorly about a fellow cop, but anyone outside the department couldn't. And he never did it where it would reflect poorly upon the badge. He forgot that not everyone thought the same way he did.

"What Adrian means," Strange said to Dave, but his eyes were on Morgan, "is Major Crimes plays by a different set of rules than us."

"I didn't have anything to do with this," Dave said excitedly. His voice rose. "I already told you what I know, which is nothing. I had a theory, is all."

Several uniformed officers turned in their direction.

Morgan moved closer to the bartender and lowered his voice. "Calm down. The detectives are going to press you about The Tiptoe. They're going to hold it over your head. Threaten you with a crime unless you tell them everything you know."

Dave muttered, "Christ." His eyes widened. "*Maggie.*"

"There's nothing you can do about her now," Morgan said. "Some assholes came looking for you, and they took a shot at me. I want to know why."

Dave shrugged. "I don't know why. I told you."

"I don't believe you." Morgan grabbed Dave's shirt and pulled him closer.

Both Strange and Thorn quickly moved to block the line of sight of nearby officers. Morgan didn't care who saw this interaction. Time was short—Parker and Johnson were on the way.

Morgan continued "You told me about the other joints, but I think you're still holding out. What are you a part of?"

"I'm not part of anything." Dave tried to pry Morgan's hand off his shirt but to no avail. "I swear."

"I still don't believe you." Morgan twisted his fist into Dave's shirt, pulling the big man closer. Now the two men were nose to nose.

Dave lifted his hands in surrender. "It's the truth."

"Here's the thing." Morgan jerked his head toward Strange then Thorn. "My guys like you. If you're jammed up in something, we can help. We only want the shooters, but those Major Crimes boys are about scoring points and social climbing. They'll take all the bips they can get. You understand?"

The bartender nodded.

"They're gonna hang charges on you until you cooperate. After a while, they're gonna make you believe you were the one who killed those people at The Shortstop."

"But I didn't."

"It's what they do, Dave. We can't help you if you don't help us."

Dave swallowed.

"You better start talking because they're on the way. After they arrive, it's just you and them."

"Should I get a lawyer?"

Morgan jammed his fist into Dave's chest. It was only about an inch, but it made the detective's point. "Why do you need a lawyer? Are you involved with these murders?"

"No." Dave grabbed Morgan's arm. "But you were saying—"

"What else can you tell me?"

"I swear to God, Morgan. I got nothing other than the list. That's all I can give."

Morgan lowered his voice. "That's not all, Dave. You can give me the addresses."

***

A red Chevy Impala pulled to the curb. A tall, lean man climbed out. He wore blue jeans, a plaid shirt, and an insulated black vest.

"This just got interesting," Morgan muttered.

"Who is that?" Adrian Thorn asked.

"Shane McAfee. County Major Crimes."

Morgan and Thorn stood on the sidewalk. They had just finished talking with Dave Elmendorf. Jeremiah Strange had walked him back over to his group of customers.

Sergeant Wesley Blackwell now pantomimed running down Carlisle Avenue as he went to greet the latest arrival at the crime scene. His arms pumped as if he were hurrying, but the man's legs didn't move any faster than his walk. It was an odd juxtaposition that Morgan figured the man had perfected as he'd gotten fatter.

The two men shook hands—the sergeant more enthusiastically than the moment called for.

Thorn turned entirely around to put his back to the new arrival. He lowered his voice to a whisper. "Why are they bringing the county in? Did the brass activate the OIS protocol?"

Morgan shrugged. "Maybe."

"Bunch of pansies. How can it be officer-involved when you didn't shoot back?"

"It's more likely about the first murder scene," Morgan said, "the hookah lounge. That was McAfee's investigation. Remember the Hot Sheet? Someone must have called him because of that."

A second Chevy Impala arrived. A tall detective slid out from behind the wheel of this car. He wasn't lean like the first. This one carried a calm, detached demeanor. He stood inside the driver's door for several moments as he surveyed the scene.

Thorn glanced over his shoulder. "Now, who?"

"Tim Chambers. County Major Crimes. He's working the case with McAfee."

Thorn furrowed his brow. "Are we losing this case to Scuzz-O?" That was Thorn's nickname for SCSO—Spokane County Sheriff's Office.

Chambers stepped away from his car and quietly secured the driver's door. He took his time joining McAfee and the sergeant. He scanned the crime scene as he walked. The three men briefly spoke, and Chambers turned in Morgan's direction.

Strange sauntered up. "Where are the Hotheads? And who are these jack wads?"

Morgan said, "County homicide."

Sergeant Blackwell headed over to Morgan. The county detectives walked in his wake. "Jim, this is—"

"We've met," Morgan interrupted. He shook hands with both McAfee and Chambers. "You county guys so bored that you gotta horn in on our action?"

"There was an officer-involved shooting," Blackwell said. "County is going to investigate."

"Told you," Thorn muttered.

Morgan ignored the officer. Instead, he focused on the county detectives. "That was lucky."

"How so?" McAfee asked.

"It dovetails into your investigation of the hookah lounge shooting."

McAfee crossed his arms. "You think it's lucky, huh? We heard this was an after-hours joint. Funny how that information didn't get shared across department lines. Maybe if it had, we could have avoided an incident like this."

"Why? You think your team is better than my guys and me?"

Thorn and Strange didn't chuckle. If there was ever a moment Morgan would have liked some bravado from those two knuckleheads, it would have been right then. Instead, they warily watched the two county detectives.

Chambers asked, "Did you alert anyone about this after-hours joint?"

Morgan shook his head. "The information was dynamic, and we reacted to it."

"So, had you learned something, you would have notified us?"

"Not you, but Parker and Johnson. It was their brief that inspired us to act."

"Speak of the devils," McAfee said.

Parker and Johnson walked up the street. Morgan hadn't seen them arrive. Both men wore jeans and department-issued windbreakers. The two men ate as they approached—Parker noshed on a banana while Johnson nibbled a hardboiled egg that he cupped with his fingers. It was as if the two gym rats were the punchline to some gay joke. Unfortunately, Morgan couldn't remember the setup.

The four detectives shared comradely handshakes and stupid pleasantries like, "Long time no see" and "This is starting to be a habit." Morgan wanted to punch each of them, even the eerily serene Chambers.

Parker shoved the last bit of banana into his mouth. As he chewed, he asked, "What have we got?"

Sergeant Blackwell said, "An unknown assailant fired three shots at Morgan."

"That's what we heard," Parker said. "We also heard that you were sitting off an after-hours joint. That so?"

Thorn absently pointed at Dave Elmendorf's house. Morgan glared at him, and the officer slowly lowered his hand. Strange shook his head.

McAfee clapped Parker's shoulder. "Morgan was just telling us how he was going to notify you and Johnson."

"Is that so?" Parker asked.

Morgan eyed him. "We got information on a possible after-hours bar. We thought it might be worth sitting on."

"You didn't think to call us?"

"We were doing our job," Morgan said. "It might have turned out to be nothing."

"Nothing?" Parker's face pinched. "Does this look like nothing?"

"No." Morgan glanced around. "It looks like a crime scene."

Parker's face reddened. "Why weren't we briefed?"

"There wasn't time," Morgan said.

"Bullshit, there wasn't," Parker yelled.

The outburst caused both McAfee and Chambers to take a half-step back. Sergeant Blackwell cleared his throat and took a sudden interest in his shoes. Johnson put a hand on his partner's shoulder.

"You were sitting off the house." Parker pointed at Dave's home. "You had plenty of time to call it in. You were playing it fast and loose—like you always do."

Morgan ran a hand over his mouth, then down his neck. "We weren't sure it would turn into anything, Parker. You want me to wake you up every time we run down a long-shot lead? Because nine out of ten aren't going to pan out."

"I thought that was clear."

Morgan feigned innocence. "So going forward, we should report every after-hours joint we find?"

Parker emphatically nodded. "Hell yeah, you should. You most definitely should."

"Duly noted."

Johnson patted his partner's shoulder. He faced McAfee. "How are we handling this? You guys tackle the shooting, and we run with the after-hours investigation?"

"Going to be hard to separate the two," McAfee said.

"But it needs to be done," Chambers said. "For protocol reasons, if nothing more."

The county detectives shared a knowing look.

"Yeah," McAfee finally said. He sounded disappointed. "I guess that's the way this will play out."

The four Major Crimes detectives turned expectantly to Morgan. Blackwell noticed their movement, and his head popped up like a squirrel assuming a nut was about to drop from a nearby tree.

Morgan frowned. "That's convenient."

"What is?" the sergeant asked with a goofy smile.

"These four show up, and the music starts. But the three of us who did the actual work—" Morgan waggled his thumb between Thorn and Strange. "—get forced out. We found the shooters, and now we're gonna get pushed out of this case."

"You found the shooters?" McAfee asked. "I didn't know that." His eyebrows rose in surprise, and he looked around exaggeratedly. "Where are they? We'd be happy to give you and your boys full credit. Wouldn't we, fellas?"

Parker and Johnson remained stone-faced.

Morgan twisted his lips and fought saying something he'd have to apologize for later. He wanted to label McAfee something so he'd feel better. Still, the county detective wasn't a Hothead, an Old Dog, or a Glory Hound—the terms Morgan and others in the department used to categorize SPD's Major Crimes detectives. The county detectives didn't work in teams, so Morgan needed a label for McAfee only.

At this moment, Morgan fumbled to find an appropriate one, so he went with an old standby—asshole.

"We step out of the way," Morgan said, "and let you boys take over."

McAfee nodded. "Now you're getting it. But don't leave until we've had a chance to interview you." He tapped Chambers on the shoulder. "Let's walk."

Parker turned his palms upward. "What can I say, Morgan? That's what happens when you don't play nice with others."

Morgan reached into a pocket and handed Parker a piece of paper.

"What's that?"

"It's me playing nice."

"The Down Low? Hooligan's Hideaway." Parker looked up. "What's this?"

Morgan pointed at the paper as Johnson slipped it from his partner's hand. "That's a list of all the known after-hours joints in town. There might be more, but it gives us a starting point."

"There are no addresses," Johnson said.

Morgan shrugged. "They're speakeasies. Finding them isn't supposed to be simple."

"Where'd you get it?"

"From the guy who owns this house."

Parker looked around Morgan in the direction of Dave Elmendorf. "And he didn't know the addresses?"

Morgan considered telling Parker the truth, but he shrugged instead.

"Great," Parker said. "We got a list of places with no addresses. What am I supposed to do with this?"

"You're a detective. Figure it out."

"Very funny."

"We can look into it for you."

"This is our case."

Morgan nodded. "We know."

Parker's eyes narrowed. "What's the catch?"

"No catch. We want to help."

Parker and Johnson shared a look.

"You want the county to steal our case?" Morgan asked. When the Major Crimes detectives looked at him, he clarified his statement. "Your case."

"They're not stealing it."

"Of course not. They got a multiple homicide at a valley after-hours joint and an officer-involved shooting at this one. If you don't think they'll try to roll your cases into theirs, you're crazy. And the prosecutor will back them on it, too."

Parker's jaw flexed. Morgan knew he'd just scored a point.

The smaller detective motioned to the list that Johnson still held. "You think you can make headway on that list?"

Morgan looked at Thorn and Strange. "We can try."

The two officers nodded their encouragement.

"Uh-huh," Parker said. His gaze drifted to McAfee and Chambers. "You gotta deal with them."

"You'll put in a good word?" Morgan asked.

Parker shook his head. "Not us. If you want to play, you need to pay. Stick your own neck out. This is already political enough for us." He wandered off.

Johnson held up the list of after-hours joints. It seemed as if he considered saying something but didn't. Instead, he hurried to catch up with Parker.

"Why didn't you tell them about the addresses?" Thorn asked softly.

Morgan turned his back to the Major Crimes detectives. "Because we're gonna bust this case, not them." He eyed the two officers. "You guys tired?"

They both shook their heads.

"Then let's get out of here." He spun and walked casually toward McAfee and Chambers. They were near a patrol car with its emergency lights still flashing.

"Hey," Morgan said. "We wanna wrap this up."

"When we're ready," McAfee said.

Thorn and Strange appeared at Morgan's shoulders.

"Interview us now," Morgan said, "or we're leaving."

"No, you're not." McAfee looked at Chambers, who studied Morgan. When the quiet detective didn't speak, McAfee repeated, "No."

"We've been up all day," Morgan said. "My guys still have to write their reports before they can go home and catch some sleep."

McAfee shrugged. "I don't care. There was a shooting."

Morgan flippantly waved his hand. "It's a shots fired call."

"Are you serious?"

He wasn't, but he didn't want to be at this scene any longer than necessary. "Listen, I didn't shoot my weapon, and we don't have any suspects. Let's wrap this up so we can be on our way."

McAfee's jaw set. "This incident is connected to multiple murders. We're handling it how we see fit."

Sergeant Blackwell wandered in their direction. Getting the sloth involved in the conversation was beneficial, so Morgan delayed his response. He acted distracted and turned back to McAfee. "What was that?"

McAfee sighed. "We're doing this our way, you stubborn bastard."

Blackwell's face registered surprise. "What's going on?"

The county detectives turned in the direction of the sergeant.

"This guy," McAfee said, "is interfering in our investigation."

"How's he doing that?" Blackwell asked.

"By insisting we interview him now."

"We're tired, Sergeant." Morgan suspected calling Blackwell by his rank would play into the man's vanity. "We've been at it all day, and we still have reports to write."

Blackwell nodded. "I understand, Jim, but it's their scene. They decide when and where to interview."

Morgan hated when people called him Jim. He'd have given Blackwell an earful on another day. But right now, the best thing he could do was not fight about anything. "I understand. Hey, I've been in a shooting before. Shouldn't I get a seventy-two?"

Detective McAfee straightened. "Are you for real? You think you should get three days off to collect your thoughts? Just a minute ago, you were downplaying it as a shots fired call."

"Technically," the sergeant said, "he's right. The officer-involved protocol dictates he gets seventy-two hours off."

McAfee threw his hands into the air. "What is it with you city guys?"

"Instead of arguing," Morgan said, "why don't you interview us now? I'll pass up my seventy-two so we can keep things moving."

Chambers held up a hand. "I'll interview Morgan now."

McAfee appeared upset. "Tim, no."

"It's fine," Detective Chambers said. "You interview the officers." He lifted his chin toward Thorn and Strange. "We'll knock the interviews out, then process the scene."

McAfee tsked. "This isn't how we do it."

"It is today."

Chambers waved at Morgan. "Why don't we talk over at my car?" He walked away.

Blackwell grinned. "So everything worked out fine. I like when that happens."

Chapter 14

After their interviews, Morgan and the guys met in the parking lot of the Yoke's Fresh Market on North Foothills. It was only a few minutes from The Tiptoe Lounge, but the large parking lot was mostly empty. They'd see anyone approaching. Morgan wasn't worried about some eager cop stopping by to say hello. It was simple patrol tactics.

As far as Morgan was concerned, this was now a contest to find the shooters first. His guys against everybody else. CTF versus the Hotheads. CTF versus the county assholes. Morgan didn't feel the slightest bit bad for lumping Chambers into that category—people are judged by the company they keep.

If he was going to war against Major Crimes, he would happily do it with the members of CTF. He wished he had Nayla Senai and Courtney Earley with them. His team could beat anyone the department threw at them. Being short-handed would make it more challenging, but that was no excuse for not winning.

The three men formed a triangle with their vehicles—Morgan's Dodge, Thorn's Ford pick-up, and Strange's Mazda 6. Each rig had been seized under the state's civil asset forfeiture laws and upgraded with police radios, hidden lights, and sirens.

Morgan pulled out his notebook and flipped to a page. "We're gonna skip Sneak's Tattle Tale because that's in Coeur d'Alene, and supposedly the owner bailed for one of the K states." He looked up. Neither man argued with his logic, so he continued. "That leaves three—The Down

Low, Hillyard's Rathskeller, and Hooligan's Hideaway. We each take one and contact the owner."

"Dave called them?" Strange asked.

"He did. He left messages for those he didn't talk with. We'll huddle up after we're done."

Strange moved next to Morgan to study the notebook. "Put me on The Down Low."

Thorn sidled up to Morgan's other shoulder. "I'll take the Hideaway. What do we know about the guys who own these joints?

"Nothing," Morgan said. "And we can't run their names over the air right now. Otherwise, we'll alert everyone to what we're doing."

"What if we bop into a COPS substation and check them there?" Thorn asked. "No one would see us."

"Feel free, but there will be a record of you doing that." Morgan tapped his temple. "The department tracks everything you do on the system. If you want your number associated with those name checks right now, it's up to you. I'm not doing it."

Thorn and Strange exchanged glances.

"But if you're scared…"

Both officers extended their middle fingers in the air.

"That's what I thought." Morgan smiled. "Check the houses. If your gut tells you it's too dangerous, don't approach. Wait for one of us to back you up."

Thorn appeared offended. "Why are you looking at me like I'm the one needing a six? Maybe one of you guys will."

Strange patted his friend's back. "We all know who'll need the backup."

Thorn shrugged off Doc's hand. "Are we done?"

Morgan studied them both. "You're doing this willingly. I'm not forcing you. If you don't feel comfortable without knowing their histories—"

"Step off with that bullshit," Strange said.

Thorn chuckled. "Sometimes you sound like a poet."

"Everything should be cool," Morgan said. "Dave said we only want to ask some questions." He checked his watch. "It's nearly six. Check-in by seven. Stay alert and stay safe."

***

According to Dave Elmendorf, Hillyard's Rathskeller was located on Diamond Avenue. Dustin Roseberry owned the house and bar. Even though Morgan had never met the man, his first impression of Roseberry was positive.

A primer gray Chevy Camaro was parked out front. Morgan couldn't make the year but knew it to be a late seventies model. Its front window was cracked from side to side, and it was in desperate need of a wash.

The house was a large, two-story affair. Its salmon-colored paint flaked from the shiplap siding. A few roof shingles were missing, and several others curled. The yard was dry yellow except for a small patch of green, in the middle of which lay a garden hose. A trickle of water escaped its opening.

Morgan walked up the broken sidewalk and then ascended a small set of stairs. The front porch had seen better days. The wooden planks were warped and gray. Portions of the rusting railing were twisted and broken.

With spiking house prices, the home would fetch a handsome price if fixed up. However, its owner apparently had no interest in doing such a thing.

Morgan didn't expect to enjoy Dustin Roseberry's personality—he'd probably hate it, but he appreciated how the man lived. Morgan liked things a certain way. Or, more specifically, he wanted things as they used to be.

He hated how Spokane had changed with its rampant upgrading and beautifying in recent years. It allowed the region's scumbags to hide behind the better. They lived in nicer apartment communities, drove newer cars, and wore finer clothes. Criminals were chameleons and society was helping them change their colors.

But not Roseberry. Morgan's gaze swept over the front yard once more. He already had a good idea who this man would be.

Morgan preferred the days when a cop could point out a dirtball by what they wore, the kind of car they drove, or how they kept their house. That's why he appreciated Dustin Roseberry for letting everyone know upfront the type of person he was.

The detective rang the doorbell. When he didn't hear a corresponding *ding-dong*, it was one more thing to smile about. He banged on the door.

The longer he stood there, the happier Morgan became. This was a game all stat-fives played. Roseberry knew the cops were coming—Morgan had overheard Dave's conversation with the man—so this was Roseberry trying to upset the power imbalance. The guy didn't realize Morgan enjoyed the game in all its forms.

The detective incessantly banged on the door with the bottom of his fist and the toe of his boot. The whole neighborhood would now know that a cop stood in front of Roseberry's house.

Heavy footfalls hurried toward the front door. It sprang open, and a heavy-set white male stood in the entry. His gut hung over a pair of dingy white boxers. Faded tattoos littered his skin. His hair was disheveled, and his face was puffy.

"Dustin Roseberry?"

The man scowled. "No."

"I'm the detective Dave called about."

"You got the wrong guy."

"Funny. Step back."

Roseberry's scowl deepened. "Get a warrant." He swung the door, but Morgan caught it. Roseberry dropped his shoulder against it to force it closed, but Morgan performed the same action on the other side. They were two bull elk fighting for dominance.

"You can't..." Roseberry struggled to say, "do this." His face was near the opening in the door, only inches away from Morgan's. His breath smelled horrible—a combination of old beer, stale onions, and sleep. "I know... my rights."

Morgan poked him in the eye.

Roseberry howled in pain and released the door. He stumbled backward into the house and pirouetted with his hands covering his left eye. "Son of a bitch! You can't do that!"

"Do what?" Morgan entered the house.

"That's assault!"

"What'd I do?"

"Police brutality!"

Morgan shut the door behind him.

When Roseberry heard the door latch shut, he spun. "That's illegal entry! I'm calling the cops."

"I am a cop," Morgan said, "but by all means, feel free to call them. Let's get some uniforms in here. You tell your story, and I'll tell mine. Who they gonna believe?"

Roseberry stared at him with his one good eye. His left hand covered the other. "What's your story?"

"That you assaulted me."

"That's a goddamned lie!" Roseberry's face flushed red.

"And you got poked while I defended myself. Look at how much bigger you are than me."

"That's not what happened! You can't *lie*."

Morgan cocked his head. "You gonna stand there all morning telling me what I can or can't do, or are we gonna talk about the Rathskeller?"

Roseberry angrily waved his free hand about. "I'm gonna punch that Dave in the mouth is what I'm gonna do."

"I wouldn't blame you."

The big man stared at him with that one blinking eye.

"Show me your club," Morgan said.

A moment passed as Roseberry seemed to consider a plan of action. Eventually, he said, "I need a coat and some shoes." The heavy-set man shuffled toward the back of the house.

Morgan followed him. "Put on some pants while you're at it."

The guy awkwardly looked over his shoulder with his good eye. "You gonna watch me get dressed?"

"Not because I want to."

Roseberry grunted. He grabbed a pair of dirty jeans and pulled them on. His left eye remained pinched closed while he dressed. The gut hung over the pants now. He slipped his feet into a pair of orange rubber shoes. He didn't bother with a shirt but slid his arms through a leather jacket. Fonzie, he wasn't.

"I don't know why you're harassing me," Roseberry said. "I didn't do nothing."

"Except run an illegal club and not report a robbery."

"That's how it's going to be?" Roseberry frowned. "Dave said you would be cool."

"This is me being cool."

The two men exited the house. Just to the left side of the back steps were two wooden doors built into the ground. Roseberry lifted them to reveal a set of stairs into the basement. "There's no access from inside the house."

As Roseberry descended, he crouched so as not to hit his head. Morgan did the same. Roseberry flicked on the light.

Hillyard's Rathskeller was an unfinished basement. Basalt rock formed the walls, thick wood beams crossed overhead, large timber posts supported the house, and exposed light fixtures hung from the ceiling. At first glance, Morgan thought it looked like hundreds of other basements around the city. However, he quickly realized two things made it completely different.

First, Morgan stood at his full height with a couple of inches to spare. He'd been forced to crouch in those other basements. The second odd thing was the level cement floor. Other basements of this ilk often featured uneven dirt floors.

Four tables were spaced about the basement. A simple bar stood in the corner. Space heaters sat in a couple of the corners, and thick, orange electric cords ran to outlets secured on the support posts.

"I don't run the club in the winter," Roseberry said. His left eye remained pinched, and tears ran from it. "I can't keep it warm enough down here because of those doors. Even now, it's chilly. That's why I got the heaters. But on a hot summer night, there's no place better to come and drink. Bet your ass on that."

"How did you meet Dave?"

"He didn't tell you?"

Morgan stared at him.

"No need to be a hard ass, man. We met in the business. We've both been in it for years. You meet a guy you like, and you keep track of each other regardless of where the other bounces to."

"What about the others?"

When Roseberry's brow creased, he looked like a fat pirate. "Who we talking about?"

"The after-hours joints?"

"I don't know nobody else." Roseberry's face relaxed. He blinked his left eye, which was red and swollen. "Besides Dave's, I only know about Ahmet's, although I never been. Me and Ahmet never really got along. Can't say as I was surprised to hear that someone shot him up."

"Why would you say that?"

"Guy was a dick. This was back when he was working downtown. Before he opened The Kedi." Roseberry absently stuck his finger in his belly button. "I heard about his hookah lounge and wanted to check it out. I was just starting to put together this joint and wanted to get some ideas, but he wouldn't let me near his place."

"How'd you hear about the hookah lounge?"

"A friend of a friend, I guess. Maybe Dave." He paused, thinking. "Nah, wait, it wasn't him. The guy is a vault. Hell, I don't remember. Anyway, don't matter none because Ahmet wouldn't let me come over. I thought it was a racial thing. Him being an Arab, and me being white. It didn't bother me none to tell you the truth. Everyone is welcome here—" He muttered, "except cops," under his breath, but Morgan heard it.

"Where do you bartend?"

Roseberry scratched the edge of his belly button with his thumb. "At the Drinkery. Why?"

"Anybody ever give you a hard time?"

"I work in a bar. What do you think? But if you're asking if I think there's a connection between these murders Dave told me about, I say no."

"Why's that?"

"Because we don't talk about what we do." Roseberry waved his arm about. "How many other joints are there in town like this?"

"None."

Roseberry chuckled. "Thank you, but there are a few, otherwise, you wouldn't be here. How many? I don't know. And I don't *want* to know. Get it? I do my thing. Let them do theirs. Live and let live."

"Tell me about the robbery."

Roseberry shoved his hands into his jacket pockets. He spread the jacket wide and gave Morgan a good look at his belly. "They didn't get much."

"How many were there?"

"We had a full house. Seven, maybe eight of us."

"No, the robbers."

Roseberry nodded. "Oh, I get you. A couple guys."

"What did they look like?"

"I don't know. They wore ski masks."

Morgan scowled. Was this guy being purposefully obtuse? "Were they tall or short? Skinny or fat? What about their hands? Their necks? You must have seen some skin.”

Roseberry shrugged. “Average height, I guess.” His hands were still in his coat pockets, but he’d stopped swinging them now. “Normal weight. They were white.”

“What did they sound like?”

The question confused Roseberry. He cocked his head.

“Did they have an accent?” Morgan asked. “You know, like were they from the south? Or did one of them have a low voice? A squeaky one? Maybe a lisp. What did they sound like?”

“They sounded white.”

This guy, Morgan thought. He should have poked him in both eyes. “What’d they take?”

“What do you think?” Roseberry said. “They took our money.”

“Did they take any jewelry, credit cards, or cell phones?”

“No.”

“Did anyone have those items?”

Roseberry’s lips pursed. “What do you think we are? Poor or something?”

“If you were going to rob a joint, wouldn’t you take everything you could?”

“I’d never rob anyone. I got a job. I pay my taxes.”

Morgan shook his head. “Anybody lose a car?”

“How do you lose a car?” Roseberry furrowed his brow. “Oh, you mean— No. Why would they take one of our cars? Someone probably would have called the cops.”

“Why didn’t you?”

“Because SPD wouldn’t look for our shit. Besides, calling you guys would be like telling on myself. Hell, you’re probably going to shut me down now.”

Morgan dismissively flicked his hand. "I don't care what you do."

Roseberry's face relaxed. "For real?"

The detective turned to leave, but a thought came to him. "How'd they find your club?"

"Yeah, that's a good question. Way I figure it is somebody talked. My club is by invite only. It might not look like much, but the people who hang out here think it's pretty damn special. Know what I mean?"

"Who do you think talked?"

Roseberry shrugged. "I don't know, but if I did, there'd be a thumping coming and not from me. The regulars here are protective of this place."

"Did the guys who robbed you ask about other clubs?"

"They hit us and left—in and out. Like an afternoon quickie."

Morgan's cell phone buzzed once—the signal for a text message. He pulled the phone from his pocket to find a group message from Adrian Thorn. MORGAN, I THINK YOU SHOULD GET OVER TO THE HIDEAWAY.

A moment later, Strange sent NO ONE AT THE DL. I THOUGHT THESE GUYS WERE SUPPOSED TO BE HERE. I'LL HEAD TO THE HIDEAWAY.

Morgan wanted to crack this case. He didn't want to lose to the Hotheads or the county. He felt he did his best work when his back was against the wall—when all other options were removed.

He was tired. He'd taken a short nap the previous evening, but he was going on almost twenty-four hours of being awake now. Despite his weariness, Morgan wasn't willing to quit; he wanted to win this war.

"I need the names of your customers," Morgan said. "Especially the regulars who weren't here the night you were robbed."

Roseberry rubbed his belly. "You know I can't do that."

"Then I'll shut you down."

"Do what you got to do because if I give you the names, I might as well shut it down myself."

The two men stared at each other for several moments.

Eventually, Roseberry put his hands on his hips which shoved his jacket to the side and pushed his white belly out prominently. "Are we done here?"

Morgan grunted. "Yeah, we're done."

Chapter 15

"I want a lawyer," Charles Caruso said.

He sat at his kitchen table with his hands folded in front of him. Caruso was in his late thirties with pale skin, thinning hair, and a slight paunch. His T-shirt read *Brews on Washington*.

"This." Adrian Thorn waved at Caruso. "This is what I've been getting since I arrived."

Jeremiah Strange smirked. "Told you about that backup."

Morgan crossed his arms and studied the kitchen. Its oak cabinetry and tan sink dated it, but it was extremely tidy. Recently washed dishes dried in a nearby rack. A large spice holder hung on the wall. Morgan moved forward to check the little bottles out. He opened a cabinet door and discovered various sized dishes.

"You can't do that," Caruso said. "Stay out of there."

Morgan knelt and opened a lower cabinet door. Inside were various canned items—soups, chilis, beans, and vegetables. Morgan shut the door and stood. "Who's the hooligan?"

Caruso looked away. "I want a lawyer."

"You said that, but I asked a question you don't need an attorney for. This is a pretty nice pantry for a hooligan."

"Lawyer," Caruso said.

Morgan eyed Thorn. "Did he show you the Hideaway?"

"I only made it this far."

"Has he tried anything hinky?"

"Besides repeating his demand?" Thorn shook his head. "I walked in, told him what I was after, and that's it."

Morgan studied Caruso. "We're not leaving until you talk with us."

"I want a lawyer."

Thorn clucked his tongue. "A broken record."

"Smack him upside the head," Strange joked. "See if the needle skips."

Caruso looked up, and his eyes briefly widened. He quickly caught himself, though, and his face hardened again.

Violence, or at least the threat of it, could be helpful if need be. Morgan had applied physical pressure before but never in front of his teammates. He was willing to do things that pushed the limits, yet he never wanted to put the team in a questionable position.

Morgan pulled out a chair and sat across from the man. "Here's what we know, Charlie."

"It's Charles." It was said flatly as if he'd made this correction throughout his life. "Charlie is my dad. Chuck was my grandfather." Caruso never looked up when speaking to Morgan.

"All right, *Charles*." Morgan rapped the table with his knuckles. "Here's what we know. Several murders occurred at two after-hours joints. You've heard about those because Dave Elmendorf called you. Right?"

It was barely perceptible, but Caruso nodded once.

Morgan continued. "Another joint was robbed. Maybe you know about that, maybe not. But you were robbed, too."

Caruso's head came up slightly, and his eyes darted about the room.

"Dave told us," Morgan said. "I don't understand why when my man shows up to talk about this situation, you start with the *Law and Order* routine."

"Lawyer."

Morgan waved his hand over the Formica kitchen table. "One of the things we're trying to determine is where it all started. Ground zero, so to speak. We know where the last one happened because of the murders, but it sounds like this string of terror might have been going on for a while. See what I'm saying?"

Caruso remained silent.

"If we can't find the shooters," Morgan said, "we'll pin the whole thing on the source. You know, the guy who put the killers onto all the after-hours joints. The prosecuting attorney has got all sorts of ways to call that behavior, but since you're a *Law and Order* guy—I'm assuming you are since you talk like it. Anyway, we'll arrest the guy who talked and call it aiding and abetting the killers. You ever wonder how much prison time would fall to a guy who aided and abetted nine murders? It's gotta be a lot."

"A whole lot," Strange said.

"A lifetime," Thorn agreed.

Caruso didn't look at Morgan, but his eyes flicked toward the wall.

"Someone's gonna pay, Charles. That's the way the system works. Somebody always pays. Checks and balances. The system needs a fall guy to sit next to the judge. Right now, you think you're playing it smart by asking for an attorney. But does that ever work out that way in those shows? The defense attorneys always lose."

"Lawyer." Caruso stood, and his chair scooted back. "You have to let me call. It's the law!"

Thorn and Strange moved toward him.

"I'm sorry." Caruso lifted his hands into the air. "I'm sorry." He grabbed his chair and sat again.

"So we're going to talk?" Morgan asked.

"Not without a lawyer," Caruso said.

"Why don't you show us the Hideaway? Let us see your club."

"I have my rights."

"We're not going to bust you for having a club. That's not what we're here for."

Caruso crossed his arms and shook his head.

Morgan leaned back in his chair and drummed his fingers along the edge of the table. "All right." His gaze shifted to the two officers. "See if you can find his bar. Check for outside entrances. Maybe it's in the garage."

"You can't do that," Caruso said. "It's an illegal search."

Thorn furrowed his brow. "You don't want us to hang here and witness his statements?"

Strange patted his partner's shoulder. "Let's leave them alone." He stepped toward the back door. "Let us know when you're done, Morgan."

"Good luck," Thorn muttered to the homeowner.

Caruso watched the officers go. When the back door closed, he faced Morgan. "I want a lawyer," he said.

"It's just us now."

"Doesn't matter. I still want—"

"You gave the list of the clubs to the shooters."

"No." Caruso shook his head. "I didn't. I wouldn't."

"You did. It was in alphabetical order." Morgan stood. "They hit your place first. I don't know why but they did. Who were they?" He moved over to the spice rack.

"I couldn't see their faces."

"Had they been here before?"

"I don't know who they were."

Morgan read the labels of the jars on the rack. "Allspice, anise, basil, brown mustard." He looked over his shoulder to Caruso. "Did they threaten you for the list, or did you just hand it to them?"

"I never—"

"Cayenne pepper, celery seed, coriander, cumin." Morgan turned back to Caruso again. "What do you do with cumin? Never mind. I've got a few spices, but mine are tossed in a drawer. Keeping them this way is so much more efficient. Is everything in your life as orderly as this?"

Caruso didn't speak.

Morgan bent and opened the lower cabinet door. "So this list of clubs—was it already written down, or did you keep it in your head? I like what you did with your cans here. Labels faced out, so they're all easy to read. Like at the store." He chuckled. "I just noticed this. You alphabetized them by category, too. Beans, chili, soups, and vegetables. Nice. Were your parents this way, too?"

He glanced over his shoulder at Caruso. The man stared back at him.

Morgan closed the cabinet before straightening to his full height. "You're not exactly a man built for violence, are you?"

Caruso's tongue darted out between his lips, and it appeared he had trouble swallowing.

"When those men walked in, you told them about the other clubs. Why?"

Morgan could see it now. Caruso teetered on the edge. If Morgan pushed too hard, Caruso might resist and return to demanding the lawyer. Sometimes the best thing an investigator could do is give a man a little silence to throw himself over the edge.

"They already knew about the clubs," Caruso said. It was as if a valve had been turned and the pressure released. His whole body slumped.

"By name?"

Caruso waved a hand. "Not by name, no. But they knew they existed."

"How?"

"Because of how they asked."

Morgan frowned. "Which was?"

Caruso's face pinched, and he lowered his voice. "*Where are the other fucking clubs?*" His face relaxed. "That's how they asked. Demanded would be a better word. They flashed their guns in my face."

"That's how they sounded? Deep voices?"

"One of them, yeah."

"Did you notice anything else?"

"While I was writing the list, one of them pushed the sleeves of his shirt up. They were both wearing long-sleeve T-shirts. I think he did it absently. Like he wasn't thinking about it."

"Did he have a tattoo?"

Caruso nodded. "An S with a dagger through it. Might have been a sword."

"And you've never seen these guys before?"

"They had masks on."

"Why didn't they shoot you?"

Caruso blanched. "Maybe because I gave them what they wanted."

"How many other people were in the club when it happened?"

"None."

"Why not?"

"Some nights are like that. I was all alone. I was listening to music, drinking by myself, when they walked in."

"How did you find out about the other joints?" Morgan asked. "I spoke with the owner of Hillyard's Rathskeller. He didn't know about your club."

Caruso shrugged. "I collect things. You haven't seen it yet, but I've got a music and movie collection, all alphabetized like—" He motioned toward the spice rack. "When I realized there were more clubs like mine, I started paying attention, keeping notes. It seemed like a fun thing to do."

"You don't seem much like a hooligan."

"I'm not, but my club—" Caruso's shoulders slumped. "I'll show you."

He stood and headed for the back door. Morgan followed.

Adrian Thorn and Jeremiah Strange stood in the middle of the yard. They watched as Caruso led Morgan to a rear door at the back of the attached garage. "The entrance is through here."

A stone footpath led from the alley to the garage. Caruso unlocked the door and swung it open.

Inside looked like a swanky nightclub. A bar stood in the corner. A leather L-shaped couch was tucked against the far wall. A crystal ball hung from the ceiling. Pictures of gangsters and criminals hung on the wall. Morgan knew a few of them by sight—Al Capone, Pablo Escobar, and Bonnie Parker and Clyde Barrow. There were several photographs of individuals that Morgan didn't know.

"These are my hooligans," Caruso said and motioned to the pictures. "It seemed a fitting theme to what we were doing here."

Thorn and Strange stepped into the homemade bar. Their eyes swept the room, and both men nodded appreciatively.

Caruso seemed an odd type for a bartender. Morgan thought he might have been better fashioned to be an accountant or a librarian.

"Where do you work?" Morgan asked.

"The Chili's inside the airport."

Morgan expected a disdainful grunt from one of the officers, but they both stood by silently.

"How do you think those guys found you?" Morgan asked.

"You mean, how did they know I had a list?" Caruso shrugged. "Luck of the draw."

"Luck only goes so far," Morgan said. "Someone knew about your list. Who did you tell?"

"No one. I swear." Caruso looked at Thorn and Strange before turning back to Morgan. "I promise. I wouldn't have told them hadn't they stuck their guns in my face."

***

"I'm fading," Morgan said. "How about you guys?"

The three men stood in front of the Starbucks at the corner of Division Street and Buckeye Avenue. They were about to go in, but Morgan had stopped them on the front sidewalk.

"I'm good," Thorn said.

Strange patted his chest. "I can go all day."

The two men didn't look any better than Morgan felt, but they were nearly a decade younger than him. He didn't want to admit that would make a difference in this matter, but it was clear the guys spent many late nights out together. He'd grown soft by hitting the rack early. It might have been with the occasional woman, but that didn't help his ability to operate at a high level for more than twenty-four hours. He needed some sleep.

Vehicles stopped for the red light at the nearby intersection. A truck with a missing muffler loudly rumbled.

"Take off," Strange shouted. "We'll take it from here."

Thorn hollered, "We got you covered."

Morgan shook his head. He wouldn't leave now and let his guys continue to work. He led from the front.

The stop light changed to green, and the truck accelerated. Its engine roared into the distance. Morgan waited until it was a block away before speaking.

"We've still got reports to write."

Thorn and Strange shared a questioning look.

"We either do it now, or we do it later."

"I'd rather run and gun," Thorn said.

"Me, too," Morgan said. "But I'm thinking how tired I am now is only going to be worse in a couple hours. Trying to finish that report then is going to be murder."

Strange dejectedly nodded. "The man is right. If we don't cut paper now, the administration has something to hang over our heads."

"This sucks," Thorn muttered. "I wanted to get into the mix today."

"There's still time," Morgan said. "But first, we oughta do our homework."

***

Morgan's chin repeatedly bounced against his chest as he struggled through his report. His fingers slowly wandered about the keyboard. The word processor frequently highlighted misspelled words. Initially, he backspaced and corrected them. After a time, though, he stopped and merely forged ahead. He would use the program's spell checker when he finished.

He was in the Criminal Task Force's office in the Monroe Court Building. It sat adjacent to the Public Safety Building. Morgan was usually thankful that the CTF remained separated from the rest of the department, but this morning it would have been nice to be in the PSB.

The department had a couple of rooms set aside for officers to sleep in. They were for occasions like now when Morgan needed to rest. He could have walked to the end of the hall, closed the door, and climbed into bed for several hours. When he emerged, he could hit the streets again. He wouldn't be as refreshed as if he had a whole night's sleep, but he would be much better than he was now.

At the end of the office, the chattering between Thorn and Strange had quieted. The only thing he heard was the clicking of their keyboards. Maybe they were finally fading.

Morgan turned his attention back to his report. He would often proofread his work, but this morning, he didn't. He ran the spell checker and accepted all the suggested corrections. Then he sent his report to Parker and Johnson with a copy to his sergeant.

He stood. "How you coming?"

Thorn grunted.

"I'm hurting," Strange said. "Gonna need a nap."

Morgan checked his watch. It was nearly seven. "Finish up, and let's meet back here at noon. Doable?"

Thorn lazily waved a hand. "Copy that."

"Yeah," was all Strange said.

Morgan left the office without further comment.

***

Morgan walked into his apartment.

He briefly paused in the hallway so a memory of Alyssa could haunt him. The two had never lived together, but she was often at his apartment. He gave her a key, but she didn't have a drawer in any dresser. A key was as committed to any relationship as Morgan wanted to get.

But here he was—wrung-out and nostalgic.

Morgan didn't miss her in the way poets wrote about suffering love's loss. And he didn't long for her while he was at the job. He simply missed her presence.

Weak, Morgan thought. He was growing old.

He headed for the bedroom.

PART IV

Chapter 16

"When did they move you down here?" Parker asked.

Officer Mason Hoerner leaned back in his chair and interlaced his fingers behind his head. His light blue shirt pulled tightly across his puffy chest. "Pretty sweet, huh?"

They were seated in a cubicle on the seventh floor of city hall. Around the corner was the mayor's office.

"The chief suggested I move down here, what with all I do for city hall." Hoerner smiled brightly. "Where's your partner?"

"He had stuff to do."

Johnson was back at the department assembling the backbone for The Tiptoe Lounge shooting report. Parker had been the primary on The Shortstop shooting, so this was Johnson's turn to step up.

Parker glanced around city hall. "I thought you were the department's liaison to liquor control."

"That's only a part of my duties."

"But the biggest part, right?" Parker asked.

"Not that big."

Hoerner's chair fell forward. The man's buttoned collar pushed against his neck, and a roll of fat now appeared. Hoerner set his hands on the edge of the desk and did a quasi-push-up. It seemed as if he kept leaning backward so his feet didn't touch the floor. It was something a kid might do. Hoerner's face reddened. Parker wondered if it was from the exertion of keeping his fat ass off the ground or if the collar was cutting oxygen from his brain.

The officer continued with his bragging. "I'm also the liaison to the gambling commission, the towing and taxi industry. Being the department's contact with city hall is just one thing I do."

Parker smirked. "Chief Dillon is the department's contact with city hall."

"Well, yeah, of course, but when he's not available, that's where I come in."

Mason Hoerner was assigned to the Office of Special Police Problems. Parker thought it a dumb name because Hoerner was the only guy in that office. Since Parker had joined the department, only a few guys had held the role. The rare turnover in the position showed two things.

First, most officers didn't want the job. It put them in a role that reported directly to the chief, making most people uncomfortable.

Second, it wasn't a high-speed, low-drag assignment. It was a lot of paperwork and glad-handing. Most cops wanted to do a job that held the potential of driving fast and getting into an occasional scuffle. A Special Police Problems officer would have to go out of his way to do either of those things.

Hoerner seemed more than comfortable sitting behind a desk—except right now. His face reddened further, and his arms wobbled. He let go, and the chair fell back into its rightful place.

"The chief didn't want to keep paying that crazy high rent for my office at Monroe Court," the officer said, "but he didn't want me in the downtown precinct either, so he worked out a deal with the mayor to put me here." Hoerner smoothed his tie, and his face returned to its standard color. "All in all, I think it works better for me and the department."

Parker disliked Hoerner. Most officers did. The guy was arrogant, and it wasn't because Hoerner was talented in one of the areas cops respected, such as investigation, fighting, or shooting. No, Mason Hoerner was a prick because of the jobs he'd maneuvered himself into. The guy was barely out of the Field Training Officer's car when he managed to get temporarily assigned to the Front Desk. It was a position typically reserved for injured officers or those late in a career. No one wanted it, but Hoerner took it with aplomb.

After that gig, Hoerner wriggled himself into yet another temporary assignment as a Neighborhood Resource Officer. Once more, it was a role usually set aside for tenured cops. Hoerner filled in for an officer recovering from major back surgery. When that job eventually returned to its appropriate designee, Hoerner found himself at the SPP desk.

"So, what can I do you for, Detective?"

"What do you know about after-hours clubs?"

Hoerner ran his hand underneath his tie and let the tail slip from his fingers. "Liquor service ends at two."

Parker frowned. "That's it?"

"Nobody serves after that. It's the law." The officer reached into a small metal tray on the corner of his desk and lifted several papers from it. Hoerner's gaze swept over them, but he didn't read the documents. It was an act designed to show how important he was. Parker fought the desire to chuckle.

The officer continued. "There aren't any clubs operating outside standard hours. Restaurants serve food at that time." Hoerner's head bounced from side to side. "Denny's and Shari's and such, but no clubs. We'd know about it if they did."

"You didn't see the Hot Sheet?"

Hoerner looked up and wiped a thumb over his lower lip. "I don't read it every day. No reason to do so in this office. You know how it is."

"Yeah," Parker said. "I know how it is."

"So, what about the Sheet? Was there something I should know?"

"Jessie and I caught a multiple in an after-hours club. One that served alcohol."

Hoerner appeared offended. "They're doing it illegally, then."

"No kidding."

"We didn't know."

"I've gathered that," Parker said.

Hoerner put his hand on his chest. "Why are you making this about me?"

"I'm not." Parker leaned forward. "What I'm asking is if you knew—"

"I didn't," the officer interrupted. "I don't."

"You don't what?"

"That's liquor control's responsibility—not mine. I don't have much to do with the bars."

Parker smirked. "You're the department's liaison. You just said."

Hoerner waved glibly and turned his attention back to the papers. "I get a notice is what I get. It says some jerk wants a liquor license." Hoerner snatched a document and waved it as an example. "Then I run a background check and pass it along to the local liquor guys. That's it. That's what I do. Nothing more."

"You always make it sound like a big deal."

The officer swallowed and followed it with a quick shake of his head. "Well, it's not."

"You don't go out on liquor checks?"

"Yeah, sure. But they're not that special."

"I don't know about that," Parker said. "The tales about your rounds with liquor control and the fire marshals on St. Patty's Day and other big nights are getting to be—dare I say—legendary."

Hoerner looked at his cubicle wall. A certificate for something hung there. Parker couldn't read it from where he sat.

"There are some stories, yeah," Hoerner said. "Sure." He faced Parker once more. "But that doesn't mean I'm responsible for the whole freakin' industry." Hoerner pointed out of his cubicle. "That's the LCB's bailiwick, not mine."

"Okay, Mason, relax. Just what are you responsible for?"

"Now, what's that supposed to mean?"

Parker shrugged. "I'm responsible for finding who murdered four people in an after-hours club. If the LCB is responsible for licensing the industry—" He thumbed over his shoulder in the same direction that the officer had pointed. "What are you responsible for?" Now, he motioned at Hoerner.

The officer stared at him.

"Nothing?" Parker asked.

Hoerner's cheeks flushed. "What do you want me to say? I don't know anything about any illegal clubs. Nothing was ever reported to me."

Parker stood. "Good chat." He left the cubicle and headed toward the elevators. He was about to press the down button when a thought occurred to him. Parker headed back.

Hoerner's head was bowed, and his fingers drummed an anxious rhythm along the edge of the desk.

"Hey," Parker said.

The officer jumped in his seat and looked up. "What?"

"Contact the liquor board. Ask them about these clubs. If they know anything, call me."

Hoerner hesitated briefly, then reached for his phone.

***

Morgan turned off the ignition and rested his forearms against the steering wheel. He'd only gotten a few hours of sleep before leaving the bed and showering. The coffee and ibuprofen weren't helping. He had a splitting headache now.

He rubbed the palms of his hands into his closed eyes. It relieved the pressure slightly, but the headache wouldn't go away. Only a full night's sleep would alleviate this pain, and for that, he'd have to wait until the end of the day.

The detective reached wearily for the car door.

Morgan felt like a zombie as he trudged up the sidewalk. Or Frankenstein, he corrected. His feet were heavy, and his boot heels scuffed the ground. He never dragged his feet—only stat-fives and sailors did such a thing.

The yellow Craftsman home was in the Perry District. White columns supported the open porch roof. Chipping gray paint covered the floor.

He stepped to the side of the door and rang the bell.

Light footsteps approached. The lock didn't slide open, and the knob remained unturned. Morgan imagined someone staring at him through the peephole.

"Who's there?" a woman called from the other side.

Morgan stepped in front of the door. "Police." He croaked the word. The detective cleared his throat and repeated, "Police."

"How do I know?" It sounded as if she were younger. Her voice was strong and forceful.

"Lady, if I wasn't a cop—" But Morgan didn't bother to finish the statement. He removed his wallet and flipped it open to reveal a small badge and department-issued ID card. The photograph showed a younger version of himself.

"Anybody can fake those."

What is it with people these days? Morgan wondered. He shook his head and stared into the peephole. "If I wanted to hurt you, I wouldn't have rung the damn doorbell. Dave Elmendorf called you. Open the door. We need to talk."

The lock slid back, and the door cracked open. An eye peered through.

"I'm a cop," Morgan said wearily. "Open up."

The door swung wide, and a dark-haired woman stood before him. "You could have said that to begin with."

"I did."

Her brow furrowed. "Yeah? Well, anybody can say it."

She appeared to be in her mid-thirties. Her hair fell to her shoulders, and she had smoldering dark eyes under heavy natural brows. She wore a gray sweatshirt, faded blue jeans, and flip-flops. "But Dave is good people." Reluctantly, she stepped back. "Come in."

Morgan moved by her. She closed the door and relocked it.

When she faced him, she hooked her thumbs into the pockets of her jeans.

"Taylor Kingford?" he asked.

"That's right."

"Detective Morgan," he said. He didn't bother giving her a card. "Why did you take off earlier?"

"When was that?"

Morgan stared at her. He was too tired to play word games.

"You mean this morning?" She appeared embarrassed. "I was with someone."

She was an attractive woman. If she didn't have a steady man, she probably spent many nights away from home. Morgan corrected himself—or a steady woman. He needed to think more progressively.

Kingford rolled her eyes. "Not like that. I went to stay with my mom. It's stupid, I know, but I freaked out after Dave's call. I didn't want to be here by myself."

Morgan feigned his understanding. He didn't get scared like that and preferred to be alone.

"Dave said you were robbed."

She nodded. "If I talk to you about this, am I going to get in trouble?"

"About your club?" He shook his head. "I couldn't care less about it."

"But will you write a report about it? I mean, will the liquor board see it? They see everything, and those bastards are vindictive. They'll take away my server's permit. If they do that, I'm out of a job. I'll have to work in another industry. I don't know what I can do. Wait tables, I guess. Answer phones, maybe? Can you see me doing that?"

"I'll keep your name out of it."

Her eyes narrowed. "Promise?"

The throbbing in Morgan's head worsened.

"Right," she said. "Okay. What other choice do I have? And Dave said to trust you. Do you want to see where it's at?"

They walked through her house until they stepped into the backyard. Once there, they climbed a set of stairs to an apartment built above a detached garage. "This was my grandparents' house. After my grandmother died, she left it to my mom, but she didn't want to sell it to anyone, so she sold it to me below market and on contract. I'm sorry for babbling." Kingford forced an awkward smile. "I'm nervous, and I'm tired. I ramble when I'm tired."

They walked into the unit, and it looked like hundreds of other apartments that Morgan had been in during his career. Oak cabinets in the kitchen. A sofa and chairs in the living room. Pictures of major American cities hung on the wall—New York, Chicago, and San Francisco.

"This is your club?" Morgan asked.

"What's wrong with it?"

"It doesn't look like a club."

"That's the point. That's why it's called The Down Low."

"We're on the second floor."

She smiled. "Ironic too. My thought was if the LCB ever did find it and they wanted to bust me, they'd show up and see it's just an apartment. I even have a lease."

"With who?"

"A friend. She doesn't pay rent or anything. It's just a piece of paper to pretend I have a renter."

"Why all the trouble?"

Kingford cocked her head. "I don't understand?"

"Why not rent this out to someone for real? Probably save a lot of money worries."

"But that's my house, and this is my club."

Morgan studied her.

"I don't want people coming into my house, using my toilet, eating out of my fridge. Would you be cool with that? But my club, yeah, I can party here. It's like my social space. You know? Where I can meet friends and whatnot."

Morgan squinted. The headache bothered him, and this woman was making it worse. Her rationale didn't make sense, but he didn't care about her life choices. He only wanted to know about one thing. "The robbery," Morgan said. "Tell me what happened."

Kingford nodded. She backed away from the entry door as she spoke. It was as if she were envisioning the crime as it took place. "These two guys came in and demanded our money."

"How many were here with you?"

She shrugged. "About six, maybe."

"About?"

Kingford bunched her lips as she thought. "Six, including me."

"And what did these guys do?"

"They made us empty our pockets and put everything on the table. They took all our cash."

"That's it? No jewelry or credit cards?"

"They smacked one of my friends for trying to talk tough. Gave him a pretty good gash on the forehead, but that's it."

"Did they steal anyone's car?"

Kingford shook her head. "No. Why would they do that?"

"Why didn't you report the robbery?"

"And confess to running an illegal bar?" She stared at him. "No, thank you. Everyone was cool with it. Well, except for the guy who got thumped. He deserved it if you ask me. As for the robbery, it's happened to me before where I worked. I never expected such a thing would happen at my own joint, but they only took cash so what's the big deal? It's almost like they did us a favor by not taking the credit cards because that would have been a huge hassle."

"Did you see any marks or tattoos on these guys?"

Kingford shook her head. "No. They were covered up." She ran her hand along her forearm. "Long sleeves and gloves. They were pretty smart that way. Got to give them credit for planning ahead."

"Could you tell which race they were?"

"Well, sure." She rolled her eyes. "They were white. I could see a little peek of skin every now and then, but that's all. Not like I can give a great description. They were like six feet tall and trim and white. That's all I can say."

"Did they say anything you remember?"

"Oh, sure." Kingford nodded. "One of them said, 'Keep your fucking mouths shut, or we'll be back.'"

***

"After-hours joints?" Debra Voller said. "You mean like Sam's Pit?"

Shane McAfee crossed his ankle over his knee. "I have no idea what that is."

"Young bucks." Voller laughed. "No sense of your history."

They were seated in Voller's office on West Broadway. She was the regional director for the Washington State Liquor and Cannabis Board. Her gray hair was cut short in an almost mannish way. She was a petite woman with large round glasses that needed frequent repositioning on her nose.

She continued. "Sam's was an after-hours joint that troubled the city of Spokane about the time I came on. The business served barbecue, and folks came from all over after the bars closed."

"Were they serving liquor?"

"Just food, but the business attracted a rough crowd. This was the early nineties, so the crack epidemic was in full swing. Dealers used to stand on the corner and sell to those arriving for some late-night noshing. Gang members hung around there, too,"

"Sounds like a bad scene," McAfee said.

"Shootings. A couple of deaths. So yeah, you could call it a bad scene. And we couldn't get involved because it wasn't liquor related."

"What happened to it?"

"The city shut it down under the nuisance law. It took a while for it to happen finally, and it upset many folks until it did. The city took the owner to court. Made the newspaper and the evening news. You were probably a kid then, huh? Anyway, the action finally made the locals happy, but it irked other businesses because it pushed the criminal activity into new areas like West First. You know what happened down there, right?"

McAfee shook his head.

Voller chuckled. "Geez, Detective. You'd think they'd give you guys a history course, but you didn't come here for that. What do you want to know about after-hours clubs?"

"We had a multiple at one of them in the county a couple of days ago. The city had one yesterday."

The director's face hardened. "We haven't gotten copies of those reports."

"How do you normally get notified?"

"County records flag any report concerning an alcohol-related business. Or the city's Special Police Problems officer sends it to us. Are you sure they were after-hours clubs? Because I've got to tell you they're rarer than a three-dollar bill."

McAfee smiled politely. "We're sure."

"Let's be clear," Voller said. "An after-hours joint isn't easy to find. They've got to be reported, and before they do, most of the operators of them willingly shut down. A neighbor gets upset and talks to the offending party. They think the cops will respond when, in all likelihood, it would be us. But the offenders knock it off pretty darn quick, either way."

"I'm here to learn and discuss, not make accusations."

Voller smiled. "My feelings aren't hurt by your questions, Detective. I'm only trying to explain how rare it is to find these clubs. I'm interested to hear what you know. Tell me about the first one."

"It was a hookah club."

"Now, that's interesting." Voller interlaced her fingers and set her hands on her desk. The WSLCB was also responsible for regulating the tobacco industry in the state. "But it might not be a violation. Depends on what was being done. Were they selling tobacco?"

"I don't know. From what we've learned, the attendees gathered there after the bars closed to smoke and drink."

"Sounds like a clubhouse. It wouldn't have been illegal if they weren't selling tobacco or alcohol."

McAfee waved his hand. "We're playing a game of what if. Let me give you the addresses." He opened his notebook.

Voller jotted down the information as McAfee spoke. He also provided the names of the clubs and the homeowners. When McAfee finished, Voller set down her pen and turned to her computer.

"None of that sounds familiar." Her fingers jumped around her keyboard. She shook her head. "Nothing on this Shisha. I like that word, by the way. Sounds like a pretty foreign girl." Voller's fingers danced some more. Once again, her head shook. "And a big zero for The Shortstop. I'm not surprised, though. Like I said, they're rare."

"But you *have* run across them?"

"Oh, sure. The last one was a few years back in Stevens County—Loon Lake, to be exact." Loon Lake was about forty minutes north of Spokane and on the other side of the county line. "An arrest came out of it, which is still odder."

"A four-dollar bill?" McAfee asked.

Voller tilted her head at him.

"What happened?" he asked her.

"The area we cover out of this office is massive. We run from the Canadian border down to Old Town. A field office out of Pasco helps with the southern coverage, but we run all the way east to Ellensburg. Trust me when I say we've got a lot of ground to cover. So we don't hunt for after-hours clubs. Someone needs to put them on our radar, and then we'll work with local law enforcement to shut them down."

"How did you discover the Loon Lake club?"

"The marshals."

McAfee's expression flattened. "The feds?"

"They were watching the house. The homeowner was involved with a white supremacist splinter group called the Silent." She rolled her eyes. "The marshals were looking for a way to get inside and couldn't find a legal one until they realized there was a lot of after-hours activity occurring in the barn."

Voller shifted in her seat and crossed her legs.

She continued. "One night, the marshals had a Stevens County deputy stop one of the boys who left the house. The guy blew a one-point-six on a portable Breathalyzer. Double the legal limit. The kid drove delivery truck for a local bakery, so a DUI would cost him his license and job. That boy wouldn't admit to anything concerning the Silent, but he copped to being at an after-hours club inside the barn. It chapped his hide that he had to pay for his drinks even after paying an entry fee. We later learned the club was a way to fund the cause, but the kid wouldn't admit to such a thing right then. Anyway, that's when the marshals got us involved. You want some coffee?"

McAfee shook his head. "I'm good."

"I won't bore you with the nitty-gritty of us getting up there, but we did prove there was after-hours activity and arrested the homeowner with the help of some Stevens County deputies. The homeowner was some ding-dong— Elias Richter." She spelled the last name phonetically.

McAfee jotted the information into his notebook. "Why was he a ding-dong?"

"He wasn't all that bright, and that's not a comment on the whole supremacy thing, but there is that, too."

McAfee nodded.

"Yeah, so," Voller continued, "the marshals used our arrest of Richter as their crowbar to enter the house. They found a bunch of supremacist literature and paraphernalia.

Nazi flags and that type of stuff. None of that is unlawful, mind you. They found knives, hatchets, you name it for edged weapons, but none of it was necessarily illegal. What finally did Richter in was an AK-47 that a marshal found hidden in the barn. He wasn't allowed to own a firearm."

"Richter was a felon?" McAfee asked.

Voller nodded. "First-degree burglary, from what I remember. Stole a neighbor's gun collection or some such when he was right out of high school. He pled guilty to that incident in exchange for a deferred sentence. Part of the agreement was he couldn't own or possess a firearm for ten years."

"What happened to him after the barn raid?"

"Richter got another deal. Funny how that works. The prosecuting attorney sent him to Coyote Ridge."

"A state facility?"

"That was the plea. I guess he didn't want the kid to go to a federal penitentiary. Richter was sentenced to a shorter time than I expected with years deferred as parole."

"When's he get out?"

"I imagine he already is. I haven't bothered to keep track of him. He's the feds' problem. Let's be honest. He got on our radar because of an after-hours club in the backwoods that no one complained about. Hard to stay worked up over that."

McAfee closed his notebook and stood. He reached across the desk and shook Debra Voller's hand. "Thank you for your time."

Out on the sidewalk, McAfee removed his phone and called Tim Chambers. The other detective answered on the third ring.

"Tim, it's Shane. I need you to look up a name."

"You got something?"

"I don't know. It might be nothing."

Keyboard clicking came through the phone line. "Go ahead," Chambers said.

A patrol car activated its siren and sped by. McAfee covered his open ear with his free hand and waited for the wailing to fade into the distance.

"Elias Richter," McAfee said. "That's Richter with a C-H-T."

"Got it."

"He went away on a weapons charge."

Chambers tapped on his keyboard. "Found him."

"He recently got out of prison, right?"

"Yeah. He was in Coyote Ridge until, oh, three months ago."

"Where's he living now?"

"He's got an address over on West Dalton." Chambers recited it.

McAfee stiffened. That was only a short distance from where he was now. "What about a P.O.?"

More clicking came through the phone. "Probation officer is… Yvette Oliver."

"Where's she out of?"

"Looks like she's on Broadway." Chambers gave him the address. "I think that's the COPS substation over there. Why's this guy important?"

"He might not be, but he had an after-hours joint up in Stevens County."

"Had?"

McAfee watched a Spokane Police Department patrol car zoom by. This one did not have its sirens activated. "Richter's weapons charge came out of an after-hours investigation."

"And you're thinking about talking to him like he's some sort of Hannibal Lector? Maybe he'll give you some insight into what's going on?"

"No. I've got a feeling. You ever get those?"

"Yeah," Chambers said. "If you want to go over to his house, I'll go with."

"Not yet." McAfee headed for his car. "Let me talk with this Yvette Oliver first, and then I'll let you know."

***

"You look like dog shit," Officer Courtney Earley said.

Morgan yawned. "Coming from you, that's saying something."

Earley was a beast. In his college days, he played on the defensive line for the University of Montana. His height would never change, but his midsection had softened over the years. Luckily, his strength remained. His hair and beard were always long, but they desperately needed washing. The man's skin looked greasy and was flecked with dirt.

He sat sideways on his motorcycle—a Harley-Davidson something or other. Morgan didn't care about bikes, and he wasn't going to pretend by asking Earley about his.

The two men were behind the Grocery Outlet on Lincoln Road. Earley didn't want to meet out in the open, and he didn't want to drive down to the Monroe Court Building. Therefore, Morgan agreed to meet him at this north-side location.

"I don't mind dressing this way," Earley said, "It's the not showering that bothers me. I can smell my stink." He lifted his left arm and sniffed his pit. Earley crinkled his nose and animatedly shook his head. "I can't wait to rotate back to CTF."

For the past several weeks, Earley had been assigned to the Special Investigations Unit.

While the Spokane Police Department used the Criminal Task Force as a hammer to bludgeon various problems, it wielded SIU like a scalpel when it came to eradicating criminal gangs.

Morgan liked blunt force better; it seemed more reliable and was easier to see immediate results.

Courtney Earley was one of the few guys who could easily fit into the world of motorcycle gangs. The leaders of SIU also wanted Adrian Thorn for this assignment due to his skeevy appearance, but the man didn't know how to ride a motorcycle. There wasn't enough time to train him, and Thorn wasn't motivated to learn.

It was just as well because Morgan would have cried holy hell if he had lost two men to SIU. No love was lost between the two teams as both stepped on the other's toes due to mission creep. SIU had argued since before Morgan's time that the CTF should be dissolved and its objectives and staffing rolled into their team. Empire building was a long-established practice at any level of government, and the police department wasn't immune to it.

"How much longer have they got you?" Morgan asked.

"Couple more days. The rally is ending, and I'll debrief with Hackworth. Then I can get out of Dodge and back to the real world."

The Wasted Souls Motorcycle Club had developed the Spirit Run Rally which they billed as the "Sturgis of the Northwest." So far, it had been a bust in the eyes of local law enforcement. The threat of thousands of bikers camped out in Pend Oreille County brought a lot of agencies together. Yet only a couple hundred bikers affiliated with outlaw clubs had shown up. It mainly was weekend warriors looking to bask in the outlaw lifestyle for a few days before returning home to the safety of their corporate jobs and gated communities. Still, the turnout of the criminal element was enough to warrant SIU's continued attention, even if it was with less enthusiasm than initially expected.

Morgan lifted his chin. "You called me out here for a reason."

"One of the Souls," Earley said, "got a call from a brother in Coyote Ridge. He said to be on the lookout for this cat named Bodean Kirkwood."

"And he's telling you this why?"

Earley shrugged. "They're playing me."

"This isn't good intel?"

"Oh, it's good. That I believe." Earley waved a hand. "But they know I'm a cop. I can look as scruffy as I want, but I'm not patched in with any club. I might as well stand around pulling my pud. The Souls and their brothers cut me out of the interesting conversations and let me join in the ones about bikes and harmless nonsense. It's a game to them. The only ones willing to talk are the citizens, who don't know any better."

Morgan crossed his arms. "So this Soul got a call from Coyote Ridge about a cat named Bodean?"

Earley nodded. "Seems Bodean and his buddies got sideways with a couple of the Souls."

"What's all this got to do with the CTF?"

"Hear me out," Earley said, "I'm getting to it. So Bodean is a supremacist, a real race war type."

"Was he hooked up with the Brotherhood?" Morgan meant the Aryans. He knew Earley understood his question.

The big man shook his head. "That's the thing. Bodean claims affiliation with the Silent. You ever heard of them?"

Morgan hadn't.

"They've been around a few years, but they're still one of the newer sects. They got the same general message as the others—whites are oppressed, the blacks are coming for our women, the left is giving away our rights, yada yada yada." Earley mimed jerking off.

"Where's this term 'the Silent' come from? I've never heard of it."

"That old nugget about the silent majority. It's just that these guys are sprinkling their racism into the soup. From what I understand, the Silent originated in Boston. You'd think most of these white-makes-right groups start in the south, but they come from all around. Hate has no ground zero."

Morgan cocked his head. "You're a philosopher now? Where'd you get this background?"

"From SIU." Earley raised his eyebrows. "They got this whole library over there. Lots of amazing stuff. We should do something like it."

Morgan frowned. "I thought you didn't want to go downtown to meet, but you went to SIU?"

"Because I didn't want to fight the traffic. Don't get your panties in a bunch. I went to SIU last night. Hackworth let me in."

"He gave you a code to their office?" A thrill flashed through Morgan's chest; he'd love unfettered access to SIU.

"No. He met me there. The guy doesn't trust me enough for a code. Anyway, they got binders of printed material from the Southern Poverty Law Center. You know them, right? It's kind of stupid that SIU printed all that info when they could have just left everything online. Hell, I could have pulled it from the cloud and would never have had to leave the rally, but you know how the department is."

Morgan might have agreed if he didn't prefer to have things printed himself.

Earley continued. "But SIU also has the books that those heel-clickers read. *The Turner Diaries*, *Mein Kampf*, you name it. They got it. It's weird to think that those bastards actually read. When I heard about the Silent, I figured it would be worth spending a few minutes in SIU's library. Hackworth agreed."

"One of the shooters had a tattoo on an arm," Morgan said.

"Was it an S with a dagger through it?"

"That's how the witness described it. How'd you know?"

"That's the Silent." Earley snapped his fingers. "Although, it's not very original, is it? I think there's even a Swedish metal band that uses something like it. Maybe they're German. I can't remember."

"Back to Bodean," Morgan said. "What'd he do that got him crossways with the Souls?"

"This is hearsay—"

Morgan twirled a finger to tell Earley to speed up his story.

"Bodean told the Wasted Souls who were incarcerated with him that they should become affiliated with the Sadistic Souls."

Morgan shook his head. He hadn't heard of the other group.

"They're an Aryan Nations biker gang. They use that Nazi lightning bolt for their Ss. You got to appreciate when they're upfront about their mission."

Morgan knew a little about the Wasted Souls. He didn't find them to be an idealistic club beyond the renegade concept—*laws don't apply to us*. Morgan thought they would do business with anyone regardless of race or religion as long as the job paid. He doubted the Wasted Souls would ever get into bed with a supremacist sect because it would limit who they could do business with later.

"Are the Sadistic Souls even in our state?"

"No," Earley said. "They're primarily in the Midwest, from what I gathered. I think it was just Bodean making noise. You know how those zealots can be. Whatever it was, it didn't go over well with the Wasted Souls. They clashed at Coyote Ridge. Both sides went to the infirmary."

"White-on-white violence," Morgan said. "You'd think Bodean would have wanted to avoid that."

"The Silent don't think that way."

Morgan crossed his arms. "How do they think?"

"That the silent majority needs to stop being quiet. That the whites need to make a stand no matter the cost."

A delivery truck pulled along the backside of the building. Morgan and Earley stopped talking as the vehicle backed toward the loading dock. A loud beeping occurred while the truck reversed. When the large vehicle finally stopped, the driver exited the cab and entered the rear of the store.

Earley turned back to Morgan. "The Silent don't have any hierarchal structure, no national leadership. It's basically a group rallying around an idea. Decentralized hate. Anyone can call themselves the Silent and spout whatever crap they want. If it goes off the rails, who's gonna stop them and tell them it's not the party line?"

"And you're telling me this why?"

"Bodean's out. As of a month ago."

Morgan still didn't see how this affected him or the team. "Okay, and?"

"Supposedly, that shifted the power balance in Coyote Ridge. The Wasted Souls—the guys still behind bars—grabbed one of Bodean's boys and messed him up. To save his skin, the guy talked."

"About?"

"Bodean's plans."

"Let me guess," Morgan said, although he didn't want to speculate. Getting the CTF involved in any supremacist garbage wasn't something he'd ever want to do. His father and grandfather spouted that nonsense when he was a kid. It took him years to get it out of his head. If he could keep the white-is-right crowd in SIU's purview, he would happily let them have it.

"Race war, that's what you're thinking." Earley smirked. "But no. Bodean's got a hard-on for the Souls." The big man pushed off his bike and stood. "According to the jailhouse rat, Bodean wants to knock over the Soul's clubhouse. To practice, he's been hitting after-hours joints. That sounds like what you been dealing with—right?"

Morgan stared at Earley.

"Or am I wrong?"

"It doesn't make sense."

"Why not?"

Morgan closed his eyes as he tried to envision the clubhouse on Sprague Avenue. "The Souls have a fortified structure with cameras on the corners." Morgan pointed to his left and right. His eyes were still closed. "Reinforced doors on the front and back." Morgan opened his eyes. "These after-hours clubs were sitting ducks in comparison. The killers walked right up to them. Practicing on them is like a heavyweight fighter training with kids before a championship bout."

Earley shrugged. "That's the intel they gave me. But here's something else that won't fit. One of the SIU guys—Calhoun, know him?"

Morgan did.

"Calhoun's on light duty and not working the rally with the rest of the team up in Newport. He saw Booster and a couple prospects clearing some stuff out of the Wasted Souls clubhouse. The guy drove by at the right time and noticed the activity. Just got lucky."

"When was this?"

"Yesterday."

"Did you see Booster leave the rally?"

Earley shrugged. "I don't know how we missed him leave."

Morgan rubbed his temples. The headache he had was lessening, but it still bothered him. "What were they pulling out of the clubhouse?"

"Calhoun passed along the intel to Hackworth, who passed it along to me, but none of it is great. Supposedly, everything was in boxes. Calhoun said it looked like moving day."

"How did Calhoun know they were prospects with Booster?"

"They weren't wearing colors, and he hadn't seen them before. They must be really new because the prospects we have on the books were at the rally with me. I had eyes on them the whole afternoon. I know they didn't leave."

Morgan's eyes narrowed. "Did Calhoun follow the van?"

Earley smirked. "The guy was out for lunch with his wife. He wasn't prepared to follow it. Hackworth asked me to poke around the rally, but I got nowhere with my questions. Most wouldn't acknowledge the matter. One of the guys finally told me they were fumigating for bugs. I figured I should stop asking, or they'd freeze me out. I can only push so much without coming off as an asshole. I need to walk the line up there."

"I get it." Morgan briefly looked away. "Why would the president leave his club's rally?"

"He's been there most of the time, but I noticed him gone before. Not for long, but he disappeared. If I had to make a read on Booster, I'd say the guy is pissed, and my being there doesn't make him happy, either."

"If Booster is spending time at the clubhouse moving stuff out, then maybe there is something to this threat." Morgan patted Earley's shoulder. "It sounds weird as hell, but you did good."

"Listen, man, I gotta run. It was good to see you." Earley climbed onto his motorcycle. "Don't give away my spot on the team."

The motorcycle roared to life.

Morgan remained where he stood and watched the big man ride away.

Chapter 17

"Your neighborhood is party central," Parker said.

"Like I'm responsible for what people do." Roderick Wright leaned back against his patrol car and crossed his arms. "That's like me saying… Hell, Parker. I don't know how to make this about you."

Wright stood six and a half feet tall and tipped the scales at two hundred seventy-five pounds. The big man had let his afro grow over the past year. Up until then, Parker thought the man was bald. His black head had always glistened as if freshly shined.

Now, Wright's hair showed heavy flecks of gray. The white hash marks along his sleeve revealed his years of service. Roddie Wright was a Neighborhood Resource Officer based out of the COPS West office.

Parker had called him after visiting with Mason Hoerner in Special Police Problems. Wright had been at the neighboring Gardner Building. They agreed to meet at Wright's car in the department's parking lot.

"And why exactly is my neighborhood party central?" Wright said.

"The murder at Drumheller Springs Park. That was an after-hours joint."

Wright laughed. "That's Shadle, man. That's not my neighborhood. Know your map."

Parker frowned. He didn't know how the COPS program divided their neighborhood responsibilities, but he thought it would have been separated the same way the patrol division divvied up the city.

"What about the one this morning?" Parker asked.

Wright furrowed his brow. "There's another after-hours joint?"

"The shooting on Carlisle. You heard about it, right?"

"Of course, but I didn't know it was related." Wright whistled. "What's the world coming to?"

"Party central," Parker said.

"I guess people are trying to kill the bad times."

"When haven't they?"

Wright kicked a pebble, and it skittered away. "What's the deal with these illegal clubs? Is everyone running one now?"

"They're like speakeasies."

"But booze isn't illegal." He kicked another stone. "For that fact, weed isn't either. The way things are going, they're going to decriminalize shrooms next. You hear about that?"

Parker nodded. They were getting off track. "So you haven't gotten any complaints about after-hours joints?"

"From disgruntled neighbors, you mean?" Wright stuck out his lower lip and shook his head. "Nope, and that's something I would remember. What'd they look like?"

"Who?"

"These joints." Wright's eyes sparkled with curiosity.

"The first was a rinky-dink set-up," Parker said. "Like you might see at a lake place."

"I don't have friends with a lake place. You detectives must hang with some rich folks."

Parker ignored the comment. "It wasn't anything special. Plastic chairs. Card tables. But the second—" He whistled. "That place was cool. I could see why someone would want to do some drinking there."

Wright shoved his butt against the side of his patrol car and stood fully upright. He towered over Parker but not in a menacing way. He seemed excited about the after-hours idea. "Man, it would have been great to see. Doing something like that had to be like sneaking out of your parents' house."

Parker didn't know; he had never done that.

His phone buzzed, and he removed it from his pocket. It was a blocked number. That meant it was the department—likely the brass. Only a few departments, such as dispatch, came through as unblocked. Guys knew to call each other from their cell phones due to the blocked number business. Parker wanted to ignore the call, but it might be important.

He held up a finger for Wright to wait. "Parker," he said after answering.

"It's Mason."

Hoerner, Parker thought. That weasel got a blocked number assigned to him at city hall.

"I did what you asked. I called my contact over at liquor control."

Parker looked up at Wright. The big officer shoved his hands into his pockets and again leaned against his patrol car's side.

Hoerner continued. "She said after-hours clubs must be the topic du jour."

"What's that mean?"

"Of the day. It's French."

Parker lowered his head and pinched his nose. His face warmed. "I know what the phrase means."

"Then why did you ask?"

"Mason." Parker dropped his free hand and clenched it into a fist. "What did this person mean by their statement?"

"A county detective stopped by earlier to talk about the same thing."

Parker looked up and made eye contact with Wright. The bigger man cocked his head.

"Crazy, right?" Hoerner asked. "Anyway, she sent him to talk with Yvette Oliver about one of her parolees. You know her?"

"Yeah. I know her."

"Tell her I said hi. Man, I've wanted to go out with her since—"

"Gotta go," Parker said. He ended the call.

"Good call?" Wright asked.

Parker shrugged a single shoulder. "Just some info I needed."

"On the after-hours thing?"

"Yeah."

"I gotta tell you," Wright said. "I haven't heard this much about after-hours joints since Sam's Pit got shut down. I was little then, like real small, but my folks—" The look on Parker's face must have given Wright pause because the big man interrupted his own story. "You never heard of it? Great barbecue, but the city didn't like the crowd it attracted."

"Rough?"

Wright exaggeratedly rubbed the back of his hand. "Let's not fool ourselves. Spokane isn't as progressive as it likes to pretend."

As much as he loved the city, Parker couldn't argue with the man. He wouldn't even try.

"There were some lowlifes that visited Sam's, no denying." Wright shrugged. "It was the times, man. But the city shut it down, and we lost a place that served some decent grub."

"But it was an after-hours joint?"

"Not like you're saying these others are. They didn't serve booze."

"Are people talking about Sam's Pit lately?"

Roddie Wright cocked his head. "Like how?"

Parker waved a hand. "You said you haven't heard about after-hours joints this much since Sam's Pit closed down. I figured maybe people are talking about it."

He smiled. "No, man. Your multiple from yesterday showed up on the Hot Sheet. Then you stop by to chat about another shooting at one. And before all this mess started, I don't know, maybe a few months back, Yvette had some turd get out of Coyote Ridge on a weapons charge. You know Yvette Oliver?"

He nodded. "We go way back."

"She's in the office next to me. Hell of a lady. Don't go getting any ideas about her."

Parker held up his hand to show his wedding band.

"That's one of the things I like about you, man. You should see how some of the guys act around her."

"The turd," Parker said. "The one who got out of Coyote Ridge. What happened?"

"Right. Supposedly the guy had some after-hours joint up in Timbuktu. Anyway, the feds used the liquor board to bust him. Isn't that something? The federal government uses a state agency to do the dirty deed and then takes all the credit. Good work if you can get it, I guess."

"What'd they bust this guy for?"

"Weapons possession or something. You should stop by and talk with her. Get the full story."

"I think I will," he muttered. He wandered off toward his car, lost in his thoughts.

"Good talk," Wright called after him.

Parker raised a hand and absently waved.

***

"Bodean Kirkwood?" Adrian Thorn asked.

Morgan nodded.

"Never heard of him." Thorn looked to Jeremiah Strange. "You?"

"Nope."

The three men were in the CTF office. Thorn rested on the corner of Morgan's desk. Strange stood next to him.

Sergeant Ken Bynum sat at his desk with a telephone receiver pressed between his shoulder and an ear. "Uh-huh. Yeah. Sure." His pen danced across his notepad.

Detective Nayla Senai's desk remained empty. It always felt strange when a team member was gone, but Morgan thought it most noticeable when she was out of the office. He liked her for many reasons. Chauvinistically, it was nice to have a woman around. Senai brought a different vibe to their discussions, an essential viewpoint to their investigations, and she helped with female suspects. Selfishly, Morgan thought of Senai as his friend, and he looked to her as a moral compass.

Morgan often pushed beyond the limit of what the law would allow. He knew that. But he would never do anything to get the team into trouble. However, the guys would often get closer to that line than she would.

He'd never admit it to her—or anyone—but Senai had grown into something of an ethical anchor for him. And when she was gone for an extended period, he missed her.

Morgan pointed at his computer monitor. He had called up Bodean Kirkwood's history and learned the man lived off North Freya Street in an industrial area. "Look at his picture."

Both Thorn and Strange leaned in. Their faces registered a lack of recognition.

Morgan turned his monitor back to him. "He did time for possession of meth but is out now. He's got a PO up in Hillyard."

"Which one?" Thorn asked.

"Stillwell," Morgan said. "Never heard of him."

"Her," Strange said. "She's all right."

"Yeah?" Thorn asked with a lascivious smile.

"Not that way. She's what they call asexual."

The grin vanished from the other officer's face. "The hell does that mean?"

Morgan rubbed his chin. "Courtney said this Bodean character might be involved with the after-hours murders."

Strange sniffed. "How would he know?"

"The Souls told him." Morgan laid out the story then. Strange and Thorn paid close attention as the tale progressed. During the retelling, Sergeant Bynum ended his call and leaned back in his chair to listen.

When Morgan finished the recap, he said, "And that's when Courtney called me."

Thorn slid off the edge of the desk and shoved his hands into his pockets. "I don't know, man. It sounds fishy."

Strange nodded. "Like fish left to rot on the dock."

"That's what I thought," Morgan said.

Bynum scooted his chair over to his team members. "What we have to ask is, where's the profit in them telling Courtney this story?"

Morgan eyed the sergeant.

"Look at it this way," Bynum said, "what do the Souls get by spinning this tale?"

"Extra scrutiny," Thorn said, "that's what."

Strange clicked his tongue against the back of his teeth. "We're gonna post up on their clubhouse and watch for Kirkwood. The Souls couldn't come or go without us knowing."

Bynum leaned forward and rested his elbows on his knees. "And if they didn't tell us?"

"Maybe there's a shootout," Thorn said.

Strange shrugged. "It would be self-defense, and they got those cameras. No way the prosecuting attorney would take it to court."

Morgan shook his head. "Kirkwood would never get in there. It's fortified. There would be a conflict outside, but never in."

Bynum cocked his head. "So again, I ask, where's the profit in them telling Courtney this story?"

"I was thinking," Strange said but paused. The others stared at him. "Maybe the Souls discovered what Kirkwood was about to do because his boy ratted him out. You know, after the beating at Coyote Ridge. And maybe the Souls don't want to be rats by telling us."

"But they did," Thorn said. "They told Courtney."

Strange waved a dismissive hand. "But he's supposed to be undercover. They can act like they didn't know."

Morgan leaned back in his chair. "If the Souls thought Kirkwood was coming after their clubhouse, they would grab him off the street and deal with him. They wouldn't involve us."

Bynum clapped his hands once. "See? That's what I'm thinking, too. This is out of character for them. There's another play here we're not seeing."

"What do the Souls get by acting the victim?" Morgan asked.

"Legitimacy," Thorn said.

All three turned to him.

"If they need our help, maybe they develop a narrative where they aren't outlaws."

A thought came to Morgan then, and he dropped his chair forward. He tapped his finger against the top of his desk. "We're not thinking about the activity at the clubhouse correctly. It would have been missed if a guy on light duty hadn't caught it. Booster slipped away from the rally to remove whatever was in there before Courtney was fed that information. The timing means something."

"Okay," Thorn said. "What?"

"I don't know, but I trust the Souls as much as I trust this Bodean guy. You two—" Morgan pointed at Thorn and Strange. "—get out to Kirkwood's place. He lives up in Hillyard." He read the address from the monitor. "See if you can find him coming or going."

"Where are you going?" Sergeant Bynum asked. "To talk with his PO?"

"What good would that do?" Morgan asked as he headed for the door. "I'm going to talk with someone higher up. I'll call you in a bit."

Chapter 18

"Elias Richter," Yvette Oliver said. "Oh Christ, what's he done now?"

Shane McAfee leaned forward in his chair. "I don't know. You tell me."

Oliver was a Community Corrections Officer based out of COPS West—an affiliated location with the overarching Community Oriented Police Services program. Her small office was in the rear of the building, away from most volunteers. Only the leader of COPS West sat further back than her.

Oliver's blond hair fell to her shoulders, and her face was mostly free of makeup—only a touch of mascara was applied. She wore a blue polo shirt with the CCO logo and dark blue jeans. A gun and badge rode on her hip.

Her desk was cluttered with a computer, stacks of files, and the detritus of years in a single location—knick-knacks, framed photos, a travel coffee mug, and various candy wrappers. A low-rise cabinet sat behind her.

Oliver shook her head in response to McAfee's question about Elias Richter. "The guy's a moron—one of those can't-get-out-of-his-way types. You've heard about those guys who land in a pile of dog crap and find a diamond? That's not Elias. He's more likely to land in a pile of diamonds and come out with the turd."

"What would he find if he fell on your desk?" McAfee asked.

"Funny." She smirked. "We can't all be as perfect as you, Shane. By the way, how's that girlfriend? Are you guys getting ready for prom?"

McAfee forced a smile. This was the problem with joking now—he had a tender spot that anyone could drive their fingers into.

A bell rang in the cop shop. Someone had just opened the front door to either enter or leave.

"Elias Richter," Oliver said, "that's who you came to talk about." She spun her chair to face the low-rise cabinet. Like the desk, it was gun-metal gray. McAfee doubted either was state issued. He suspected that someone donated them to the COPS organization and the CCO program made use of it. It seemed an odd symbiotic relationship to McAfee.

The state could waste millions of dollars on a legislator's pet project, but the supervision of released offenders relied on the help of a volunteer organization like COPS. McAfee knew that the CCO program paid rent for the small offices, but that was a cheap alternative to securing sites from private landlords, staffing the front with paid employees, and acquiring new furniture.

Oliver returned to her desk with a thin, brown file. She flopped it open. On the left side was a piece of yellow, lined paper with handwritten notes that appeared to be in a woman's writing. McAfee surmised it to be Oliver's.

She was about to speak when a male voice said, "Look who it is."

Detective Andrew Parker stood in the doorway. He still wore jeans and the department-issued windbreaker he had on from earlier in the morning. McAfee had met the man before today and thought him an intense sort. Parker probably needed to be that way to maintain the lifestyle associated with bodybuilding. Knowing the man was compensating for something didn't take a leap of imagination. He cupped a bag of mixed chocolates in his left hand.

Things had gotten testy with Parker yesterday, but their interaction earlier today was more cordial. McAfee raised his chin in greeting. Parker nodded back.

"What is this—a workshop?" Oliver asked. She looked between Parker and McAfee. "Should I get paid a stipend or something?"

"I come bearing gifts," Parker said. He tossed the chocolates onto the desk before flopping into the seat next to McAfee. "Happy belated birthday. I would have come a couple of days ago, but I had this thing."

"You remembered! That's what matters." Oliver's face brightened. "This is why I love you, Andrew."

McAfee cocked his head, then slowly eyed Parker.

She ripped open the bag and smiled broadly. Oliver was about to stick her hand in but paused. Her eyes went to Parker. "I know you're not going to eat these—"

"They're all yours."

Oliver extended the bag to McAfee. "How about you?"

He shook his head. Goddamned Parker, he thought. He screwed up the flow of conversation that McAfee had just started with the community corrections officer. He had no idea why Parker was there, but McAfee was sure the other detective wouldn't sit back and wait for him to finish. No, he would want to jump to the front of the line. Parker had brought candy, after all.

Oliver pulled out a miniature Mr. Goodbar. She didn't speak as she took her time unwrapping the little chocolate like it was a birthday gift. Oliver studied the chocolate with appreciation when it was free of its covering. "Andrew" was all she said before gently placing the bite-sized morsel onto her tongue. She flung the wrapper onto her desk, closed her eyes, and moaned in ecstasy.

Parker glanced at McAfee and raised his eyebrows twice. "How *you* doing?" he asked in a low voice.

"Fine," McAfee said flatly. He stared back at the other detective.

"Did I interrupt anything important?"

"As a matter of fact." McAfee didn't add anything further. It was petulant not to do so. He was fully aware of that, but the bag of chocolates irritated him. McAfee had no idea about Oliver's birthday. How could he have known? But sitting there while Oliver joyfully sucked on the candy and Parker looked smugly on made McAfee feel small. He disliked that feeling.

Parker faced Oliver. "What's my friend here bothering you about?"

Oliver opened her eyes and smiled dreamily. She patted the brown file. "One of my boys," she said around the chocolate. "Elias Richter."

"Well, well, well." Parker frowned the way Robert DeNiro did. "Ain't that a coinkydink?"

McAfee furrowed his brow. "You know about Richter?"

"Why do you think I'm here?"

Oliver feigned being hurt. "You didn't come by just to wish me happy birthday?"

Parker covered his heart. "Of course I did."

"Aww." Oliver beamed.

McAfee's brow furrowed deeper. "How'd you come by Richter?"

"The same funnel as you," Parker said. "The liquor board. What have you learned so far?"

"I just got here." He motioned to Oliver. "Yvette was just about to share."

The two detectives turned toward the community corrections officer.

"I feel so special with all this attention." Oliver said it without sincerity. Her attention was on the bag of candy. "Being my birthday and all."

Parker smacked McAfee's leg and jerked his head toward her.

"Happy birthday," McAfee muttered.

Oliver's fingers waggled inside the bag. "I don't normally eat candy, you understand."

Parker glanced at McAfee and rolled his eyes.

"Only on my birthday and Christmas." Oliver reached inside and removed a miniature Krackel chocolate bar. "And Halloween." She proudly held up the small red candy. "Andrew, I swear to God, if Brooke hadn't locked you down—"

Parker smiled.

McAfee felt oddly jealous. He didn't have any physical interest in Yvette Oliver, but he really wanted to bust Parker in the mouth. Plus, his arrival had slowed everything up. "Can we?" he said impatiently.

Oliver's eyes slid to him. "What's wrong, Shane? Maybe you should have a chocolate."

"I don't want one."

"It'll make you feel better."

Parker motioned to the bag. "What if I ate one?"

"I don't care what you do," McAfee said. "Can we get back to why we're all here?"

"I'm here because it's my office," Oliver said.

"I'm here for your birthday," Parker said.

Her eyes flared with excitement. "You're the best." Oliver extended the bag to Parker, but he waved off the candies. She dropped the bag and proceeded to unwrap the Krackel candy bar. After she put it in her mouth, Oliver said, "You're not going to make me feel bad for eating this, Shane." Her words were muffled because she sucked on the chocolate as she spoke.

"I don't care what you eat. Just tell me about Richter."

"Ugh," Oliver grunted and flipped open the file. Her cheeks sunk inward as she sucked on the chocolate. "Divorced parents." Now the chocolate moved about her mouth. "Abusive, alcoholic father." Her lips pursed as she read from her notes.

McAfee had previous interactions with Yvette Oliver and always liked her, but watching her gleefully eat miniature chocolates annoyed him. He wasn't sure why. Maybe it was Parker's presence. Would he care if she noshed if the other detective wasn't there? And if that was true, why did it bother him?

Oliver looked up and swallowed. "His mother took off. She left the state to escape that relationship. If you want my opinion, I think that's the heart of the guy's problems. I'm no psychologist, but Elias couldn't go to his mother when things got bad for him. He talked to me a little but stopped when the emotions started. Some of these guys only want a shoulder to cry on—" She abruptly ended the thought and returned her attention to the file. She held her hand over the right side of the folder. "The guy's a law enforcement cliché. Juvie since shortly after he could walk. Petty crimes mostly until he got zapped for a burglary right after his eighteenth. Then he got involved with some hatemongers and was caught with an AK."

McAfee held out a hand. "Can I see that?"

Oliver gave him the file. He dropped back into his chair to read Richter's criminal history.

She searched for another chocolate which caused the plastic bag to crinkle loudly. "Making more babies?"

McAfee didn't bother looking up. She wasn't talking to him.

"Brooke doesn't want me to even think about it," Parker said. "She says if the thought passes through my brain, she gets pregnant."

Oliver chuckled. "You two are a couple of teenagers." She unwrapped yet another chocolate.

McAfee's face pinched as he struggled to concentrate. Oliver had Richter's juvenile record—probably because it was never sealed due to his continued criminal activity. The guy's first contact with law enforcement happened when he was twelve years old—Third Degree Theft. McAfee wondered what a kid would steal. Candy, probably—maybe a toy. The charges were never filed. The case was dropped. Presumably not worth the hassle by all involved.

"What do you know about Richter?" Parker asked. "Tell us something not in the file."

"When I first met him," Oliver said. Her voice was muffled due to another chocolate in her mouth. "I thought I was going to have a hard ass on my hands."

"Is that so?"

"Uh-huh." The plastic bag rustled again. "I don't know why I eat the dark chocolates. I always think I should like them because my dad did, but then I eat one, and they're never as good as I expect."

"I understand," Parker said.

"No, you don't. Talking to you about chocolate is like trying to explain algebra to my dog."

"I've eaten candy."

"When you were a kid."

McAfee squinted as he further concentrated. Richter's petty crimes continued throughout his childhood. Several more arrests occurred over the next couple of years—all for minor theft. McAfee knew that if these were what he'd been caught for that Richter had likely gotten away with much more.

When he was thirteen, Richter was arrested for malicious mischief. McAfee wondered what Richter broke. Windows of a vacant building, perhaps? Or had he graffitied something? No charges were brought, whatever it was. Maybe Oliver would know, but the guy's childhood didn't seem important. Why he turned bad didn't matter. The fact was that the guy did.

Oliver unwrapped yet another chocolate.

McAfee stopped reading long enough to wonder how many she'd eaten now. For a woman so fit, she sure pounded a lot of candy. Maybe it was like she said—she only did so on three days a year. But he'd seen wrappers on her desk when he arrived. Her birthday was a couple of days past, so did others know about her sweet tooth? Maybe someone else brought her some. He didn't bother to look up and continued reading.

"Elias," Oliver said, "didn't turn out to be so tough. He's a wuss—a pushover."

"Yeah?" Parker asked. "Like that boyfriend you used to have?"

"Close, but no."

McAfee flipped a page in the file.

Six years passed in Richter's life, and he accumulated the same number of arrests. Not quite one a year, but it averaged out that way. No charges were brought against him. The lack of charges wasn't likely due to a wealthy and connected relative. Rather, it was because all his crimes were misdemeanors. A prosecutor wasn't going to bring charges against a kid for a pilfered candy bar or a stolen Hot Wheels car if that's indeed what he took.

"Maybe it *is* me," Oliver said.

"You?" Parker asked.

McAfee stopped reading and looked up.

"Because I'm a woman." Oliver glanced between the two detectives. "Maybe Elias acts the way he does around me because I'm a woman. His mother took off when he was young. He told me his dad was a real winner."

"I don't know," Parker said disbelievingly.

"What do you think it is?"

"Maybe he acts like a wuss around you because he thinks that's what'll get him into your pants."

She scowled. "Thanks, buddy."

"You done with that?" Parker asked McAfee.

He looked back down at the file. "No."

"Read faster, then."

"Stop talking."

"We're not talking to you."

McAfee grunted.

Richter's first charges were brought when he was fourteen. He'd been charged with second-degree burglary and was remanded to juvenile detention. It didn't look like it lasted long. That same behavior played out until he was an adult—petty crimes and arrests followed by short stints of incarceration. Then he got popped for a felony—First-Degree Burglary which sent him away for a stretch in the Airway Heights Correctional Center.

Parker shifted in his seat. "You're going to get a cavity."

"Worry about your own teeth," Oliver said as the bag rustled again. "So, Detectives, you gonna tell me what you're both doing here, or am I supposed to pretend that I know what this is about?"

McAfee raised a finger. "Hold on."

"I'll give you something to hold on to," Oliver said.

He looked up and then glanced at Parker.

The other detective shrugged. "She's dirty."

"What?" Yvette said. "Cut me a break. I'm on a sugar high, and you would have said the same thing, Andrew."

"Not me. I'm an angel."

Yvette pshawed. "Since when?"

Parker looked at McAfee. "You done?"

"Almost." McAfee's gaze dropped to the file. He repeatedly tapped his finger on Richter's listed burglary charge.

Robbery and burglary were on the same spectrum but on opposite sides. A lot of activity could slide under the umbrella of those two charges. However, McAfee believed the individuals associated with those crimes fell into different categories. Burglars tended to be nonviolent individuals who broke into structures to steal things. They avoided people, and conflict often came from being surprised. On the other hand, robbers were violent individuals who used force to take something directly from a person. They couldn't avoid others as their crime demanded they contact a victim.

It might be a simplistic way to consider the subject, but it gave McAfee a starting point when considering the two crimes. If Elias Richter was involved in the after-hours murders, he had significantly jumped from burglar to robber-cum-murderer. What was the catalyst for that jump?

Parker said, "While Captain Speed Reader takes his time, answer me another question—what gave you the impression that Richter was going to be a hard ass?"

"Because of his affiliation with the white supremacy movement."

"What affiliation?" Parker asked.

"Something called the Silent," McAfee mumbled. His finger settled on a note at the back of Richter's file. He looked up and met Oliver's gaze. "You think that affiliation turned him violent?"

"You don't?" She raised her eyebrows. "They're not a book club. He's a quiet guy, sure. But I've seen plenty of quiet guys who went inside for some heinous things."

Parker tapped the file that McAfee held. "You done now?"

McAfee handed the folder to him. "What do you make of his history?" he asked Oliver.

She squinted. "I already told you about his mother. According to Elias, his father brought him up in the hate movement, although he doesn't call it that. He calls it the truth. And he certainly doesn't resent his father for exposing him to it. It's as if another person were brought up in the Mormon or Catholic church—it's just part of their upbringing. Get it?"

McAfee nodded.

"I'm not sure how much peeling back this onion will help. What you need to know about Elias is this—he's not the sharpest tool in the shed."

"Because he's a pushover?" McAfee asked.

"Not mentally challenged or anything, but he was one of those kids raised with the philosophy that education didn't matter. He'll believe whatever garbage is fed to him.

The person doing the feeding is more important than the meal itself."

"He's a follower," McAfee said.

"And that's the problem," Oliver continued. "He's hanging around Bodean Kirkwood."

Parker looked up from the file to eye McAfee. The other detective shook his head. He'd never heard the name before, either.

"Bodean is a real shitbag," Oliver said. "He bunked with Elias in Coyote Ridge."

"What'd he go in for?

"Possession of methamphetamine."

"Anything violent in his past?"

Oliver shook her head. "No, and trust me, I looked. I wanted a reason to keep Elias away from him because that boy is crazy. He's not right in the head. I wish I could have gotten a parole condition that he couldn't hang out with known felons, but there wasn't justification."

"Are you Bodean's PO, too?"

She shook her head. "That's Stillwell up in Hillyard. She's got his file. That's how I checked into him."

McAfee's shoulders slumped, and he glanced at the file that Parker now read. The discussion about Elias Richter felt like it wasn't going anywhere.

"I'm still waiting," Oliver said, "for you two to tell me why you're here. What's your interest in Elias?"

McAfee waved at the file. Parker batted his hand away.

"I was hoping—" McAfee started, but Parker interrupted him.

"*We* were hoping."

"We were hoping," McAfee restarted, "to make a connection to some recent murders."

"Murders?" Oliver asked.

"At two after-hours spots. Nine victims total. We're assuming at least two killers involved."

Parker looked up from the file and nodded.

Oliver glanced between the two men. "So you came here because Elias had an after-hours joint in Stevens County? That's a thin connection to start looking at Elias, don't you think?"

McAfee shrugged. "I haven't heard about them for my entire career, and suddenly we've got dead people at two. Then someone mentions your boy was arrested a couple of years ago for running one."

"Are you thinking he has a vendetta against them or something?"

Parker closed the file and set it on the edge of Oliver's desk. "That doesn't sound right." He reached out and tapped the file. "Especially after reading this." He eyed McAfee. "Is that what you think?"

McAfee shook his head. "I don't see the nexus."

"Richter had an after-hours club," Parker said, "but big whoop, right? Like what makes a guy who's mostly small-time, graduate to robbery and murder?"

"Bodean Kirkwood?" Oliver offered.

McAfee turned his palms upward. "But he doesn't have a history of violence." Frustration welled in his chest. "I guess it's a lead."

Parker stood. "Not a good one, though." He motioned toward Oliver's desk. "Enjoy the chocolates."

"Oh, I will," Oliver said. "Every last one."

McAfee stood. "Thank you for letting us look at the file."

"Good luck with your case." Oliver extended the chocolates to him. "For the road."

He slipped his hand into the bag and pulled out a dark chocolate. "Thank you."

"You can have all of those." She scrunched her nose. "Yuck."

Chapter 19

Morgan pressed the doorbell and looked up at the camera hanging from the east edge of the building's soffit. He then looked at the camera at the opposite end of the building. He waited a moment so anyone inside could get a good look at him.

After a minute, he stepped off the sidewalk to study the only motorcycle parked there. It sat perpendicular to the curb. Morgan didn't know much about bikes. It was a Harley-Davidson—it said so in beautiful orange script. And the motorcycle was full of chrome. Leather saddlebags hung over the back—the name *Booster* was stitched into them. Morgan assumed nothing was inside the bags—its owner wouldn't be foolish enough to leave anything in them. Not in this neighborhood. Not even with the reputation of the Wasted Souls standing guard over them.

Morgan looked toward the clubhouse and the two cameras again. He wondered if they could see him in the street. There were cameras at opposite ends of the building. The members would likely want to keep a watch over their bikes. Morgan caressed the motorcycle's gas tank.

The club's gathering place sat on Sprague Avenue just east of a freeway overpass. It was a squat gray building—nothing anyone could get excited about. Had it not been for the metal bars covering the windows, no one would have a reason even to notice the thing.

Upon closer inspection, a metal plate reinforced the front door. A sign hung above the entrance—*Abandon Hope All Ye Who Oppose*.

Morgan didn't have any heartburn with grown men gathering as a club. He fully understood the allure. He had understood it since he was in the Marines. Hell, that's why he loved the Criminal Task Force—it was them against the world.

He walked around the bike and pretended to be interested in the engine. When he stood, he grabbed the handlebar. Still, no one came to the door.

Maybe he had it wrong. Perhaps Booster wasn't at the clubhouse. What if he'd caught a ride somewhere else? It's not like Morgan had the man's phone number. He had no other way to go about contacting him.

Morgan looked down the street.

The area had gentrified over the years as part of the city's efforts to turn it into a thriving business community. The arterial had been revamped with something the city called a traffic diet, and new bus turnouts were added. Aesthetically pleasing, low-income housing projects cropped up along the road. Outreach centers and a community activity hub were added. Developers beautified two-story brick buildings into thriving economic opportunities.

And Morgan hated it all.

Citizens and do-gooders moved into an area they knew nothing about with catchwords like "revitalize" and "restore." They tried unsuccessfully to rebrand it as the International District before settling on the Sprague Union District. But it was new paint over battered, moldy drywall. Those bleeding hearts didn't know the true legacy of East Sprague, and they sure as hell didn't know its value to the city as it was.

That's why Morgan liked the nearby clubhouse. Its squat ugliness refused to be bullied by gentrification. It was a reminder of the neighborhood's history. Of whom and what still lay beneath the recent application of hope.

Morgan swung a leg over the Harley-Davidson and sat on it.

A bolt noisily slid from inside the clubhouse, and the door opened. A graying, pot-bellied man stepped out. He wore a leather vest covered with patches. "Get off, Morgan, before someone sees you."

"I'm thinking about getting one."

"The hell you are." Booster angrily waved at him. "Now, goddamn it. I'm serious."

Morgan slowly slid off. "What's one of these things cost?"

"More than you got."

Booster looked up and down the block. He scratched his unshaven face. "If one of the boys saw—"

Morgan clucked his tongue. "But they're all up at the rally, aren't they?"

"What do you want?"

"Heard you were packing up. Wanted to know where you were moving to."

"You heard wrong."

"That wasn't you and a couple prospects loading a delivery truck?"

Booster rubbed a hand over his mouth. "House cleaning. That's what we were doing."

"You? The charter's president? I don't know."

"If you want things done right, you gotta do them yourself."

Morgan smiled. "Ain't that the truth? Still, it's a strange time to be doing such a thing, what with the big rally going on. How's that going, by the way?"

Booster rested a wrist over the motorcycle's handlebar. "It's going great."

"Yeah?"

"Yeah," he said emphatically.

"Then why are you down here?"

"Came for supplies."

Morgan put his hand on the seat of the bike. "Going to take them back in the saddlebags?"

"What of it?"

"Rumor has it you guys are worried about Bodean Kirkwood hitting your clubhouse."

"Maybe we are."

Morgan smirked. "I don't buy it."

"Nothing to buy. We told your guy what we knew. Bodean has a beef with us. It started on the inside. He brought it out."

Morgan lifted his chin in the direction of the clubhouse. "You got cameras, reinforced doors, steel bars over the windows. He's not getting inside unless you want him in. If you know about the beef, why aren't you taking care of it yourself?"

Booster shook his head. "That's the problem with cops. Even when we try to help, you get suspicious."

"Let's walk through the clubhouse," Morgan said.

"No."

"Why not?"

"Outsiders aren't allowed."

"What did you pull out of there?"

"Odd and ends. I told you we were cleaning."

Morgan lowered his head as he thought.

"Listen, man." Booster looked up and down Sprague Avenue. "I got things to do. Are we done here?"

"This is a smoke screen."

"What is?"

"All of it." Morgan crossed his arms. "You're the president. You should be up at the rally, but you're not. One of our guys saw you with a couple of prospects he'd never seen before. You're not worried about being hit. You needed a story for being gone. You needed a reason to load that delivery truck."

"I don't know what you're talking about."

"So what was it? You ripping off the club?"

Booster barked a single laugh. "You got brain damage."

"No, that doesn't sound right. Drugs, maybe."

Something in Booster's eyes told Morgan he was close, but he hadn't hit the mark. "I'm done. Have a good day, Detective."

"What about guns?"

Booster had turned, but there was a hitch in his movement when he heard the word "gun." A coldness hit Morgan's belly.

"That's what this whole thing is about—guns."

Booster turned around and forced a smile. "What are you babbling about?"

"Those men who helped you load weren't prospects, were they? They were from another club." Morgan slapped his hands together. "That's what this rally is about, too. You got SIU up in Newport watching a fake rally while you moved some guns under their noses."

Booster opened his palms. "I don't know what you're talking about."

"I can find that truck."

"You think you can." Booster's smile appeared natural now. "I'll tell you this much. They're no longer in that truck."

"Then why the story of Bodean Kirkwood?"

"Because he's a real piece and your boy, Earley, needed something so he'd stay out of our business. What's with you cops thinking we'd be cool with a narc at our rally?"

Morgan shrugged. "You opened it to the public. You don't think there are cops at Sturgis?"

"Ours is a private event for lovers of the lifestyle. Not cops."

"It's on public land."

Booster sniffed dismissively. "I'll remember that when I crash the Policeman's Ball."

"By all means. So everything you told Courtney about Bodean was just a story to keep him busy?"

"Him hitting our clubhouse was bullshit, but the rest was real. Bet your ass on that."

"How'd you find out about the scheme?"

Booster rubbed the seat of his Harley. "After Bodean and his cellmate left, a couple of ours got the scoop from one of those Silent boys left behind. Freaky little bastards."

"What's with you and the supremacists? I thought that would be right up your alley."

Booster stuck his tongue up under his lip. "You know, Morgan, you're an asshole."

"Bikers and the lovers of the master race seem to go hand-in-hand."

"Not us." Booster's face hardened. "Not us."

So, Morgan had been right in his earlier assessment. It didn't make him feel better; it just helped push a puzzle piece into place.

"What are you doing in there now—" Morgan motioned to the clubhouse. "—with all the guns gone?"

"I don't know what you're talking about."

"Sure, you don't." Morgan watched a dilapidated Honda sedan drive by. Loud rap music emanated from the car. Smoke drifted from the windows. "If you're not into the master race, why don't you hang a rainbow flag in the window? Maybe get together in the park and sing kumbaya."

"Like I said, Morgan. You're an asshole."

"Enlighten me about this new-age attitude of yours. I want to know."

"As long as people stay out of our way, we don't give a damn what they do."

"That's very forward-thinking."

"To each their own." Booster flicked his hand. "Even you, Morgan."

"How'd you know Kirkwood hit an after-hours joint? It hasn't made the news."

"Not your news, Morgan, but ours—the whisper stream. Bodean and his partner can't keep their mouths shut. Word got around."

* * *

Andrew Parker sat behind the steering wheel with his elbow resting on the door. In the passenger seat was Shane McAfee. Neither man had said anything for the past several minutes.

They were parked on Dalton Street, several houses away from the last known residence of Elias Richter. McAfee's car was behind Parker's. Upon their arrival, they attempted to contact the man, but no one answered the door.

The afternoon sun seemed hazy, but that might have been due to the dirtiness of the car's windshield. Parker flipped down the visor above the driver's seat. It immediately cut the sun from his eyes.

"How long do you want to hang out here?" McAfee asked.

"I don't know. Few minutes maybe. This might be a total circle jerk. You can take off."

McAfee shrugged. "I'll wait."

"Chambers knocking the paper out?"

"Yeah."

"How's he to work with?"

"Good." Now, McAfee flipped his visor down. "I like the guy."

The silence returned to the car.

A moment later, McAfee asked, "What about your partner? How's he to work with?"

"Good," Parker said. A couple of seconds clicked by before he felt the need to add, "I like him."

Both men nodded and let the conversation die after that. Five minutes passed. The only noise in the car came from the patrol radio. Officers called out traffic stops and requested name checks. Neither detective felt the need to comment on any of the activity.

Parker's phone rang and he languidly pulled it from his pocket. The screen read *Morgan*. "Look who it is," he said, turning the phone in McAfee's direction.

McAfee smirked. "Our favorite."

Parker swiped his thumb over the screen and switched it to speaker phone. He announced his last name.

"It's Morgan. Where are you?"

"In my car." He eyed McAfee.

"We got a problem."

"And what's that?"

"I know who's behind these killings."

Parker bent his head over the phone. "How do you know?"

"They're talking."

McAfee leaned in. "Who's they, and what are they talking about?"

"Wait," Morgan said. "Who's that?"

"McAfee."

"Cute. You two sharing a romantic moment somewhere?"

"Don't be an asshole," Parker said.

"I'm getting accused of that a lot lately."

"Maybe take that as a sign."

"Who is *they*?" McAfee prompted. "And what are they talking about?"

"Bodean Kirkwood and some jerkoff named Elias Richter. You two desk jockeys ever hear of them?"

"We have," Parker and McAfee said at the same time.

Morgan chuckled. "Will wonders never cease?"

"How do you know they're involved?" Parker asked.

McAfee leaned over the phone. "And for the third time, what are they talking about?"

"Guns."

"They already have guns," Parker said.

"Not these," Morgan said. "They're trying to get assault rifles."

The two detectives stared at each other.

A moment passed before Morgan asked, "You guys still there?"

Chapter 20

Everyone stopped talking when Morgan entered the department's conference room. Four homicide detectives, SPD's Special Investigation Unit sergeant, and SPD's Investigative Unit captain turned their heads to the brutish detective.

That irritated Parker, especially since McAfee was briefing everyone on what he and Parker had learned from Yvette Oliver.

Morgan dropped heavily into the chair next to the captain. It squeaked in protest. A five o'clock shadow lined the detective's jaw, and redness filled his eyes. His gaze swept the table. When it landed on the captain, he lifted his chin in acknowledgment.

The bastard didn't apologize for being late, Parker thought. It was ten minutes after five, and he was the one who called this meeting. He better not try and blame a long day for his tardiness. Everyone at this table had worked long hours.

Except maybe Captain Gary Ackerman. The guy looked like he stepped off the Brooks Brothers website. Parker furrowed his brow. Did Brooks Brothers even sell suits anymore? He didn't know—he bought his from Men's Wearhouse. Wherever Ackerman shopped, they tailored their offerings. The captain always looked squared away.

"Good of you to join us, Detective," Ackerman said.

"Had to set something up."

Ackerman motioned to the others present. "We all had things to do."

"I get that."

"You know McAfee and Chambers from the county?"

Morgan nodded at the two detectives. Neither returned the courtesy.

"McAfee," Ackerman said, "was bringing us up to speed on what they learned from the liquor board."

"I heard," Morgan said.

"Well, I haven't." The captain turned to SIU Sergeant Trevor Hackworth, who sat on the opposite side. "You?"

"Nope." The conference room's fluorescent lights gleamed off Hackworth's bald head. He eyed Morgan with apparent disdain.

Parker smiled. It was official—everyone disliked Morgan.

The CTF detective leaned back in his chair and looked at McAfee. "I don't want to hold you up."

"I'm done." He faced the captain. "We didn't have any direct information linking Richter or Kirkwood to anything until Morgan called."

That information seemed to dissatisfy the captain. He stared at McAfee for a second longer before sliding his gaze to Parker. "Anything to add?"

Parker wanted to say something—anything—to help Ackerman out, but it would have been inconsequential. Less was more in situations like this, so he remained silent and shook his head.

The captain's lips puckered. His eyes swept over Johnson and Chambers. Both men shook their heads. Ackerman breathed in deeply, then faced Morgan. "All right, Detective. Your turn. Why are we here?"

Morgan laid his hand on the table. His thumb tapped three times. "I visited Troy Misterek."

Hackworth bolted upright. "What were you thinking?"

Ackerman looked over his shoulder. "Who are we talking about?"

"The Wasted Souls." Hackworth pointed at Morgan. "He talked with Booster, the club's president. We're running an operation against them in conjunction with the Kootenai County Sheriff's Office. He knows that."

The captain eyed the CTF detective. "Is that true?"

"Me talking with Booster? I just said it was."

Ackerman's face reddened. "That you knew about Hackworth's operation."

Morgan's thumb repeatedly tapped the table again. "Yeah. I knew."

"Of course he knew," Hackworth angrily said. "His teammate is assigned to us."

"Which one?" the captain asked over his shoulder.

"Earley."

"The big guy with the beard?"

"That's the one."

Ackerman's gaze returned to Morgan. "Why did you approach Misterek when you knew SIU had him under surveillance?"

"They weren't watching him. He was at the clubhouse. SIU was up at the rally in Pend Oreille County."

The captain opened his mouth to say something but slowly closed it. He looked over his shoulder to Hackworth. The SIU sergeant stared back at him.

"Great," Ackerman muttered. When he faced Morgan again, he asked, "Why did you approach Misterek?"

Morgan shrugged a single shoulder. "A hunch."

"A hunch?" Hackworth blurted.

Ackerman held up a hand to quiet the sergeant.

"We're dealing with private clubs," Morgan said. "I figured I'd talk to one of the longest-running private clubs in town."

Parker scoffed. Johnson shook his head in disbelief. McAfee and Chambers eyed one another.

The captain looked around the table. "Nobody believes that story, Detective."

Morgan turned to McAfee. "Tell me something. How'd you end up at liquor control?"

The county detective stared at him.

"Did someone provide you reliable intel, or were you playing a hunch?" Morgan tapped his gut. "Well?"

McAfee's jaw flexed before reluctantly saying, "I went with my intuition."

"A five-dollar word for hunch." Morgan eyed Parker. "What about you, Muscles? What motivated you to see that parole officer?"

Parker wanted to tell Morgan to shove it up his fat ass, but the man was right. Maybe it wasn't exactly a hunch that led him to see the Special Police Problems officer, but it was close. It might have been good police work that also led him to the Neighborhood Resource Officer, where he was referred to talk with Yvette Oliver. However, it could all be argued to be a gut feeling. In the end, Parker chose to remain silent. He looked at the captain and disappointedly shrugged.

Ackerman rolled his eyes.

"You're letting him get away with that behavior?" Hackworth whined.

"Whatever information he has is why we're here," the captain said. "Let him fill us in on what he knows."

Morgan nodded several times. "I'll skip the whys and wherefores and get to the good stuff."

"Please do," Ackerman said.

"Bodean Kirkwood and Elias Richter want to buy assault weapons."

"And they contacted the Souls?" Hackworth asked. The SIU sergeant was suddenly happy. "That's great. Let's bust them all."

"No," Morgan said. "Kirkwood hates the Souls. Maybe Richter, too."

Parker glanced around the table, but everyone was as confused by that statement as he was.

"Why does Kirkwood hate the club?" the captain asked.

"Because he insists that the Wasted Souls should align themselves with the Sadistic Souls, a Neo Nazi biker gang from the mid-west."

Ackerman furrowed his brow before looking over his shoulder to Hackworth. The sergeant shrugged.

"They're not in Washington State," Morgan continued, "but that's how their beef started while in Coyote Ridge."

"Booster gave you all of that history?" Hackworth asked. "I'm crying foul if none of you are."

Ackerman didn't look back. His attention remained on Morgan. "So if there's this beef between the Souls and these two men, how do we know Kirkwood and Richter are involved?"

Hackworth flopped back in his chair and sighed audibly.

Morgan's phone buzzed, and he removed it from his pocket. He looked at it briefly, then put it away.

"The beef?" Ackerman prompted. "Kirkwood and Richter?"

"Those two morons are broadcasting their success," Morgan said. "They've told people what they've done."

"Robbing after-hours clubs?"

Morgan nodded.

"To what end?"

"They're getting a stake together to buy bigger weapons and more ammo."

"For what purpose?"

"Isn't it obvious?" Morgan asked.

Ackerman's face flattened.

Parker eyed McAfee. "Your victims were Turkish and black—right?"

"And of Russian descent," Chambers added.

Parker nodded. "I'm sure they saw that as fraternizing with the enemy."

"A race traitor," McAfee said.

Johnson leaned forward. "Several of our victims were gay."

"Maybe Richter and Kirkwood discovered this," McAfee said, "and shot them?"

Ackerman waved a hand. "You guys are getting ahead of yourselves. Maybe they intended to kill everyone, and race and orientation had nothing to do with it."

"They robbed several other clubs," Morgan said, "and no one was hurt."

All the men at the table turned to stare at the CTF detective.

"You talked to those clubs?" McAfee said.

Parker shook his head. "Son of a bitch. You could have told us this on the phone."

"My guys and I talked with them this morning."

"After the shooting?" McAfee asked.

Morgan motioned to Parker. "He knew we were going to look into them."

"But you didn't have the addresses," Parker said.

McAfee's eyes narrowed. "Or did you?"

"We had to get them from the guy—" Parker repeatedly snapped his fingers.

"Elmendorf," Johnson said.

"Yeah, Elmendorf. Either he gave them to you before you turned us onto them, or you did some high-speed police work. None of us have had a chance to go out and talk with them."

Morgan turned his palms upward. "What can I say?"

Parker's face warmed. "You can say you sandbagged us."

Ackerman frowned at Morgan, then turned his chair to face the group. "Here's the problem as I see it. Two suspects have been identified in the after-hours killings. Morgan believes they're trying to raise funds to buy weapons to further a supremacist agenda. The question we've got to ask ourselves is do we believe his intel?"

The men at the table looked at each other. Begrudgingly, each of them nodded.

"So," Ackerman asked, "how are we going to stop them?"

"Patrol officers are sitting off Richter's house now," Parker said. He looked to Morgan. "And you said your guys are watching Kirkwood's last known residence."

Morgan nodded. "Thorn and Strange." He checked his phone once more and smiled. Parker thought the CTF detective looked oddly serene.

"We should get SWAT on standby," Hackworth said. The man was a former leader of the specialty team. He'd promote any opportunity to deploy them.

Ackerman nodded. "I'll alert them, but we need a way to flush Kirkwood and Richter out from wherever they're hiding. Anyone have a way to get in contact with them?"

"What about their POs?" Chambers asked.

Morgan looked up from his phone. "If Kirkwood and Richter are called in by their POs, they'll know they've been made."

"You think they'll run?" Ackerman asked.

"Based upon nine murders—" Morgan said.

Parker interrupted, "Don't forget they drove around in a stolen car."

"They weren't trying to be subtle," McAfee said.

The captain shifted in his chair. "They're looking for trouble?"

"Maybe it didn't start that way," Chambers said, "but after the first murders, something changed."

Johnson knocked on the table. "If they get caught, they are going back inside for life. They have to know it."

Morgan cleared his throat. "We need a different tack than a frontal approach."

"SWAT is trained specifically for this type of threat," Hackworth said. "This is our wheelhouse."

Ackerman ignored the sergeant's input. He cocked his head and asked Morgan, "I suppose you've got an idea on how to lure them out into the open."

"That's why I was late. It's already in play."

The clock on the wall ticked loudly. No one said anything.

Ackerman visibly struggled to control his anger. "You took action without consulting us?"

"I didn't know we were running this investigation as a committee. My bad." Morgan didn't even bother to feign his innocence. Parker wanted to slug him.

The redness returned to the captain's face. "It's Parker and Johnson's case."

McAfee cleared his throat.

Ackerman extended a hand toward the county detectives. "And theirs, too."

"I understand," Morgan said, "but maybe all this isn't really connected. Maybe it's just a couple felons talking out of their asses about buying assault rifles."

"Is that what you believe?" Ackerman assessed the others in the room. "Is that what any of us believe?" When no one argued with him, the captain faced Morgan again. "So what did you do?"

"We offered them some guns."

"*What?*" the captain said.

"Are you kidding me?" Parker murmured. Several others were talking simultaneously, so no one commented on his question.

"That's entrapment," McAfee said.

Morgan lifted a hand. "My guy called Kirkwood and said he heard they wanted weapons. That's all. He said he could put them in contact with a guy selling."

Hackworth slapped the conference room table. "You better not be talking about Earley." He leaned forward to speak into Ackerman's ear. "He's assigned to us, Captain. He's my guy until I say he's not."

Morgan focused on Ackerman. "Earley's working the bikers, but it's not like he's undercover. The Souls know he's a cop and are treating him like one. They cut him out of important discussions and let him in on the conversations they want him to be part of."

"But he's our eyes and ears on the inside," Hackworth said. His brow furrowed. "That's where you got this lead. He fed it to you. If the Wasted Souls gave him something while he was out there, then it should be our dance. Whatever you're proposing, we should be the lead dogs."

"They fed it to him to keep him busy. Probably because none of their other stories were working. Booster slipped away while your guys were watching to make an arms deal with some of the boys attending the rally."

"That's horseshit."

Morgan smiled in that cruel way of his. "You think so? Even one of your boys saw Booster loading a van. What did you think he was hauling away? Furniture?"

Ackerman looked over his shoulder to Hackworth.

The SIU sergeant appeared confused. "You can't believe a word this guy says, Captain."

Morgan rested his elbow on the table. "We're meeting Richter and Kirkwood at The Well tonight. Midnight."

Ackerman turned around. "A public place? No. This needs to be done in private."

"They set the terms. The best we could do was control the bar. I know the owner. She'll work with us. She won't like it, but she'll stay out of our way and let us do our thing. She owes me."

Parker leaned forward. "Kirkwood and Richter hated the Wasted Souls. Earley couldn't have told them he was working with the bikers. Who'd he use for a reference?"

Morgan tapped the table. "Good catch. Courtney said he sold to the Souls and the Dead Boys. Kirkwood and Richter aren't going to call the bikers to get a recommendation, and they sure as hell aren't going to call the blacks."

McAfee shook his head in disbelief. "So these two are playing this on faith?"

"Sometimes," Morgan said, "all you get is a little faith."

"And a hunch," Parker added.

Chapter 21

Elva Lightly stopped by the table that Morgan sat at. "Oh, you two don't look suspicious at all."

He broke away from his conversation with Courtney Earley to look up at the bar owner.

She was in her sixties with tired eyes and a wrinkled face courtesy of years of smoking and hard living. Her stringy hair fell to her shoulders. Elva wore faded blue jeans and a black T-shirt that read *Educated Redneck*.

Elva swung an arm as she motioned to the other patrons. "You ain't in disguise like the others. How come?"

Morgan shook his head. "Beat it, Elva."

Her eyes narrowed. "You should be nicer."

"I'm trying to save you from trouble."

"Then you should have gone elsewhere and taken your friends with you."

The bar owner walked off.

Courtney Earley chuckled. "She was probably something in her younger years."

"Don't take anything from her now," Morgan said. "She's still got a long line of suitors."

The Well was a dive bar at the corner of Washington Street and Second Avenue. It wasn't a hotbed of criminal activity, but it catered to a misfit clientele—bums, drunks, and general miscreants. Morgan stepped into the establishment throughout his years on patrol. He kept an eye on it when he made it to CTF. The type of patron who drank there was always good for information they overheard elsewhere.

Right now, there were six members of SIU and four SWAT teammates sitting inside the bar. Male and female officers were dressed like bar patrons and involved in their own conversations. Adrian Thorn and Jeremiah Strange were outside in an unmarked vehicle used for surveillance. To keep any potential conflicts with Kirkwood and Richter to a minimum, only Caucasian team members were used inside.

Strange didn't take the news well. "This is bullshit," he said earlier in the night.

Thorn was supposed to be inside the bar, but he chose to observe The Well from outside in a show of solidarity with his friend. "Total bullshit," the officer said with even more enthusiasm than Strange.

The meeting with Elias Richter and Bodean Kirkwood was scheduled for midnight. Shortly before eleven, Elva quietly cut off her regular customers and sent them on their way. The department would reimburse her for lost income. Morgan didn't expect it to be much, even if Elva padded the numbers.

A song was on the radio. It was some rock & roll crap Morgan had heard during his years in the Corps. Earley seemed to like it, though. Even though it came out before the big man was born, Earley's head bobbed in time with the rhythm.

"Two men are approaching," Trevor Hackworth said into Morgan's earpiece. *"Look alive, folks. If these are the shooters, they could be armed."*

Morgan didn't touch the earpiece as the movies showed. It was a stupid habit that would get a guy killed if he really did it. Instead, he spun the beer bottle in his hand. Elva had replaced its contents with water. She'd done the same for everyone in the joint.

All in the bar except Elva wore an earpiece. There was no need for anyone to respond to Hackworth. They all knew their assignments.

The technical guys assigned to SIU had also installed hidden cameras throughout the bar. Everything that went down inside The Well tonight would be recorded—even the men's restroom.

The front door opened, and two white men entered. From how they scanned the room, it was clear they had business other than drinking.

Earley leaned toward Morgan. "The master race."

"*Easy,*" Hackworth said.

Even before introductions, Morgan could identify the two men.

Elias Richter was a tall, lanky man with shifty eyes. He had a high forehead with close eyes and a long, thin nose. They were the tell-tale features of inbreeding somewhere in the family tree. He walked like a baby giraffe taking its first steps. He wore a red flannel shirt over a black T-shirt, blue jeans, and hiking boots.

Bodean Kirkwood, on the other hand, was oddly handsome for a guy so involved in the game of race-baiting and meth distribution. He looked like he might have been the high school quarterback, the starting pitcher, or the class president. His features were those an aspiring politician would die for. Perfect hair, bright eyes, and an appropriately shaped nose. The only thing that marred the man were the tattoos running the length of both arms. He wore a black T-shirt, camouflaged pants, and combat boots. Morgan imagined him standing in a darkened alley.

The two arrived at the table.

Kirkwood's gaze passed over Morgan and Earley. "Which one of you is Donahue?"

Earley lifted his chin. When he called about their interest in automatic weapons, he'd given the fake name. It was a name the CTF had established years ago for situations like this.

"Who's this? Your dad?"

"Gallagher," Earley said. "He's the man who's got what you want."

"You from the old country?" Kirkwood asked Morgan. "No."

Morgan believed Kirkwood was the man who shot at him at The Tiptoe Lounge. The camouflaged pants put the idea into his head, but the difference in the two men's builds convinced him. The shooter standing in the shadows hadn't appeared like an awkward giraffe.

Richter stepped forward. "What do you get out of this meeting?" he asked Earley.

"A finder's fee."

"Donahue and Gallagher," Kirkwood said. "A couple of Spokane Micks."

"You got a problem with that?" Morgan asked.

"What if I do? You gonna make a stink about it?"

"Not unless you came empty-handed."

Elva walked over. "Evening, boys, something to drink?"

"We're not drinking," Kirkwood said.

Richter forced a polite smile and shook his head once.

"What about you two?" Elva asked Morgan and Earley. "Ready for another?"

"We're good," Morgan said.

"I'm not so sure about that," Elva said before walking away.

Morgan fought back a smile. The department wanted an officer behind the bar, but Elva refused to let anyone work the counter except her. If the SPD wanted to use her establishment to sting Kirkwood and Richter, she insisted on being where she could ensure nothing was vandalized or stolen. "I don't trust cops," she had said to Captain Ackerman. "Least of all the ones who ask me for a favor."

Kirkwood leaned in. "We got the money. You bring what we want?"

"Depends on what you want," Morgan said.

"We told him." Kirkwood lifted his chin to Earley. "He didn't tell you?"

Earley had, but Morgan needed either Kirkwood or Richter to say it for the recording. "Maybe he got it wrong."

Kirkwood frowned. "Goddamned greenies." His gaze briefly shifted to Richter before settling back on Morgan. "AKs. Two of them. Untraceable."

"See?" Earley said to Morgan. "I told you. Message delivered just as requested."

"You got them?" Kirkwood asked.

Morgan nodded.

"Then let's do this."

"No," Morgan said.

Kirkwood stiffened. "Why not?"

"Because they're not here."

"Where are they?"

"Outside," Morgan said. "No offense, but we don't know you. Therefore, we don't trust you."

"Fuck you, and you're knowing," Kirkwood said. He smacked Richter's arm with the back of his hand. "We don't trust you either."

Richter nodded his support.

"Show us the cash," Morgan said. "We'll have the guns brought inside."

Richter looked toward the door. "You got another guy?"

"He's outside waiting for our call."

"That's not how we do things," Kirkwood said

"But that's how we're doing them tonight." Morgan inhaled deeply. "If you want the guns, that is."

Kirkwood shook his head. "This doesn't feel right." He eyed Richter. "Let's get out of here." He headed for the door.

"*Don't let them walk,*" Hackworth said into Morgan's ear. "*We need them to pay for the guns.*"

Morgan didn't move, however. Richter didn't either. He watched Kirkwood walk away, then turned his attention back to Morgan. "He's leaving."

"I see that."

Richter's lips twisted as he thought. "Tell me how this would play out. If we showed you the cash, I mean."

"My man makes a call," Morgan tilted his head toward Earley, "and the guns come walking in."

Richter glanced around the bar. "There are too many eyes. We don't like it."

"This was your idea."

"We didn't want it done inside. We wanted a public place."

"It's not like you're buying a pallet of them. You're buying two. It was hardly worth our time to come down here."

"Yeah?" Richter's eyes narrowed. "Where'd you come down from? Maybe I know your people."

Morgan frowned. "After we make the call, our guy will go straight for the head. One of you follows him in. The other stays with us."

Kirkwood returned to the table. He turned his back to Morgan and Earley before he asked Richter, "Why're you standing here?"

"He's explaining how it would go down."

"I'm telling you, man," Kirkwood whispered. "This doesn't feel right."

Richter eyed him. "It's worth asking a question. If you don't like what he says, we'll go." He faced Morgan. "Explain it again so he can hear."

Kirkwood hesitatingly turned around.

"You show us the cash," Morgan said, "and this guy makes a call." He pointed his beer bottle to Earley. "Our guy brings in a duffel and goes straight for the head. One of you follows him to confirm the product. The other stays with us. All these people in the bar bear witness to us being civilized to each other. Simple."

The two men exchanged a questioning glance.

"See?" Richter asked.

Kirkwood studied Morgan for a moment, then Earley. "You, I like." He pointed at Morgan. "But Gallagher smells like a cop."

Morgan jumped from his chair and sent it rolling behind him. He started around the table, but Earley grabbed his wrist and held him. Richter lifted his hands in defense as Morgan was closest to him.

"Eat those words," Morgan said, "or I'll make you."

Kirkwood leaned forward. "I'd like to see you try."

Several in the bar turned their way.

"*Nobody move,*" Hackworth shouted through the earpieces. "*Go back to your drinks.*"

"Hey!" Elva moved toward the end of the bar. "Knock that off, or you're all outta here!"

Morgan said, "Let go," and angrily jerked his hand free from Earley. "You two—we're done."

"*Don't let 'em walk, Morgan. Reengage.*"

He grabbed his chair and rolled it back to its original spot. Morgan dropped into it.

Richter and Kirkwood remained where they were.

"Are you deaf?" Morgan wriggled his fingers in the air to mimic sign language. "I said, get out."

Kirkwood took an unsure step toward the door but kept his eyes on Richter. "What?"

"We made it this far."

"Trust me," Kirkwood said, "I know what I'm talking about."

Richter tilted his head. "Let's do it my way for once."

"Are you two retarded?" Morgan asked.

"*Morgan!*"

Hackworth might lose his mind over many things, and Morgan's use of an inappropriate word might be one of them. Nevertheless, two felons stood in front of him. They were suspected killers and white supremacists. The last thing they would respect was his proper use of language. These two men thought they were a couple of junkyard dogs set loose on society. In Morgan's estimation, the only thing that Richter and Kirkwood would respect was a bigger dog.

"Our money is still good," Richter said.

Earley leaned on the arm of his chair. "Listen to him."

Morgan curled his lip. "Shut up, you."

The big man angrily flicked his hair back and sipped his fake beer.

Kirkwood's eyes darted about the bar. "Okay, fine. Give us another reference. Nobody could confirm two Limey pricks dealing hardware."

"This is my last warning," Morgan said.

"*Let out some line, man,*" Hackworth said. "*They're nibbling the bait.*"

"What if we pay a premium?" Richter asked.

Kirkwood turned to his friend. "What are you doing?"

"Getting what we came for." To Morgan, Richter said, "How's an extra ten percent sound? Would that ease things?"

"Two hundred bucks," Earley said.

Morgan scowled at Earley. "I can do the math."

Kirkwood shook his head. "You gotta be kidding me."

"Well?" Richter asked.

Morgan slowly faced the taller man. "An extra two hundred." He pointed at Kirkwood. "And he apologizes."

"The hell I will," Kirkwood said. He backed away. "Not a chance."

Richter sat at the table. He dug into his front pocket and pulled something out.

"*He's counting cash,*" Hackworth said through the earpiece.

Kirkwood moved forward and leaned into Richter's ear. "What're you doing?"

"You asked me to get this done, I got it set up, and we're here. Sit down." Richter set several bills on the table. "There's your ten percent." From his back pocket, he pulled out a crinkled white envelope. He put that on the table and slid it across. "There's your money."

Morgan didn't reach for it. When Earley did, the detective grabbed his arm. "Not yet."

Richter eyed Kirkwood. "Dean, do it."

Bodean Kirkwood's jaw flexed, and he closed his eyes.

"For the cause," Richter said.

When Kirkwood opened his eyes, he stared at Morgan. "I apologize for calling you a cop."

Morgan nodded once, then tilted his head toward Earley. "Make the call."

Earley slipped a flip phone from his pocket, dialed the only number on it, and said, "Now." When he hung up, he reached for the loose cash and the wrinkled envelope on the table. Earley discretely counted all the money under the table. "We're good."

Kirkwood rested his elbows on the table. "You ever serve time anywhere, Gallagher?"

"The Corps," Morgan said.

The man appeared confused. "Where's that?"

"Everywhere."

Kirkwood must have gotten Morgan's reference because his face relaxed. "No, man. Prison. You ever do time?"

Morgan shook his head.

"What about you, Donahue?" Kirkwood asked.

The Gallagher and Donahue aliases had been used in the past, but they didn't have deep histories attached to them. They were shadow covers—something the CTF could use in a pinch. Neither Morgan nor Earley were going too far off from the path of those covers. There wasn't a need tonight.

"What's with the questions?" Morgan asked.

"Making conversation. You got a problem with that?"

The door to the bar opened, and Adrian Thorn walked in. He wore a faded denim shirt, greasy blue jeans, and work boots. A baseball hat was pulled down low over his eyes, and he carried an awkward-shaped duffel bag over his left shoulder. Thorn didn't look at nor stop at Morgan's table as he walked toward the back of the bar.

"Restrooms are for paying customers only," Elva called.

Thorn said over his shoulder, "Gimme a beer," but didn't stop walking.

"You gotta pay first!"

The officer stepped into the restroom.

Elva muttered to herself and angrily slapped a rag against the bar counter.

Richter looked to his friend. "Me or you?"

Kirkwood pushed back from the table. "I can use the change of company." He headed toward the restrooms.

A new song came over the radio. It was another annoying number that Morgan remembered from his days in the military.

"Where'd you get the guns?" Richter asked.

Morgan raised an eyebrow. "What do you want them for?"

Richter lifted a hand in deference. "Dumb question. Never mind."

"*All right,*" Hackworth said through the earpiece. "*Here we go. Thorn is showing the guns to Kirkwood.*"

"What about flak jackets?" Richter asked. "Do you have any?"

Morgan glanced at Earley before responding, "You mean Kevlar?"

"Don't get excited. We're tapped out now, but if you get your hands on a couple, we'll call you when we're ready."

Morgan nodded. "We can do that."

"Cool." Richter leaned back in his chair and pointed into the air. "You like this song?"

"I don't know it," Morgan said. And he didn't. He just knew it was irritating. One of the guys in his unit had played this type of music, and Morgan never stuck around long enough to listen to it.

"It's 'Brown Sugar,'" Earley said. "How do you not know the Rolling Stones?"

Morgan shrugged. His mind was still on the Kevlar vests.

"Things are looking good," Hackworth said. *"Everybody stay alert."*

"Know what it's about?" Richter asked Earley.

"Heroin."

"That's funny." Richter shook his head. "People say that, but that's because they never listen to the lyrics."

Earley's brow corrugated. "I listen to the lyrics."

"You hear the chorus." Richter sang "Brown Sugar" at the same time Mick Jagger did. "It's about slaves getting raped by their masters." A nasty smile hinted at the corner of his mouth.

"Huh," Earley said.

"You like that?" Morgan asked.

"Relax, Morgan," Hackworth said in his ear. *"They're wrapping it up in the restroom. We're almost done."*

Richter shrugged a single shoulder. "It's all right, I guess. Just found it fascinating."

"Which part?" Morgan asked. "The rape of slaves or that people don't listen to the lyrics?"

"You must be a Beatles fan." Richter chuckled. "You probably like that faggoty 'Blackbird.'"

Morgan had no idea what Richter was talking about, but he knew the racism in the man's soul. It was the same thing that had permeated his grandfather and father's existence. Those men raised Morgan with the hatred. He battled to get free of their legacy. Morgan tried to judge men and women on their character, their choices in life, but at times he knew he still fell prey to those ugly thoughts he was raised with. He despised that part of himself.

"*Deal is done,*" Hackworth said. "*Everyone get ready.*"

The bathroom door opened, and Adrian Thorn walked out without the duffel bag.

As he passed the bar, Elva said, "You owe for your beer."

"Don't need it now."

Elva once again whipped the rag against the bar. "Don't come back, asshole."

Thorn didn't bother looking at Morgan or Earley as he headed toward the exit. He pushed the door open and entered the night.

The bathroom door opened a second time, and Kirkwood stepped out with the duffel slung over his shoulder.

Richter stood. "Looks like things went okay. I suppose we have a deal."

Morgan nodded. "Suppose we do."

"I'd say it's been a pleasure, but—"

"*Now,*" Hackworth said into the earpiece.

The room erupted in motion. Men and women jumped from their chairs with guns drawn. "Spokane Police!" several of them shouted.

Kirkwood clutched the bag with both hands as he ran for the exit. An officer grabbed the bag's strap as Kirkwood ran by. He was yanked off his feet and landed on his back, still clutching the duffel. Several officers leaped on him. They yelled, "Stop fighting" and "Quit resisting," though Kirkwood didn't seem to be doing much of either.

As for Richter, he hesitated when the commotion began. It was as if he were waiting for Kirkwood to get nearer to him before acting. Courtney Earley left his chair like the defensive football player he once was. He hit Richter around the waist, lifting the man off his feet, and drove him into the far wall.

Richter cried out, "Dean!" before crumbling to the floor.

Morgan remained seated and watched everything unfold with satisfaction. It was then he realized his headache was gone.

Chapter 22

Shane McAfee sat in a chair across from Bodean Kirkwood. He set a file on the small table between them. They were in an interview room in the Spokane County Sheriff's Department wing of the Public Safety Office. Standing in the corner was SPD Detective Jessie Johnson.

On the opposite side of the building, through a set of secured doors, was the Spokane Police Department's wing. Parker was interviewing Richter. Chambers was observing that interview.

McAfee admitted it was an unconventional way to proceed with the interviews, but the murders had occurred across jurisdictional lines. A stink could be made that everything happened inside Spokane County, but his job was as much about political considerations as it was enforcement.

The administration of both departments only cared about results—results they could take credit for later. If his department fought for control of nine murders and it blew up on them, they would own that failure solely. McAfee once heard police leadership schools taught only two things—how to steal credit and correctly assign blame. If that were true, spreading the risk had to be a sub-course.

Bodean Kirkwood's left wrist was chained to a metal bar that ran the wall's length. His hand gripped the bar, and he rested his elbow on it. He leaned back in his chair and tried to affect the appearance of a man with nothing but time to worry about.

McAfee set his hand on the manila folder. Usually, he'd pull out the white Miranda Warning card inside and read it, but Kirkwood was advised of his rights after his arrest at The Well. If he was going to ask guilt-seeking questions outside the illegal gun buy, he'd reread the warning. Instead, he was going to ease into the interview. "My name is Detective McAfee." He jerked his head toward the corner. "That's Detective Johnson. We're being recorded right now." He pointed to a camera lens that stuck out of the wall. "You've been advised."

"Like I care," Kirkwood said. "This is entrapment." He picked at something imaginary on the wall. "All of you did it, but I'm not worried about it. My lawyer'll get me off."

Kirkwood hadn't requested a lawyer at The Well, and McAfee wasn't going to ask if he wanted one now. "I don't want to talk about what happened at the bar yet."

"Yeah? You should. I'm gonna get a big-ass settlement out of it." He glanced at Johnson. "I'll probably own this joint."

"Tell me about prison."

Kirkwood's gaze slid to him. "What for?"

"I'm curious."

"Why? You wanna go? Looking to be somebody's bitch?"

"Is that where you met Elias?"

Kirkwood glanced at Johnson again. "What about it?"

"Tell me about your relationship with him."

"There ain't no relationship."

"You're not friends?"

"Are you messing with me?" His face reddened.

"I'm trying to establish who you were to each other."

"We're nobody to each other." He blinked faster. "Just a couple of guys."

McAfee looked down at the file. He didn't bother to open it. "So you weren't in prison together?"

Kirkwood's chair fell forward, and the handcuff slid forward on the bar. "What's your problem? You know we were, or you wouldn't have asked. You trying to say something? Well, say it." His voice raised. "Go ahead and say it."

"I'm not saying anything."

"Yeah, you are." Kirkwood smacked the table with his free hand. "You know you are."

"I'm trying to establish that you and Elias Richter are friends."

Kirkwood's face pinched, and he faced the wall.

"Will you admit to that?" McAfee asked.

"Friends? Sure. Are you happy now?"

McAfee ignored his question. "You're a member of the Silent."

Kirkwood rolled his eyes. "Nobody's a member of the Silent."

"But you believe in it."

"You should, too." Kirkwood faced him. "If you knew what was good for you."

"Tell me about it."

"You don't wanna know," Kirkwood muttered. He sounded like a petulant child.

McAfee opened the file and pulled out a couple of sheets of paper. It had been gathered by one of SIU's team members. He didn't know which. "The Southern Poverty Law Center says—"

"Race traitors," Kirkwood interrupted.

"—that there aren't any major philosophical differences between the Silent's agenda and groups like the KKK or skinheads."

"You're missing the point."

"What's the point?"

Kirkwood stared at him.

"I want to know," McAfee said. "Educate me. I'm trying to figure out why you did what you did."

Kirkwood slapped his chest. "And what did we do except get entrapped? When a jury hears what you cops pulled, I'm walking away with bank. Just like Randy Weaver did."

Weaver was a rallying cry for extremists in the area. In 1992, he barricaded himself in his north Idaho compound for eleven days against federal agents who wanted to arrest him for attempting to sell illegally sawed-off shotguns. By the time the siege ended, Weaver's wife and son were dead. A jury acquitted Weaver of almost all charges—only two minor gun charges stuck, and one was set aside by the judge. He served eighteen months. Weaver also sued, and the US Government settled for $3.1 million—a million each for his daughters and $100,000 for Weaver.

McAfee didn't want to discuss Randy Weaver. He generally knew enough about the subject, but Kirkwood likely had a fanatical view of the man. "What's the point of the Silent? What am I missing?"

"The point is—" Kirkwood shifted in his seat. He glanced at Johnson and then down to his shoes. Several seconds passed before Kirkwood seemed to calm himself. He lightly set his hand on the metal table. "The Silent is us. It's inside. We don't hold meetings. We don't need stupid haircuts or to hide our faces. The message is us, and we're the message."

"That sounds like the bible," McAfee said.

A malicious grin spread across Kirkwood's lips. "Amen. Glory be."

***

Andrew Parker rubbed a thumb into the palm of his other hand as he consulted his notes. "How long after you got out of Coyote Ridge did you hook up with Bodean?"

"We never hooked up," Elias Richter said.

The response surprised Parker, and he looked up from the manila folder.

Richter blushed. The man's left hand dangled in a handcuff that was chained to a rail bolted to the wall. He sat upright in his chair. His other hand was tucked under a leg that nervously bounced.

Parker glanced at Tim Chambers, who stood in the corner. The county detective's expression didn't change. A freaking robot, Parker thought. His attention returned to Richter. "You didn't hook up?"

"That's what I said. You think we're gay or something?"

Parker cocked his head. "Being gay is a weakness in the nationalist community." Parker was careful not to say 'supremacist.'

"It's a disease." Richter looked to Chambers, then back to Parker. "A plague. And I'm not gay. Neither is Dean."

"All right, then."

"We're not."

"I said okay, but it's considered weak, right? A defect of some sort?"

Richter's jaw flexed. "A defect. Sure."

Parker didn't push that topic any further. He could come back to it later if need be.

"So, back to my question—"

"I told you," Richter interrupted.

"After you got out of Coyote Ridge, how long was it before you met up with Bodean?"

Richter's eyes widened slightly before shaking his head.

"Yeah," Parker said. "How long?"

"Right away, I guess."

"He was waiting for you?"

Richter stared at him.

"Like a friend does when they go to the movies or something."

"I got out first. When he got out, we hooked—" Richter stopped. He glanced to Chambers. "We met up."

Parker made a note in his file. "Where did you get the money to buy the guns?"

"What guns?"

"The guns we have you on video buying." Parker had already read Richter his rights. He wasn't going to dance around guilt-seeking questions. Since they had already arrested Richter for illegally purchasing weapons, he was going directly after the man.

Richter blinked. "You had video?"

"Covering all angles. Even had one in the restroom when Bodean went in to inspect the guns."

"Cops lie." Richter looked to Chambers. "Everybody knows it. You even get trained to do it."

"No lie," Chambers said. "The picture was clear as day."

"Crap," Richter muttered to himself.

Parker tapped the table. "So, the money? How'd you get it?"

"We worked for it."

"Doing what?"

"Odd jobs."

"Like what?"

Richter shrugged. "Stuff. Helping move things, I guess. I don't know."

"You don't remember how you and Bodean made twenty-two hundred bucks?"

"Odd jobs. Why? Do you know how you made all your money?"

Parker nodded. "I do. Every dime."

"Well, I don't." He glanced to Chambers. "We don't. I guess that's how we're different."

"How'd you pay for things?" Parker asked. "Food, rent, gas."

"Cash."

"And you don't know where it came from?"

"How many times do I have to say it?"

Chambers grunted and shifted his standing position. He crossed his arms and leaned a shoulder against the wall.

Parker reconsulted his notes. "What kind of car do you drive?"

"I don't have a car."

"What about Bodean?"

"He doesn't have one either."

"What'd you guys do? Take a bus to a gun buy?"

Richter shrugged—a single shoulder this time.

"Well?" Parker asked.

"Maybe we walked."

"There's no maybe about it. Either you did, or you didn't. Which was it?"

Richter shrugged again—both shoulders this time. "I don't know what to tell you."

Someone knocked on the door. Chambers opened it. It was one of the CTF guys Jeremiah Strange. He whispered something to Chambers.

Richter's eyes narrowed at the black officer's presence. Parker studied Richter's response. He hoped the camera recording their interaction would pick up the intricacies in the man's face. His brow furrowed, his lips parted, and his free hand balled.

Chambers said to Parker. "I'll be back." He closed the door behind him.

Richter relaxed and faced the detective.

"You all right?" Parker asked.

"Fine," Richter said. "Why wouldn't I be?"

"So, how did you get to The Well?"

"Why's it matter?"

"Humor me."

Richter thought for a second. "We just got there."

"Did you take a taxi?"

"No."

"Did you borrow a car?"

"*No.*" His denial was said with too much emphasis.

Parker's eyes narrowed. "Maybe you stole a car."

"That's the same thing as borrowing."

"No, it's not."

"Whatever. We didn't do that."

"Did someone give you a ride?"

Richter's gaze shifted to another part of the room. When he looked back, he said, "Yeah. That's what happened, and that's why I don't wanna tell you about it. I don't wanna get her in trouble."

It was a lie, and Parker made a note about it. There would be time to circle back to it. Right now was about setting up the boundaries for Richter's story. Then Parker would move the fence posts in little by little until the man had no room to move. "What did you want the guns for?"

"Target practice." Richter nodded. "Recreational use. You know, maybe to go deer hunting or something."

"With an AK-47?"

"It would kill a deer."

"I certainly would expect so."

Richter pushed himself upright. "People like you force us to buy guns this way."

"Me?" Parker asked.

"And the criminal laws of this nation."

"You went to jail for illegal possession of a firearm. Why do it again?"

"If a nation's laws are immoral, should I continue to bow to them?"

Parker smirked. "Who goes hunting with a fully automatic rifle?"

"We hadn't decided on hunting," Richter said. "I was just saying. We might have only used it for target practice."

"Thank you for not trying to deny the weapons."

"You said there was video. Besides, there was a roomful of cops. What's lying going to get me? I was busted for it once. I know how it goes. I'll serve some time and get out. Okay, so you got me. Let's wrap this up and get the clock started."

"Why not buy the guns through your previous source? The guy who got you one a couple years ago."

Richter tsked. "If only I could. Cancer caught him. Left us looking for a new source."

"Why did you want the Kevlar vests?"

"We didn't—" Richter stopped speaking. His eyes lowered as he thought. Eventually, he shrugged. "I was talking through my ass."

"You weren't looking to purchase body armor?"

"Why would I want that? I was wondering what those gun runners could get their hands on. I didn't know they were cops. Had I, I wouldn't have come at them with a stupid question like that. What if I asked if they could get their hands on a stealth bomber? Would I be in trouble with the Air Force?"

The door opened, and Tim Chambers stepped back in. He held a piece of paper. Both Parker and Richter faced him. He said, "Patrol found a 2012 Ford Fusion down the block from The Well. It's registered to Jarrod Stone."

Richter stared unblinkingly at Chambers.

"Did they search the vehicle?" Parker asked.

"Not yet. They've secured it, and it's being towed to the property room."

"Do you know what's going to happen now?" Parker asked Richter.

He turned to Parker. "With what?"

"The Ford registered to Jarrod Stone. He was murdered with three others at an after-hours joint called The Shortstop. The killers stole Stone's car from that crime scene. We'll write a warrant to search that vehicle. Then our technicians will search it top-to-bottom for fingerprints, fibers, and anything that can tie the car back to you and your buddy. I'll bet you've watched those CSI shows. You've seen what those crime scene techs can do—especially with DNA."

While murder investigation shows created unrealistic expectations in jury trials, they were a boon to detectives. Parker often held the threat of a motivated evidence technician over a suspect's head.

Richter swallowed with some difficulty.

"When we link that car to you—and you know they will, right?" Parker smiled maliciously. "When that car is linked to you, those four murders are on your plate."

"And," Chambers said, drawing Richter's attention to him, "after that case is tied to you, the vehicle left near that crime scene—an Audi Quatro—will likely tie you to the five killings at The Shisha Room. We wrote the search warrant on that one and the lab techs processed it today."

Richter's left hand grasped the metal railing while his right clutched the table's edge. His head bobbed repeatedly.

"I've got to ask," Parker said, "what was with the cars? You had to know it was stupid to drive around a vehicle taken from a homicide scene? Why push fate?"

Richter lowered his head. He took several deep breaths as if to steady himself. He looked up at Parker then to Chambers. Tears welled in his eyes. "Dean."

"What about him?"

"The cars…They were his idea."

***

"I figured the hell with it," Kirkwood said. "If we got stopped, we'd go out blasting. Help advance the cause."

"But you'd be dead," McAfee said.

"Maybe not. You never know."

A moment ago, a CTF officer—the long-haired one who carried the duffel bag into The Well—had interrupted the interview to tell Jessie Johnson that the Ford Fusion stolen from the second murder scene had been recovered. Prior to that, Kirkwood was reluctant to admit any participation in the robberies.

Now, the man couldn't brag enough. It was like he knew something was inside that Fusion which was going to seal his fate once it was searched.

"You stole the Quatro because your car broke down?" McAfee said. "What did you do with your vehicle?"

Kirkwood chuckled. "We left it where it died—that little grocery store on Argonne. We almost didn't hit that hookah joint after it crapped out because we had to hoof it in."

"What was wrong with the car?"

"Something with the exhaust system, I think. I don't know. We rolled some guy living in it down by the courthouse. The damn thing smelled like piss, but it ran decent enough."

McAfee eyed Johnson to see if he'd heard anything about an incident like that, but the other detective shook his head.

Kirkwood continued. "We should have gotten a different car from the jump. Probably wouldn't be sitting here if we went for quality instead of ease. Live and learn."

"Why go through with it?"

Kirkwood flicked something imaginary from the table. "Who would talk? We'd already ripped off three of them. No one knew it was us. We had a foolproof plan."

"Until you killed someone."

"That was a bonus." Kirkwood patted the table three times. "We never expected to stumble into something like that."

"Like what?"

"You want me to say it? You think we don't know about the kicker you're gonna shove down our throats. You protect their lives but not ours. That's the problem with this country—it's broken. It's upside-down. Their lives are more important than ours."

McAfee studied Kirkwood. "You killed them because they were people of color."

"Listen to you—so politically correct. People of color. I bet they taught you that term in some class." Kirkwood glanced at Johnson. "What about you? Were you in the same class? Did you learn all the approved words? Microaggression. The patriarchy. Cisgender. Who made up those words?" Kirkwood laughed. "Let me ask you something. Did they make you announce your pronouns before the start of the class? What's yours, Detective? Because mine is bad motherfucker."

Parker didn't bother correcting the man about his pronoun question.

"And so we don't have any miscommunication," Kirkwood continued, "there was a wigger in the room. That Russian should have known better."

"Why steal the Quatro, though? It stood out."

Kirkwood rolled his eyes. "We didn't know it was that goofy looking car. Elias took it because he said it was an Audi. Once we were outside, it didn't make sense to go back for a different set of keys. It also didn't make sense to run out of the neighborhood. We had the cash, and it was time to jet."

"Was the plan to go out in a firefight with the cops?"

Kirkwood waved cavalierly. "We didn't have a plan."

"You were robbing after-hours clubs to raise money to buy AK-47s."

"Says you." Kirkwood smirked. "You got no proof of that."

"Other than the two of you buying AKs from a couple of cops."

"Says you," Kirkwood repeated.

"Where did you get the revolvers you had with you?"

"Friends of the cause, and that's all I'll say about that."

McAfee would work on getting that detail another time. It wasn't necessary information. He had more than enough now.

***

"Why did you steal the Fusion?" Parker asked.

Richter tapped the metal railing with a single finger. "Because it wasn't owned by one of them."

Parker lifted an eyebrow.

"We didn't want to drive in their cars, so we took the dude's. You know the guy who wasn't."

"Were you afraid of catching the disease or something?"

Richter shrugged. "We weren't taking any chances. That's why we took that hunk of junk."

"Why not stick with the Audi?"

"It was almost out of gas."

Parker cocked his head. "But you had all that cash."

"We weren't robbing those joints for gas money."

"And you took the Audi because?"

Richter inhaled deeply. "We may not like those commie bastards, but when push comes to shove..."

"They're the right color."

"Listen. I'm not a racist. Neither is Dean. We're just for the separation of our people. They can live their lives, and we'll live ours." He looked to Chambers. "Why can't everyone have their own space?"

Parker's job wasn't to argue the semantics of racist ideology. It was to develop enough probable cause to arrest

Richter for the murders at The Shortstop. Chambers was there to observe Parker's interview and establish probable cause for the homicides at The Shisha Room.

Chamber's asked, "Why didn't you search Sidorov's apartment?"

Richter's face pinched. "Who?"

"You had his keys and the registration to his car. Why didn't you search his apartment?"

"Right, right." Richter nodded. "The Russian. We thought about it, but by the time we arrived at his apartment, there was already a cop car sitting in the parking lot."

"And you didn't want to get into a shootout like Butch and Sundance?"

"If we had to, yeah. But I keep telling you that wasn't the plan."

"What *was* the plan?" Chambers asked.

Richter frowned but didn't answer.

"Where'd you stash the revolvers?" Parker leaned forward. "We will find them. Either when we search your apartments or the Ford we towed. Why not tell us?"

"You're gonna find them." Richter sighed. "They're in the car—that Ford. We left them under the seats."

"Why?"

"Because you're not supposed to have them inside a bar."

Parker stared at Richter for a moment before shifting his glance to Chambers. The county detective remained stoic.

"What?" Richter asked.

"You were buying guns. You'd already committed robbery and murder but left your guns in the car?" Parker shook his head. "Help me understand."

"It's a bar. Everyone knows you can't bring a gun inside there. You can get into real trouble for it. That's why we chose to leave them outside."

"Why'd you pick a bar?"

"We thought we'd be doing an exchange in a parking lot. We wanted a little coverage from bystanders, but your guys messed us up by saying we needed to do the deal inside. But then we thought it was a smart choice because none of us would have guns. Sort of like sanctuary."

There were often times in cases where a suspect said or did something that made little sense to Parker—this was one of them. "But you could have brought your guns inside."

Richter seemed disappointed that Parker wasn't getting it. "You can't have guns inside a bar. It's a law."

Parker stared at him.

"I learned the hard way not to mess with the liquor board." Richter looked to Chambers, then back to Parker. "What's going to happen now?"

"Right now, you'll be booked for buying the firearms."

Richter's lips twisted. "And the other things?"

"I'll come over in the morning and add those charges."

"Do you think…" Richter's voice trailed off.

"What?"

"Do you think they'll let Dean and me go someplace together?"

Parker knew there was no way that a prosecutor, a judge, or a warden would agree to that after what these two men had done. But Parker knew he or one of the other detectives would want to talk with Richter again in the coming days, so there was no need to unnecessarily upset the man.

"I don't know, Elias. Maybe."

Richter nodded. "If you promise that, I'll tell you whatever you want me to."

"I just want the truth."

"Yeah, okay."

Parker walked around the table and removed the handcuff from around the bar. He put his hand on Richter's shoulder, and the man turned around. He placed both hands behind his back, and Parker secured the second cuff.

"I'll walk him over," Parker said to Chambers.

The county detective nodded and opened the interview room door.

"Do you know how Dean's doing?" Richter asked.

Parker shook his head. "No."

"You think he blames me?"

"For what?"

"I was the one who told him to stay at the bar. I even made him say he was sorry to that guy." Richter shook his head. "Man, that cop fooled the fuck out of me."

"Yeah, he does that to us all."

Chapter 23

Morgan pulled into the apartment community's parking lot just as the sun broke over the horizon. The Dodge Charger slowly wound through the complex on its path to his garage.

A crew was out cutting the grass. He couldn't hear the engines of the lawn equipment, but he imagined its incessant hum. Morgan had slept through the whirring mechanical sound before. It was a skill he'd honed since the Marine Corps.

He exited the car, closed the garage door, then trundled up the stairs to his apartment. It felt as if he carried sandbags on both shoulders and like weights were tied around his ankles.

Silence greeted him inside the apartment. He didn't expect anything else. He slowly closed the door behind him and stood in the entryway.

Nostalgia rolled over him in the form of memories of Alyssa.

She often greeted him like an eager puppy—with an open mouth and a wagging tail. His hands would wander her lovely curves and effortlessly evoke soft moans and satisfying giggles. Those were the "pull" moments when he worked to show her how much she meant to him. He could just as easily induce harsh rebukes and slaps across the cheek. Those were the times he "pushed" her as reminders of how easily he could live alone.

Maybe he'd been shortsighted in treating her so poorly near the end. She had been a satisfying woman to have around. He grunted. That was the danger of wistfulness.

It made him feel weak. It also made him feel a little stupid. But mostly, it made him feel old.

Move it, maggot.

Morgan shuffled forward, down the hallway, and into the kitchen. He took off his gun and badge and set them on the counter. He removed everything else from his pockets—keys, wallet, and pocketknife—and tossed them up there, too.

Then he lumbered into his bedroom. He didn't bother undressing.

There was no reason to do such a thing.

***

"Daddy!"

Parker closed the door to his home and turned to find three smiling girls waiting for him. He knelt and hugged them all.

"Long night," Brooke said as she walked past. She tousled his short hair. "Breakfast?"

"Please," Parker said. He stood and lifted all three girls at once. They squealed in delight.

"Girls, give Daddy some room. He just got home."

Parker set the children down. He waded through them on his way to the kitchen.

"What kept you?" Brooke asked.

"Bad guys." It was a simple answer while the girls were in earshot.

"Did you catch them?"

"We did."

"Are these the ones—" Brooke eyed the children who played nearby. She faced Parker and whispered. "Are these the ones responsible for the murders a couple of nights ago?"

Parker nodded.

"I'm proud of you." His wife kissed him.

He closed his eyes and held her for a moment.

When they broke their embrace, he patted her behind. "I love you."

Brooke moved to the refrigerator. "You doing okay?" She pulled out a carton of eggs and set it next to the stove.

"I'm beat."

"Are you going back in today?"

"After I get some sleep. We've got to finish the paperwork."

Brooke removed two containers of vegetables that she'd cut several days ago. "Is a veggie omelet okay?"

Parker didn't want anything heavy before he slept. "That's perfect."

"After I fix this, I'll get dressed and take the girls out."

"You don't have to."

"It's easier than trying to keep them quiet. You can call when you wake up."

He bent and lay his arms on the counter. His chin rested on the back of his hands. Parker watched Brooke as she tossed the vegetables into a pan. "You can come to bed with me."

She glanced over her shoulder. "You say that now. The girls will bang on the door as soon as we get in there."

"Put a movie on for them."

"They're wound up. I'll take them out to a park."

Parker groaned and closed his eyes.

"Just remember, mister. You're the one who wanted three."

"Should we have another?" he asked dreamily.

He heard the approaching footsteps but didn't bother to open his eyes until the plastic spatula slapped the top of his head.

"What'd you do that for?"

"Why do you think?"

"I was only asking."

Brooke pointed the utensil at him. "Stop thinking about it, or I'm gonna waddle around for nine months."

Parker smirked. "You only waddle for four of them."

She smacked him on the head again. "I said no. Now, let me finish your eggs."

He smiled and contently watched his wife move about the kitchen.

***

Shane McAfee opened the door to his South Hill home and entered.

He pulled his gun and badge from his belt and set it on the stand in the hallway. He checked himself in the mirror that hung on the wall. Dark bags were under his eyes, and his short hair was mussed.

He thought about food but figured he'd get something when he awoke. He planned to get a few hours of sleep and then return to the office to complete the Kirkwood and Richter paperwork. It was a multi-jurisdictional case, and both departments needed to work together. They would loop the prosecuting attorney in soon to ensure everyone did their part correctly. It was too big of a case not to do so.

McAfee walked into his bedroom and stopped long enough to get undressed. He proceeded to the shower. He didn't want to climb into bed feeling grimy. The water heated quickly, and he climbed in.

He let the hot water work the knots out of his shoulders.

They'd gotten lucky. Not only had the jurisdictions been able to come together, but Elias and Kirkwood both talked. Maybe they would recant their stories later or try to modify them, but it wouldn't matter. Both waived their rights and were on film now.

The two were sunk.

McAfee was fine that it was a team win. He cared more about the result than the accolades. He would have preferred that James Morgan hadn't been such an integral part of the solution, though. He disliked the man.

McAfee turned his face to the spray, hoping it would wash away his thoughts.

The glass shower door opened, and he turned to look. Emily stepped inside and pulled the door shut.

"Aren't you supposed to be at school?"

"I'm skipping class." She slipped her arms around his neck.

"I didn't text you for this."

"I know." She stood on her tiptoes.

"I gotta go back to the office in a few hours."

"I'm not stopping you." Emily pulled his head down toward hers.

"I need to get some sleep," McAfee protested half-heartedly.

"Whatever you say." She kissed him.

Did You Enjoy the Book?

Thank you for reading *The After-Hours War* and visiting the 509! I hope you enjoyed meeting some of the recurring characters. This is a continuing series with other characters occasionally stepping into the lead role. There are two parallel series to the 509 Crime Stories—the Flip-Flop Detective and the John Cutler mysteries. I hope you'll check them out.

I'm always grateful when a reader takes time out of their day to comment on one of my novels. If you do write a review, please email me, and let me know.

I'd love to say thanks!

About the Author

Colin Conway is the creator of the 509 Crime Stories, a series of novels set in Eastern Washington with revolving lead characters. They are standalone tales and can be read in any order.

He also created the Cozy Up series which pushes the envelope of the cozy genre. Libby Klein, author of the Poppy McAllister series, says *Cozy Up to Death* is "Not your grandma's cozy."

Colin co-authored the Charlie-316 series. The first novel in the series, *Charlie-316*, is a political/crime thriller that has been described as "riveting and compulsively readable," "the real deal," and "the ultimate ride-along."

He served in the U.S. Army and later was an officer of the Spokane Police Department. He has owned a laundromat, invested in a bar, and run a karate school. Besides writing crime fiction, he is a commercial real estate broker.

Colin lives with his beautiful girlfriend, three wonderful children, and a codependent Vizsla that rules their world.

Find out more at colinconway.com.

Also by Colin Conway

THE 509 UNIVERSE

The 509 Crime Stories

The Side Hustle
The Long Cold Winter
The Blind Trust
The Suit
The Value in Our Lies
The Mean Street
Murder by Any Other Name
Black and Blue in the Lilac City
The Only Death That Matters
The After-Hours War
The Fate of Our Years
The Night of the Dead Boys
The Path of Progress
When the Wicked Rest

The John Cutler Mysteries

Cutler's Return
Cutler's Chase
Cutler's Friend
Cutler's Cases
Cutler's Bargain
Cutler's Legacy

The Flip-Flop Detective

Strait Over Tackle
Strait to Hell
Strait Out of Nowhere

OTHER SERIES

The Cozy Up Series

Cozy Up to Death
Cozy Up to Murder
Cozy Up to Blood
Cozy Up to Trouble
Cozy Up to Christmas
Cozy Up to Danger
Cozy Up to Terror

**The Charlie-316 Series
(with Frank Zafiro)**

Charlie-316
Never the Crime
Badge Heavy
Code Four
The Ride-Along

OTHER WORKS

Some Degree of Murder (with Frank Zafiro)
Tales from the Road (with Bill Bancroft)